# BLOOD AND THE DEVIL'S DUE

*A Brutal Western Tale of Blood, Betrayal, and Redemption*

## Kimberly St. Clair

**Uncorked Publishing**

uncorked

*Dedication To the untamed spirits of the West—those who fought, bled, and endured.*

*And to every mother who would ride through fire for her child.*

*And to my family—this book is for you, with all my love.*

*"The frontier is a land of dust and blood, where the law is forgotten, and mercy is a luxury few can afford."*
— Anonymous, 1885

*"There are no heroes in the desert. Only survivors."*
— Unknown

*"Vengeance rides swiftest on the heels of the desperate."*
— Old West Proverb

# FOREWORD

In crafting this novel, I sought to capture the raw, unrelenting spirit of the American frontier—a place where survival was an act of defiance and love was often the only light in a world shadowed by violence.

The journey of Ellie Calhoun and Cullen McKenna is one that reflects the resilience of countless souls who endured the unforgiving landscape of the West. As you embark on this story, I hope you feel the weight of every sacrifice, the fire of every moment of courage, and the depth of every unspoken love.

This tale is my humble homage to the indomitable will of those who came before us.

# INTRODUCTION

The American frontier of the 1880s was a crucible of hardship and resilience, where survival often came at the barrel of a gun and mercy was a rare commodity. This introduction provides context to the world in which this story unfolds—a time when the open plains held both promise and peril, and every horizon brought new challenges. Here, amidst the dust and desolation of the Llano Estacado, Ellie Calhoun's story begins—a tale of love tested by cruelty, and vengeance forged in fire.

This is not merely a story of the Old West; it is an exploration of human endurance, driven by the unbreakable bond between a mother and her child. As you turn the pages, prepare to be transported into a world where every heartbeat echoes against the endless horizon, and every choice is carved into the unforgiving landscape. Welcome to the journey.

# PREFACE

The American frontier of the late 1800s was a place both untamed and unforgiving—a land where survival was earned through grit, sacrifice, and often, blood. This story is born from that harsh reality, inspired by the countless forgotten lives that shaped the West. It is not a tale of legends or lawmen, but of those whose stories were never told, whose battles were fought far from the pages of history books.

Here, in the dust and shadows of the Llano Estacado, you will meet Ellie Calhoun, a mother whose love for her daughter burns brighter than the desert sun, and Cullen McKenna, a man haunted by his past and bound by secrets. Together, they traverse a world where mercy is scarce, and vengeance is a bitter companion.

This is a story of survival, sacrifice, and the relentless pursuit of hope in a land where both dreams and nightmares take root. Welcome to a journey through fire and blood.

# ALSO BY KIMBERLY ST. CLAIR

We Will No Be Forgotten

Red Snow

Beneath These Branches: The Haunting of Darlington House

# PROLOGUE

The wind howled through the canyon, a hollow, mournful cry that twisted between jagged rocks like a wounded animal. The desert stretched endless beyond it, a vast ocean of dust and shadow swallowing the last dying light of day. Somewhere in the distance, a coyote's cry pierced the dusk—a lonely, desperate sound, lost beneath the rising fury of an oncoming storm. The sky above bruised purple and black, a belly full of rage, waiting to spill.

And in the heart of that desolate expanse, a little girl ran for her life.

Mercy McKenna had always been small for her age, but she was fast. Faster than most. She'd spent her childhood racing through the open fields of her family's ranch, dodging between fence posts, her bare feet kicking up clouds of dust, her laughter wild and untamed as the wind itself. But there was no laughter now. Only the sharp, ragged sound of her breath, the frantic drumbeat of her heart pounding against the fragile cage of her ribs.

Her legs burned with each desperate stride, the torn remnants of her nightdress flapping against her bruised knees, streaked with dirt and blood. Her bare feet were raw, cut by sharp stones and twisted roots, but she didn't feel it. She didn't dare look back. She couldn't. The men who had stolen her were close— close enough that she could still hear the crunch of their boots over the brittle earth, the faint jingle of spurs, the low murmur of voices thick with cruelty. They weren't shouting anymore. They didn't need to.

They knew she had nowhere left to run.

The canyon walls narrowed ahead, looming like jagged teeth. Mercy scrambled up the rocky path, her small hands scraping against rough stone for balance. The ground beneath her feet slick with rain, blood—some of it hers, most of it not. Her mind flickered with shattered images, memories sharp as broken glass.

The rough hands that had torn her from her bed in the dead of night, fingers like iron shackles bruising her arms. The sound of her mother's scream—raw, animal, a sound no child should ever hear. The gunshot that followed, sharp and final. Her father's voice—Cullen's voice—roaring her name, fierce and full of a terror she'd never heard before. Then nothing. Darkness.

When she'd woken, the world had changed. She was bound, gagged, her wrists raw from rope, her mouth dry with fear. The wagon rocked beneath her like a coffin rattling over rough roads. The men spoke in low voices, calling her by a name that wasn't hers. A mistake. A cruel, brutal mistake. But mistakes didn't matter to men like them. Mistakes still bled. Mistakes still died.

She hadn't cried.

Not then.

But now, as her strength gave out, as her knees buckled and she fell hard against the unforgiving earth, she felt the first tear slip hot and bitter down her cheek. She bit her lip until it bled. Because crying was weakness. And weakness got you killed.

A shadow fell over her.

She didn't have to look up to know.

Jed.

He wasn't the worst of them. But he wasn't the best, either. He was somewhere in between—a man with tired eyes and a gun that never left his hip, a man who carried ghosts like old debts unpaid. His face was carved from stone, but there was something in his eyes—a flicker of something almost human beneath the hardened veneer.

He crouched beside her, his shadow long and dark in the fading light, his voice low and steady. "Don't fight me, kid."

Mercy glared at him, her small hands curling into fists. She had no gun. No knife. But she had her teeth, her nails, and a fury that burned hotter than any fear.

She lunged.

Jed caught her easily, his grip firm but not cruel. She kicked, bit, screamed—fought like a cornered animal. But he didn't flinch. Didn't shout. He just held her, steady as the earth beneath them, his arms a cage she couldn't break. His voice was a whisper against the storm.

"Not yet, kid."

She hated him.

Hated them all.

But most of all, she hated herself. Because deep down, buried beneath the rage and terror, she knew he was right.

It wasn't time to fight.

Not yet.

But one day...

One day, she would make them pay.

As the first crack of thunder split the sky, lightning igniting the canyon walls in ghostly flashes, Jed carried her back down the path—away from freedom, away from everything she had ever known. The storm broke overhead, rain falling like shards of glass, mingling with the blood on her skin.

And Mercy didn't cry.

Not again.

Not ever.

Because tears were for the dead.

And she wasn't dead.

Not yet.

# CHAPTER ONE

The wind carved through the canyon like a sharpened blade, its mournful wail echoing off jagged cliffs and sweeping through the scorched Arizona desert. It was 1885, a time when the West was still wild, untamed, and dripping with blood from battles fought over land, power, and revenge. The desert stretched endless, its silence often a companion to death, and tonight, it whispered of something sinister. Against this harsh, unforgiving landscape stood the Calhoun ranch—weathered and unyielding, much like the woman who ruled it. Eleanor "Ellie" Calhoun had never bent to the land's will or the men who tried to take what was hers. She had fought drought, raiders, and whispers that doubted a woman could hold her own. And she had won—until now.

Brimstone, her black stallion, sensed the unease long before Ellie did, his ears flicking back, muscles tense beneath her firm grip. As she crested the last rise before home, the familiar sight of smoke from the chimney did nothing to ease the knot in her gut. She scanned the valley, searching for the familiar figure of Harlan Cutter, her foreman. A Confederate veteran turned bounty hunter, Harlan had been broken by war and whiskey, but never careless. Yet tonight, his absence gnawed at her nerves.

Jonas McCreedy, young and wide-eyed with fear, waited near the barn, shifting on restless feet. "Harlan's gone," he stammered, voice cracking. Ellie's blood ran cold. Harlan might have been a drunk, but he would never abandon Mercy —her daughter, her reason for breathing. Ellie dismounted, boots crunching against the hard earth, hand brushing the worn grip of her Colt. The front door swung open with a creak that scraped her nerves raw, revealing a smear of blood on the porch, dark and wet. Inside, chaos reigned—furniture overturned, glass shattered, and blood pooling on the floor. Harlan's lifeless body, crucified against the wall, greeted her, his throat slit so deeply it revealed bone. Beneath him, a single word carved into the wood chilled Ellie to her core: RUN.

Ellie's pulse roared as she tore down the hallway to Mercy's room—empty, sheets torn, blood staining the bed. A shadow shifted outside. Ellie spun, Colt raised, and locked eyes with a man cloaked in a bloodstained duster, his face painted red with a jagged grin. Mercy's doll dangled from his hand. Ellie's rage burned hotter than her fear, but before she could fire, he whistled a sharp, mocking tune and vanished into the night. Mercy was gone. But Ellie Calhoun wasn't broken. Not yet. And God help the Red Hand—because she would burn the world down to bring her daughter home.

# CHAPTER TWO

The Arizona desert, unforgiving and vast, stretched beneath the cold gaze of the silver moon, swallowing everything in its path—light, sound, and even hope. In the harsh year of 1885, the West was a crucible where only the ruthless survived, and tonight, Eleanor "Ellie" Calhoun was nothing if not ruthless. She rode hard through the darkened wilderness, Brimstone's hooves pounding against the parched earth, her heart racing with desperation that tasted like bile in her throat. Each passing moment stole Mercy further from her reach, and the desert, cruel and merciless, seemed intent on swallowing her daughter whole. Ellie's body was a knot of tension, her mind replaying every scream, every drop of blood left behind. She pushed her stallion harder, whispering promises to a God she didn't believe in, knowing full well that if she failed, the Red Hand would vanish into outlaw country where neither law nor conscience dared tread.

Ellie wasn't searching for redemption or justice. She craved vengeance, raw and unrelenting. But to exact that vengeance, she needed a monster—someone as brutal as the land they roamed. Not her father, a man long lost to drink and regret. She needed Cullen "Crow" McKenna. Once the love of her life, now a legend of violence, McKenna was a bounty hunter whose name struck fear into the hearts of even the most hardened outlaws. Ellie had loved him once, naively believing she could save him from his darkness. But McKenna never wanted salvation—only blood. His words echoed in her memory, a grim promise: "There ain't no heaven for men like me, darlin'. Just hell. And I aim to be the devil."

Ellie rode south, the ghostly shadows of cliffs and canyons looming around her, whispering of ambushes and unseen dangers. McKenna had disappeared years ago, some said dead, others claiming he had become something worse— a ghost among the Apache, a wraith in the wilds. Ellie prayed he was alive, knowing the cost of his help would be steep, but willing to pay it. As the terrain grew treacherous, Brimstone's restless movements warned her of unseen eyes. Arrows hissed through the air, missing her by mere inches. She fired back, steady despite her fear, until a shot from the darkness felled an approaching warrior.

Cullen McKenna emerged from the shadows, taller and leaner than she remembered, his cold eyes like pale flames beneath his weathered hat. Dust and blood clung to him like a second skin, his rifle still smoking. His grin was sharp, dangerous. "Ellie Calhoun," he drawled, voice like whiskey over gravel. "Didn't think I'd see you again." Ellie's grip on her Colt never wavered. "I need your help," she bit out. McKenna's grin faltered at her words. "The Red Hand took Mercy." His face hardened, the predator in him awakening. "You ain't gonna like my price," he warned. Ellie, eyes blazing, whispered back, "I don't care." McKenna's slow nod sealed their fate. "Then let's go kill some bastards."

# CHAPTER THREE

The desert was an unrelenting beast, swallowing light and life in equal measure, its endless expanse broken only by jagged cliffs and shadowed canyons that whispered promises of death. Beneath the relentless sun, its scorched earth cracked like parched lips begging for mercy, but none would come. Ellie Calhoun and Cullen "Crow" McKenna rode through this hellish landscape, their silhouettes swallowed by the waves of shimmering heat rising from the sand. The weight of the journey pressed heavy on Ellie's shoulders, her thoughts consumed by the terrifying image of her daughter, Mercy, lost somewhere within the grasp of the Red Hand. Every mile they covered was a silent war against time, and Ellie's resolve hardened with every hoofbeat that carried them closer to a reckoning soaked in blood.

McKenna's presence beside her was both a reassurance and a bitter reminder. His sharp gaze scanned the horizon with a predator's precision, his lean frame relaxed but coiled like a serpent ready to strike. The years had carved lines into his weathered face, each scar and shadow telling stories Ellie wished she could forget. The cold gleam in his eyes, like ice beneath a scorching sun, reminded her that he was not a man prone to mercy. They rode in silence, two souls scarred by violence, bound together by necessity and vengeance.

Their path southward was marked by blood. Scattered homesteads, burnt to the ground, and bodies left to rot under the unmerciful sun painted a grim trail that the Red Hand had carved through the desert. Ellie's jaw clenched as she forced herself to look, each scene fueling the storm within her. McKenna, ever the pragmatist, took it all in with the detached calm of a man too familiar with death.

At dawn, they found the first grim sign of the Red Hand's trail. A lone rider, strung up from a gnarled mesquite tree, his lifeless body swaying gently in the breeze. His face was a mask of agony, swollen and mutilated, while dark blood stained the earth beneath him. Ellie's breath hitched, her eyes narrowing as she spotted the mark seared into his chest— the unmistakable bloody handprint of the Red Hand. McKenna dismounted, approaching the scene with a calculated calm, his fingers tracing the bruises and rope burns. "This wasn't a clean kill," he muttered, pulling a bloodied knife from the dirt. "Cartel work." Ellie's stomach churned at the revelation. "The cartel?" she whispered. "They're working with the Red Hand?" McKenna's grin was humorless. "The Red Hand's made a deal with devils worse than me, darlin'. This just got a whole lot bloodier."

By midday, they reached an abandoned outpost, its skeletal buildings scarred by time and violence. The air was thick with the metallic tang of blood, and inside the half-burned saloon, bodies lay strewn like discarded dolls, each missing their hands. Ellie's knuckles whitened around her revolver as she surveyed the carnage. "This wasn't just a killing," she murmured. "This was a warning." McKenna nodded grimly, eyes flicking toward the darkened doorway at the back of the room. Ellie's pulse quickened as she followed his gaze, gun raised, knowing the fight wasn't over. Then, from the shadows, the crack of a gunshot shattered the silence—and the true battle began.

# CHAPTER FOUR

The desert devoured light and life alike, a vast graveyard where the sun scorched mercilessly and shadows twisted like silent predators. Ellie Calhoun rode through the treacherous landscape with Cullen "Crow" McKenna by her side, the suffocating heat pressing down on them as if the earth itself conspired to steal their breath. The trail south had grown harsher, the once-open plains giving way to jagged cliffs and narrow canyons that coiled through the rock like veins leading into the heart of something ancient and malevolent. Each mile was a cruel reminder of the stakes, every gust of wind whispering Mercy's name like a distant plea. Ellie's resolve hardened with every heartbeat, each moment spent imagining her daughter trapped in the hands of men who thrived on suffering.

By dusk, the sky was an unsettling canvas of crimson and violet, the horizon bruised with the weight of impending violence. The air was thick, heavy with the promise of blood, and Ellie knew they were close. The land itself seemed to hold its breath, the silence unnatural, as if warning them of the darkness ahead. Finally, they reached it—El Diablo.

The town was a hidden scar carved into the canyons, a place unmarked by any map and unclaimed by any law. Its narrow streets twisted like a serpent's spine, lined with crumbling buildings that bore the weight of too many sins. Outlaws lurked in every shadow, their eyes cold and hungry, hands never far from their weapons. El Diablo was a purgatory for the damned, where the only justice was delivered through bullets and betrayal.

They tethered their horses outside La Muerte Roja, a saloon darkened by years of smoke and sin, its warped walls echoing with the sound of drunken laughter and whispered threats. Ellie's pulse quickened as they stepped inside, the weight of countless stares settling on them like a shroud. The men inside were wolves—scarred, ruthless, and starved for blood.

At the center of the room sat El Lobo Negro, the infamous leader of Los Lobos. His scarred face was a map of violence, eyes black as midnight, and his hulking frame exuded a quiet, terrifying authority. Ellie's hand twitched near her revolver, but McKenna's low voice steadied her. "Not yet."

El Lobo's gaze settled on them with predatory amusement. "El cuervo," he greeted McKenna, his smile a dangerous thing. "I thought you were dead."

"Not for lack of trying," McKenna replied, his tone dark. Ellie stepped forward, cutting through the tension with the sharp edge of her determination. "We're looking for a girl. Fifteen. The Red Hand took her."

The room's atmosphere shifted, the mention of the Red Hand drawing low murmurs. El Lobo's expression hardened. "You're too late," he said, the words landing like a punch. Ellie's heart froze. "What do you mean?"

"They sold her. To the Colonel. Three days ago." Ellie's blood turned to ice as McKenna's face darkened. The Colonel. A name spoken only in hushed warnings. "Where?" Ellie demanded, shattering a bottle and pressing the jagged glass to El Lobo's throat. The room tensed, but El Lobo only smirked. "Hacienda de las Sombras," he whispered.

McKenna's voice was grim. "It's not just a house. It's a fortress." Ellie's eyes burned with rage. "Then we'll tear it down brick by brick." And with that, they left El Diablo behind, the devil's laughter echoing in their wake.

# CHAPTER FIVE

The desert wind keened through the night, an unholy wail that carried the promise of bloodshed across the barren expanse. Ellie Calhoun rode hard through the darkness, every muscle taut with desperation as Brimstone's hooves pounded the cracked earth beneath them. Beside her, Cullen "Crow" McKenna moved like a shadow, his eyes sharp beneath the brim of his hat, the weight of past sins etched into every line of his face. The Hacienda de las Sombras waited ahead, a fortress carved from nightmares, and within its walls, Mercy waited—if she was still alive. Ellie's grip on the reins tightened until her knuckles turned white. She would burn the world to ash before she let them keep her daughter.

The night stretched long, the stars cruel and distant, shards of cold light above an unforgiving land. Each mile they covered felt heavier, each breath a struggle against the weight of time slipping through their fingers. The badlands whispered of hidden dangers, and Ellie felt their presence, unseen eyes watching from the shadows. She kept her gaze forward, the fire in her chest burning brighter than the fear coiling in her gut.

Suddenly, the stillness shattered. Hoofbeats thundered

behind them, and Ellie's instincts screamed in warning. She turned just as a bullet whizzed past her, the crack of gunfire echoing through the canyon. McKenna cursed, drawing his revolver in one swift motion. Five riders emerged from the darkness, faces painted in crimson—the Red Hand. Ellie's heart pounded as she spun Brimstone around, her rifle steady despite the chaos. Shots rang out, sparks igniting the night as Ellie and McKenna fought back. Blood sprayed into the dust as Ellie's bullet found its mark, a Red Hand rider tumbling lifelessly from his horse. McKenna moved with deadly precision, each shot claiming another life. But the Red Hand wasn't done. An outlaw lunged at Ellie, knife gleaming in the moonlight. She fired, the shot tearing through his throat as his body hit the ground with a dull thud.

By dawn, the fight was over, the bodies left behind as silent warnings. Ellie's hands still trembled as they made camp, the fire casting flickering shadows on their worn faces. McKenna's voice was low, haunted. "The Colonel turns girls into weapons. Spies. Killers." Ellie's blood ran cold, her rage a living thing inside her. Mercy wouldn't be one of them. She couldn't be. Ellie's eyes hardened as she whispered into the fire, "Then we kill them all."

With dawn's first light, they rode south once more, into the mouth of hell, ready to carve a path through blood and fire to bring Mercy home—or die trying.

# CHAPTER SIX

The desert stretched endlessly, a scorched graveyard where the sun baked the bones of forgotten men and whispered their sins to the wind. Dawn bled across the horizon, a slow, crimson seep staining the jagged cliffs and barren earth. Ellie Calhoun rode with grim determination, her eyes locked ahead, each mile a silent vow to tear apart the world for Mercy. Beside her, Cullen "Crow" McKenna moved with a deadly calm, the weight of past deeds and unspoken truths hanging between them like the loaded revolvers at their hips. The Hacienda de las Sombras lay ahead, a fortress of nightmares where innocence was bartered for blood, and within its walls, Mercy awaited rescue—or ruin.

The journey south was brutal, the desert an unforgiving beast with fangs of jagged rock and claws of scorching heat. Dust clung to their skin, sweat streaking through grime as the sun clawed its way into the sky. Ellie's mind churned with fury and dread, every second Mercy remained in that hell tightening the knot in her chest. McKenna's silence gnawed at her, but there was no time for questions. Not yet.

By midday, they reached the crumbling ruins of an old

Jesuit mission, its walls battered by time and war. McKenna dismounted first, his boots stirring the dust as he scanned the shadows. "We need bullets," he muttered, leading Ellie inside. The scent of decay lingered, mingling with gun oil and something older, darker. In the dim light, an old man emerged —Joaquín, an Apache warrior turned arms dealer, his scarred face a map of battles lost and won. Ellie tensed, but McKenna's curt nod eased her hand away from her gun.

"You should be dead," Joaquín rasped, his eyes cold. "So should you," McKenna replied, unsmiling. Ellie's voice cut through the tension. "We need weapons." Joaquín's sharp gaze lingered on her before pulling up a hidden stash—rifles, ammunition, death waiting to be dealt. As they loaded up, Joaquín's words sliced through the air like a blade. "Does she know?" Ellie's heart stopped. "Know what?" McKenna's silence was deafening. "Mercy is his," Joaquín said bluntly.

Ellie's fury exploded. She shoved McKenna hard against the wall, her voice a raw snarl. "You knew?" He swallowed hard. "Not until now." The betrayal burned hotter than the desert sun, but Ellie's resolve was unshaken. "We ride," she ordered, grabbing her rifle. Joaquín chuckled darkly. "This is blood you're spilling." Ellie's eyes burned. "Then we bleed together." As the sun set behind them, they rode into the jaws of death, vengeance their only guide, and Mercy their only hope.

# CHAPTER SEVEN

The wind clawed through the desert, a sinister whisper weaving through canyons, carrying the scent of sweat, gunpowder, and impending death. Against the backdrop of a crimson sky, the Hacienda de las Sombras loomed like a scar carved into the earth, its high stone walls stained by centuries of cruelty. It was a place where hope died screaming, where innocence was devoured whole, and within its walls, Mercy waited—if she still lived.

Ellie Calhoun's heart hammered as she reined in her horse behind the jagged cliffs that hid the hacienda from the outside world. Her hands trembled, but not from fear—from the rage simmering beneath her skin. Her blonde hair was tangled with dust, her face a mask of grit and determination. She had been told that beauty was wasted on the West, but Ellie had never cared for vanity. Her beauty had hardened into something dangerous, something lethal. Tonight, the men who had taken her daughter would learn what that meant.

Beside her, Cullen McKenna's dark eyes flicked to the fortress. His face, weathered by time and violence, was unreadable, but Ellie knew him too well. There was a storm brewing behind that smirk, a deadly calm that always preceded bloodshed. The revelation of Mercy's paternity still hung heavy between them, but Ellie pushed it aside. Revenge first. Answers later.

They tethered their horses under the cliffs, moving like shadows toward the thick stone walls. McKenna's blade sliced through the iron lock on the side gate with practiced ease. Inside, the hacienda pulsed with life—drunken laughter, distant footsteps, and the metallic clink of weapons being cleaned. Ellie inhaled deeply, the scent of decay, sweat, and despair filling her lungs. Her fingers curled around her rifle.

"We do this fast," she whispered.

McKenna's lips twisted into a grim smile. "Fast is my specialty."

The first guard never heard them. McKenna's knife slid into his throat, a gurgling breath the only sound he made as he crumpled. Ellie's rifle silenced the second guard with a shot between the eyes. Blood sprayed the wall, but there was no time to recoil. More men would come.

Gunfire erupted. The courtyard became a battleground of smoke and shadows, Ellie and McKenna weaving through the chaos, their bullets finding targets with brutal precision. Ellie's pulse roared in her ears, every shot a promise. She caught a glimpse of the Colonel at the top of the stairs, his cruel smile unwavering. Beside him, Mercy's small frame trembled, a bruise darkening her cheek.

Ellie's vision blurred with rage. She raised her rifle, but the Colonel's pistol fired first. Pain seared through her side as McKenna tackled her to the ground.

"You don't get to die," he growled.

Ellie gritted her teeth. "Mercy—"

McKenna's eyes burned. "We'll get her."

Through the haze of pain, Ellie aimed once more.

And the night exploded with vengeance.

# CHAPTER EIGHT

The wind gnawed at the bones of the desert, howling through the canyons like the wail of lost souls. The sky bled crimson, casting jagged shadows over the Hacienda de las Sombras, a fortress carved from the earth's darkest nightmares. Each stone whispered of unspeakable horrors, of lives stolen and innocence crushed beneath boot heels. Tonight, blood would answer blood.

Ellie Calhoun crouched behind a craggy outcrop, her breathing shallow, her pulse a war drum in her chest. The revelation that Mercy was McKenna's daughter still clawed at her mind, but fury smothered everything else. Her blue eyes, sharp as a whetted blade, locked onto the fortress where her daughter was held captive. Dust clung to her sweat-slicked skin, her hands steady on her rifle despite the rage simmering beneath her calm exterior.

Cullen McKenna knelt beside her, his dark eyes scanning the walls. Time had etched hard lines into his face, but it was his past that made him dangerous. The infamous bounty hunter had spilled enough blood to drown his conscience, and tonight, his sins would fuel his vengeance. His voice was a rough whisper. "We go in quiet. Kill quick."

Ellie's lips curled into a feral grin. "Then let's make them bleed."

They moved like phantoms, slipping through the shadows to the side gate. McKenna's knife sliced through the lock with a quiet rasp, and they crept inside. The air was thick with the coppery tang of blood and the acrid bite of stale sweat. Ellie's stomach churned, but her resolve never wavered.

The first guard died without a sound, McKenna's blade buried deep in his throat. Ellie's rifle spat death, dropping another man before he could raise an alarm. The courtyard erupted into chaos as gunfire echoed against stone walls, sparks flying as bullets ricocheted. Ellie's pulse pounded, each shot a promise of vengeance. She moved with deadly grace, her rifle kicking hard against her shoulder as bodies fell around her.

At the top of the grand staircase, the Colonel watched with cold amusement. His white suit was pristine despite the carnage, his scarred face twisted into a cruel smile. Beside him, Mercy stood bound, wide eyes filled with terror. Ellie's breath caught. Her vision blurred with fury, but before she could fire, the Colonel pressed his pistol to Mercy's temple.

"Cuervo," he sneered, his gaze locking onto McKenna. "You always were a fool."

McKenna stepped into the open, guns drawn. "Let her go."

The Colonel's laugh was a blade to Ellie's heart. "You don't give orders here

# CHAPTER NINE

The desert stretched endlessly beneath the weight of an unforgiving sky, its vast, barren expanse whispering stories of blood and bone, of men who had dared to conquer it only to be swallowed whole. This was land that remembered every scream, every drop of blood spilled by Apache warriors, Spanish conquistadors, and Confederate deserters alike. And now, it claimed Ellie Calhoun's blood too, soaking it into the dust as if welcoming another lost soul to its cruel embrace. Ellie drifted between darkness and painful clarity, each shallow breath sending a searing bolt of agony through the wound in her side. The steady rhythm of hoofbeats echoed in her ears, blending with distant memories —the sharp crack of gunfire, Mercy's frightened cries, the Colonel's twisted grin. Yet through the haze, one sound tethered her to the present: McKenna's low, gravel-rough voice murmuring close to her ear, urging her to hold on, to stay with him just a little longer. And then there was only the night, vast and merciless, stretching on forever.

Ellie's eyes fluttered open to a sky littered with stars, their brilliance sharp against the velvet darkness. The cool desert breeze kissed her sweat-dampened skin, but it couldn't dull the fire that burned in her side. The jagged cliffs of the Llano Estacado loomed in the distance, their shadowy forms like silent sentinels guarding the edge of the world. This was no-man's land in 1885, a place feared by outlaws and lawmen alike, where survival was a coin tossed to fate. She realized she was draped across McKenna's saddle, her body leaning heavily against him. His arm wrapped around her waist, steadying her, his grip both protective and unyielding. She tried to shift, but his hold tightened, warning her not to move, not to tear the wound open again. Her cracked whisper demanded one thing—Mercy. McKenna's gentler-than-expected reply assured her their daughter was safe, asleep in the wagon, but the memory of blood-soaked walls and the Colonel's malevolent grin gnawed at her.

As they rode through the night, Ellie's mind drifted back to the Calhoun Ranch—the place she had fought for with sweat, blood, and sheer will. The wide plains of Kansas Territory had been her sanctuary, carved from the wilds near the Yellowstone River. She had endured droughts, raids, and the endless whispers that a woman couldn't hold land alone. But she had. Until now. All that remained was ash, scattered by the merciless wind. Her raw, bitter voice broke the stillness, confessing that nothing was left for her. McKenna's silence spoke volumes, the weight of unspoken regrets thick between them. Ellie's sharp gaze locked onto his face, searching for answers she already feared. Her accusation sliced through the quiet—he knew Mercy was his. McKenna's low, regret-tinged response admitted as much, knowing for sure when he saw their daughter's eyes. Fifteen years of raising Mercy alone, weaving tales of a dead father, were now undone by this truth.

McKenna insisted Mercy deserved to know, but Ellie, barely audible, insisted not yet. But the day would come.

The night grew darker, the desert stretching endlessly before them, when McKenna's body tensed. Ellie followed his gaze, her blood turning to ice as five riders, silhouetted against the moonlit horizon, galloped fast. His low growl confirmed what her gut already knew—they had company. Her fingers curled around her revolver, the cold steel a familiar comfort. McKenna's hand brushed hers, a fleeting touch heavy with unspoken words. 'Stay alive, darlin',' he whispered, and then, gunfire shattered the night.

# CHAPTER TEN

The desert stretched endlessly beneath the weight of an unforgiving sky, its vast, barren expanse whispering stories of blood and bone, of men who had dared to conquer it only to be swallowed whole. This was land that remembered every scream, every drop of blood spilled by Apache warriors, Spanish conquistadors, and Confederate deserters alike. And now, it claimed Ellie Calhoun's blood too, soaking it into the dust as if welcoming another lost soul to its cruel embrace. Ellie drifted between darkness and painful clarity, each shallow breath sending a searing bolt of agony through the wound in her side. The steady rhythm of hoofbeats echoed in her ears, blending with distant memories —the sharp crack of gunfire, Mercy's frightened cries, the Colonel's twisted grin. Yet through the haze, one sound tethered her to the present: McKenna's low, gravel-rough voice murmuring close to her ear, urging her to hold on, to stay with him just a little longer. And then there was only the night, vast and merciless, stretching on forever.

Ellie's eyes fluttered open to a sky littered with stars, their brilliance sharp against the velvet darkness. The cool desert breeze kissed her sweat-dampened skin, but it couldn't dull the fire that burned in her side. The jagged cliffs of the Llano Estacado loomed in the distance, their shadowy forms like silent sentinels guarding the edge of the world. This was no-man's land in 1885, a place feared by outlaws and lawmen alike, where survival was a coin tossed to fate. She realized she was draped across McKenna's saddle, her body leaning heavily against him. His arm wrapped around her waist, steadying her, his grip both protective and unyielding. She tried to shift, but his hold tightened, warning her not to move, not to tear the wound open again. Her cracked whisper demanded one thing—Mercy. McKenna's gentler-than-expected reply assured her their daughter was safe, asleep in the wagon, but the memory of blood-soaked walls and the Colonel's malevolent grin gnawed at her.

The desert pulsed with a sinister quiet as they rode through the endless night, the weight of blood spilled and secrets kept pressing down like an iron yoke. Ellie's mind, clouded with pain and fatigue, kept drifting back to the Calhoun Ranch—the place she had fought for with sweat, blood, and sheer will. The wide plains of Kansas Territory had been her sanctuary, carved from the wilds near the Yellowstone River. She had endured droughts, raids, and the endless whispers that a woman couldn't hold land alone. But she had. Until now. The embers of her memories flickered painfully—the creak of the barn doors in the early dawn, Mercy's laughter echoing across the open fields, the warmth of the hearth on bitter nights. All that remained now was ash, scattered by the merciless wind. Her raw, bitter voice broke the stillness, confessing that nothing was left for her but vengeance and survival. McKenna's silence spoke volumes, the weight of unspoken regrets thick between them. Ellie's sharp gaze locked onto his face, searching for answers she already feared. Her accusation sliced through the quiet—he knew Mercy was his. McKenna's low, regret-tinged response admitted as much, knowing for sure when he saw their daughter's eyes. Fifteen years of raising Mercy alone, weaving tales of a dead father, were now undone by this truth. McKenna insisted Mercy deserved to know, but Ellie, barely audible, insisted not yet. But the day would come.

The night grew darker, the desert stretching endlessly before them, when McKenna's body tensed. Ellie followed his gaze, her blood turning to ice as five riders, silhouetted against the moonlit horizon, galloped fast. His low growl confirmed what her gut already knew—they had company. The air grew taut with impending violence, the scent of gunpowder already lingering like a promise. Her fingers curled around her revolver, the cold steel a familiar comfort. McKenna's hand brushed hers, a fleeting touch heavy with unspoken words. 'Stay alive, darlin',' he whispered, and then, gunfire shattered the night, the desert exploding into chaos as the wolves of the desert closed in for the kill.

# CHAPTER ELEVEN

The night was a suffocating void, thick with silence, broken only by the distant howl of a lone coyote and the whisper of wind through the canyons. The Llano Estacado stretched before them, an endless expanse of desolation that swallowed even the faintest glimmers of hope. Ellie Calhoun's heart pounded against her ribs, every throb a painful reminder of the wound that still seeped crimson into the rough fabric of her shirt. Pain anchored her to the moment, sharpening her senses as she crouched beside the dying embers of their fire. The desert felt alive, its ancient bones shifting beneath her boots, its unseen eyes watching from every shadow. Her hands trembled not from fear, but from the weight of her failure—Mercy was gone, stolen from her again by hands she had not seen, by men she had not yet killed. She could still hear her daughter's scream, a haunting echo that carved itself into her mind, relentless and unforgiving.

McKenna sat across from her, his sharp gaze hidden beneath the brim of his hat. His face, hardened by years of violence and regret, was unreadable, but the tension in his shoulders betrayed him. Blood stained his duster, his skin pale beneath the dirt and sweat, and yet he seemed unbreakable, a man forged in the crucible of this unforgiving land. His voice, low and gravelly, broke the silence, a simple observation wrapped in concern. Ellie barely acknowledged him. She knew what he was thinking—that they were too broken, too wounded to chase ghosts in the dark. But Ellie didn't care. Pain was fleeting. Mercy's absence was a blade twisting in her chest, far sharper than any knife. She forced herself to breathe, to push through the ache in her ribs, her fingers tightening around the rifle that never left her side.

The darkness pressed close, the quiet too perfect, too still. McKenna's gaze flicked to her, a silent question in his eyes. How many? Who were they? She shook her head, her jaw clenched tight. It didn't matter. All that mattered was the hunt. She wouldn't let them vanish into the desert like ghosts. Not with her daughter. McKenna shifted, wincing as he adjusted the bandage on his arm. His voice, barely a whisper, warned of the dangers ahead, of the madness of tracking in the dark. Ellie's response was cold, unyielding—they would ride at dawn. No argument. No hesitation. And McKenna, despite the storm in his eyes, nodded.

The hours dragged like an eternity, the weight of exhaustion pulling at their bodies, but Ellie's mind was a battlefield of memories and rage. She saw Mercy's face in every flicker of the fire, heard her laughter in every gust of wind, felt her tiny hands in every heartbeat. She would burn the world to bring her back. Dawn crept over the horizon, bleeding soft hues of gold and crimson across the barren landscape. Ellie was already on her feet, her rifle loaded, her eyes hard. McKenna joined her, his revolver spinning once in his hand before settling into its holster. He gave her a small, sardonic smile, the kind only he could manage in the face of death. Ellie's voice, a whisper laced with venom, promised fire and blood. And with that, they rode into the maw of darkness, two shadows chasing the devil himself, ready to kill and bleed until there was nothing left but dust and vengeance.

# CHAPTER TWELVE

The first light of dawn clawed its way over the horizon, casting a blood-red glow across the unforgiving expanse of the Llano Estacado. The vast plateau stretched endlessly before Ellie Calhoun and Cullen McKenna, its cracked earth whispering tales of death and betrayal with every gust of wind. The weight of exhaustion clung to them, their bodies bruised and battered from battles fought and lost, but their resolve was unbroken. Ellie's ribs ached with each breath, the wound beneath her torn shirt still weeping, but the pain was nothing compared to the void Mercy's absence left in her chest. She gripped the reins tightly, her knuckles white, her mind fixed on one singular thought: finding her daughter.

McKenna rode beside her, his icy gaze scanning the horizon with a predator's intensity. Blood stained his black duster, his hat casting a shadow over the sharp lines of his face. The desert stretched out around them, a sea of dust and desolation that swallowed men whole, but neither of them hesitated. The faintest trail, a broken branch, a displaced rock, guided them south, deeper into cartel territory. Ellie's fingers tightened around the rifle strapped to her back, each jolt of her horse reopening the wound along her ribs, but she pushed the pain aside. Mercy was close, and that was all that mattered.

The sun climbed higher, scorching the land beneath them, until a torn piece of blue fabric caught Ellie's eye, fluttering from the thorns of a mesquite bush. She tore it free, her breath catching in her throat—it was Mercy's dress. McKenna's expression hardened, his jaw tight, as they spurred their horses forward. The trail led them to a shallow river, the muddy banks betraying fresh hoofprints heading south. Ellie's heart pounded as realization settled like lead in her stomach—they were taking Mercy to the border.

As the sun began to set, painting the sky in shades of fire, the scent of death reached them first. Three bodies hung from the low branches of a mesquite tree, their faces blackened, their hands severed. Ellie's stomach churned at the sight of the Red Hand's mark burned into their chests. McKenna, grim-faced, muttered that they were close. Too close. Without another word, they rode on, pushing through the rising exhaustion and the growing darkness.

The sun dipped below the horizon, casting long shadows, but Ellie's focus never wavered. Mercy's face haunted her every thought, her scream echoing in the silence. And as the night swallowed them whole, Ellie Calhoun rode into the darkness with vengeance burning in her veins, knowing that when she found them, there would be no mercy left to give.

# CHAPTER THIRTEEN

The sun hovered low in the sky, a molten orb sinking into the horizon, casting the Llano Estacado in an eerie glow. The shadows stretched long and lean, bleeding into the rolling hills that marked the shift from barren desert to the wilder, untamed frontier. The land had tested them, pushed them to the edge of exhaustion, but neither Ellie nor McKenna had the luxury of surrender. Every aching movement, every labored breath, was driven by a single truth—Mercy was still out there, and they would find her, no matter the cost.

The terrain had changed, the parched, cracked earth giving way to thickening vegetation. The scent of pine and juniper filled the air, mingling with the ever-present dust, a sign that they were leaving the worst of the desert behind. But the presence of more trees and uneven ground meant more places for enemies to hide, more corners for death to lurk in the dark.

Ellie shifted in the saddle, her body protesting every motion. The wound along her ribs burned, the hastily tied bandages beneath her shirt sticking to her skin with dried blood. The constant pain had become background noise, something she had learned to push past, but exhaustion clawed at her bones, wearing her down with each passing mile. She didn't dare acknowledge it, not with McKenna watching, not with Mercy's life hanging in the balance. Weakness was a luxury she could not afford.

McKenna rode slightly ahead, his frame stiff in the saddle, his movements fluid but tense. The long black coat that once gave him the air of an outlaw legend now clung to his frame, stiff with dried blood and dust. The man had always carried an air of danger about him, but now it was something different—something coiled, something ready to strike. His revolver rested easy in his grip, fingers ghosting over the trigger as his sharp gaze swept the landscape.

It was just as they crested a ridge that McKenna reined in his horse, slowing to a halt. Ellie followed his lead, scanning the land ahead. Then she saw it—a small, flickering glow in the distance, barely visible through the sparse trees.

A camp.

McKenna exhaled slowly, rolling his shoulders like a man preparing for a fight he already knew was coming. "That's them."

Ellie's grip on her rifle tightened, a fresh wave of adrenaline burning through her veins, chasing away the dull ache of exhaustion. "Then let's end this."

They dismounted in silence, leading their horses behind a cluster of rocks before creeping forward, keeping low. The camp sat in a clearing, nestled at the base of a rocky incline. A handful of men moved around the fire, their figures outlined against the flames. There were four, maybe five, but

Ellie knew better than to assume they were alone. More could be hidden in the brush, watching, waiting.

She crouched beside McKenna, her voice barely above a whisper. "We need to do this clean. We take out the sentries first, then move in before they know what hit 'em."

McKenna nodded, but his gaze remained fixed on something beyond the fire. Ellie followed his line of sight—to a figure bound and slumped against a tree.

Her heart slammed against her ribs.

Mercy.

Her daughter was there, alive, but barely. Her small frame was wrapped in tattered clothing, her hair matted, her face turned slightly to the side, hidden by the flickering shadows. Even from this distance, Ellie could see the bruises marring her skin, the slight rise and fall of her chest, the way her fingers twitched as though she were fighting to stay conscious.

Ellie forced herself to breathe, to push past the rage clawing at her throat. She wanted to storm into that camp, to put a bullet in every last one of those bastards, but she knew that would only get Mercy killed.

McKenna shifted beside her, reaching for his rifle. "I take the one by the horses. You handle the two by the fire."

Ellie nodded, already lining up her shot.

The night swallowed the crack of the first gunshot.

The sentry by the horses dropped where he stood, his body crumpling into the dirt without a sound. Ellie fired next, her bullet finding its mark in the skull of the man closest to the fire. Before the others could react, McKenna was already moving, his revolver spitting fire as he cut them down with brutal efficiency.

Ellie surged forward, her boots kicking up dirt as she sprinted for Mercy. The last man standing let out a panicked shout, scrambling for his rifle, but Ellie was faster. She slammed the butt of her gun into his jaw, sending him sprawling onto his back. He reached for his knife, but she stepped on his wrist, grinding his hand into the dirt with her boot.

"Where's the rest of them?" she snarled.

The man coughed, blood dribbling from his split lip. "You think this ends here?" he rasped. "You think you can stop it?"

Ellie didn't hesitate.

She pulled the trigger.

The gunshot echoed into the night, swallowed quickly by the silence that followed.

She turned, dropping to her knees beside Mercy. Her hands trembled as she untied the ropes binding her daughter's wrists, brushing blood-matted hair away from her face. "Mercy," she whispered, voice breaking. "It's me, baby. Mama's here."

Mercy stirred, her eyelids fluttering. She let out a weak sound, her lips parting, but her voice was too hoarse to speak. Ellie gathered her into her arms, pressing a kiss to her dirt-streaked forehead, rocking her slightly.

McKenna stood guard, his revolver still gripped tight, scanning the trees, waiting. But there was no movement. No more gunfire. Just the three of them in the stillness of the night.

Ellie exhaled sharply, pressing her forehead to Mercy's, eyes burning with unshed tears. "I got you, baby. I got you."

Mercy whimpered, curling weak fingers around Ellie's shirt, clinging to her as though she were the only solid thing in a world gone to hell.

McKenna finally turned to face them, his expression unreadable. But there was something in his eyes—something raw and unspoken.

Ellie met his gaze, holding Mercy tight against her chest.

"We're not done," she said.

McKenna nodded. "No. We ain't."

The night pressed in around them, the darkness full of unseen dangers. But for the first time since this nightmare began, Ellie felt something else.

Hope.

And she would kill anyone who tried to take it from her again.

# CHAPTER FOURTEEN

The Llano Estacado stretched endlessly under the relentless sun, its vastness a testament to nature's indifference. The horizon wavered in the heat, creating illusions of water where there was none. The land, with its sparse vegetation and rolling plains, was both a sanctuary and a snare. Here, survival was a daily battle, and only the resilient endured. Ellie and McKenna pressed on, their horses moving with a determined gait, the weight of their mission pressing heavily upon them. They had seen the distant glow of a campfire the night before, a beacon in the darkness, but the terrain had forced them to hold back. The enemy was near, and they could not afford to rush blindly into a trap. The only option was to wait, watch, and strike when the moment was right.

The temperature began to drop as the sun dipped below the horizon, casting long shadows that slithered across the plains. The once scorching heat gave way to a biting chill, a stark reminder of the desert's dual nature. They found shelter in a small outcropping of mesquite trees, their twisted branches offering a semblance of cover as they prepared for what lay ahead. McKenna slid from his saddle first, his movements slow and deliberate, his body still bearing the weight of his wounds. Ellie followed suit, suppressing a wince as the dull ache in her side flared anew. They were battered, bloodied, and running on nothing but grit, but they had come too far to break now.

The night was eerily quiet, the usual sounds of nocturnal creatures conspicuously absent. Ellie, her instincts honed by years on the frontier, felt a prickle of unease. Something was off. She exchanged a glance with McKenna, whose sharp gaze was already scanning the darkness beyond the firelight. They both knew that silence on the plains often meant one of two things—predators, or men worse than them. Her hand drifted toward the hilt of her knife, McKenna's toward his revolver, their bodies tense and waiting. Then, a low, guttural growl rose from the blackness, followed by the sound of shifting movement. A second later, a blood-curdling howl split the night, sending a chill racing down Ellie's spine.

From the shadows emerged a pack of wolves, their eyes gleaming with hunger. These were not the wary scavengers that trailed the fringes of civilization—these were gaunt, desperate beasts, driven by starvation and the cruel law of the wild. The leader of the pack, a massive brute with matted fur and a scarred muzzle, stepped forward, baring its teeth. The other wolves followed suit, their low growls harmonizing into a sound that sent dread curling through Ellie's gut. For a moment, there was nothing but the wind, the fire, and the silent challenge hanging between predator and prey. Then, without warning, the alpha lunged.

McKenna moved first, sidestepping with practiced ease

as he fired, the gunshot shattering the night. The bullet struck true, and the beast crumpled, its final snarl cut short by death's embrace. But the shot did little to deter the rest of the pack. Hunger overrode fear. The wolves attacked en masse, a blur of fur and fangs. Ellie barely had time to react before one of them leapt at her, its jaws snapping inches from her face. She twisted, driving her knife deep into its flank, feeling the sickening give of flesh beneath her blade. The wolf howled, clawing wildly, but she yanked the knife free and struck again, silencing it for good. Another lunged from her left, catching her off guard. She felt the sharp agony of teeth sinking into her arm, a burst of white-hot pain radiating up to her shoulder. Gritting her teeth, she slammed the wolf's skull with the butt of her pistol, then plunged her blade into its eye. The creature twitched once, then fell still.

McKenna fought like a man who had danced with death one too many times. His revolver barked fire, cutting down anything that came too close. When the bullets ran dry, he fought with his fists, with whatever he could grab—boots, stones, even his own damn belt. Blood slicked his knuckles, his breath coming in ragged gasps as he drove the surviving wolves back. But the pack wasn't giving up easily. One of them feinted, drawing his attention just long enough for another to lunge from behind. McKenna turned too late, and the weight of the wolf slammed into him, driving him to the ground. Ellie saw the beast's jaws snapping at his throat, saw McKenna straining against the inevitable, but before the creature could land a killing blow, Ellie raised her pistol and fired. The wolf's body convulsed, then slumped lifelessly across McKenna's chest.

For several heartbeats, all was still. Then, as if finally

realizing the battle was lost, the remaining wolves slunk back into the darkness, their glowing eyes watching before disappearing into the night. Ellie stood there, breathing hard, the metallic taste of adrenaline thick on her tongue. The fire flickered, its glow painting the aftermath in shades of red and gold. The bodies of the fallen wolves lay scattered, the scent of blood thick in the air. She swayed slightly, exhaustion pressing in from all sides. That was too damn close.

McKenna groaned, pushing the dead weight of the wolf off him. His chest heaved, his arms shaking from exertion. He glanced at Ellie, his expression unreadable. Then his gaze dropped to her arm, where blood seeped from fresh wounds. "Let me see," he murmured, his voice rough with exhaustion. Ellie hesitated but relented, letting him take her arm. His fingers were surprisingly gentle as he tore a strip from his already-ruined shirt and began binding the wound. The pain was sharp, but bearable. She had survived worse. As he worked, she found herself studying him—the lines of his face, the bruises and cuts that painted his skin, the flicker of something in his eyes that she couldn't quite name. They had been through hell together. And they weren't done yet.

"Thank you," she whispered, the words slipping free before she could stop them. McKenna paused, his fingers stilling for just a fraction of a second. Then, slowly, he reached out, brushing a strand of hair from her face. The touch was fleeting, almost hesitant, but it sent something twisting in her chest. "We'll get through this, Ellie," he said quietly. "Together."

The words settled between them, heavy with unspoken promises. She wasn't sure what they meant—not yet—but for the first time in a long time, she didn't feel like she was carrying the weight of the world alone. As dawn approached, they prepared to move on, their bodies aching, their weapons bloodied, their purpose unchanged. The Llano Estacado had tested them, but they had survived. And as long as Mercy was still out there, they would keep fighting. Because the real battle had yet to begin.

# CHAPTER FIFTEEN

The Llano Estacado stretched endlessly under the relentless sun, its vastness a testament to nature's indifference. The horizon wavered in the heat, creating illusions of water where there was none. The land, with its sparse vegetation and rolling plains, was both a sanctuary and a snare. Here, survival was a daily battle, and only the resilient endured.

Ellie and McKenna rode in silence, the weight of their mission pressing heavily upon them. Their horses, though weary, moved with a determined gait, sensing the urgency of their riders. The duo had faced numerous challenges, but the Llano Estacado presented a unique blend of natural perils and unseen threats.

As the sun dipped below the horizon, casting long shadows that danced across the plains, the temperature began to drop. The once scorching heat gave way to a biting chill, a stark reminder of the desert's dual nature. They decided to make camp near a cluster of mesquite trees, whose twisted branches offered a semblance of shelter.

The night was eerily quiet, the usual sounds of nocturnal creatures conspicuously absent. Ellie, her instincts honed by years on the frontier, felt a prickle of unease.

"Something's not right," she murmured, her hand instinctively resting on the hilt of her knife.

McKenna nodded, his eyes scanning the darkness. "Stay alert."

Suddenly, a blood-curdling howl pierced the silence, followed by another, and then a chorus. From the shadows emerged a pack of wolves, their eyes glowing with a predatory gleam. These were not the timid creatures that shied away from humans; these wolves were gaunt, desperate, and driven by hunger.

The leader of the pack, a massive beast with matted fur and a scarred muzzle, stepped forward, baring its teeth. The standoff was tense, the air thick with the scent of impending violence.

Without warning, the alpha lunged at McKenna, aiming for his throat. McKenna sidestepped, drawing his revolver and firing a shot that echoed across the plains. The bullet found its mark, and the wolf collapsed, whimpering before falling silent.

The pack hesitated, but hunger overrode caution. They attacked en masse, a flurry of fur and fangs.

Ellie fought with a ferocity born of desperation. Her knife flashed in the dim light, slashing at any wolf that came too close. One managed to clamp its jaws around her arm, its teeth sinking deep. She screamed in pain but drove her blade into its eye, feeling the shudder as it died.

McKenna, wielding a makeshift torch, swung at the

remaining wolves, the flames deterring them. After what felt like an eternity, the surviving wolves retreated into the darkness, leaving behind their fallen comrades.

Breathing heavily, Ellie inspected her wound. Blood oozed from the punctures, and the pain was intense, but she was alive.

"Let me see," McKenna said, his voice laced with concern.

He tore a strip from his shirt, binding her arm tightly to stem the bleeding. Their eyes met, and in that moment, the walls they'd built around themselves began to crumble.

"Thank you," she whispered, her voice trembling.

McKenna brushed a strand of hair from her face, his touch gentle. "We'll get through this, Ellie. Together."

As dawn approached, they tended to their wounds and prepared to move on, the bond between them strengthened by the night's ordeal. The Llano Estacado had tested them, but they remained unbroken, driven by a shared purpose and a rekindled connection.

# CHAPTER SIXTEEN

The sun hung low in the sky, casting elongated shadows over the rugged terrain as Ellie and McKenna pressed onward. Their journey had been fraught with peril, but the bond between them had only grown stronger amidst the adversity. The landscape before them was a testament to the untamed beauty of the American frontier—a land of opportunity and danger in equal measure.

As they navigated a narrow pass, the distant sound of rushing water reached their ears. Eager for a moment's respite, they followed the sound to a secluded creek, its crystal-clear waters offering a brief sanctuary. The serenity of the scene was a stark contrast to the violence that had marked their path.

While McKenna tended to the horses, Ellie knelt by the water's edge, her reflection wavering in the gentle current. The scars of their journey were evident—not just the physical wounds, but the emotional toll as well. Her thoughts drifted to the past, to a time when life was simpler, and the world seemed less cruel.

Their moment of peace was shattered by the

unmistakable sound of a rifle being cocked. Ellie's hand instinctively went to her sidearm, but before she could draw, a voice rang out.

"Hold it right there."

Emerging from the treeline were a group of men, their appearances as rugged as the landscape. At their forefront stood a man with a weathered face and cold, calculating eyes.

"Looks like we've got ourselves some trespassers," he sneered.

McKenna stepped forward, his hands raised in a placating gesture. "We mean no harm. Just passing through."

The leader's gaze shifted to Ellie, a predatory glint in his eyes. "Passing through, huh? This here is our territory. And there's a toll for crossing it."

The tension was palpable, the air thick with the threat of violence. Ellie and McKenna exchanged a glance, a silent understanding passing between them.

Without warning, Ellie drew her revolver, the movement swift and precise. A shot rang out, and one of the men fell, clutching his chest. Chaos erupted as McKenna lunged at another assailant, the two men grappling in the dirt.

The skirmish was brutal, a flurry of fists, gunfire, and raw survival instinct. Ellie moved with lethal grace, each shot finding its mark. McKenna fought with a ferocity born of desperation, his blows landing with bone-crushing force.

As the dust settled, the would-be ambushers lay defeated, their lifeless bodies a grim testament to the encounter. Ellie and McKenna stood amidst the carnage, their breaths ragged, the adrenaline coursing through their veins.

Ellie wiped a streak of blood from her cheek, her eyes meeting McKenna's. "We can't keep doing this," she murmured.

He nodded, the weight of their journey evident in his gaze. "I know. But we don't have a choice."

The reality of their situation was stark. The frontier was a land of unrelenting brutality, where survival often meant confronting the darkness within themselves. As they gathered their belongings and prepared to move on, the unspoken question lingered between them: How much more could they endure before the wilderness consumed them entirely?

# CHAPTER
# SEVENTEEN

The morning sun cast a golden hue over the rugged landscape as Ellie and McKenna resumed their journey. The events of the previous day lingered in their minds—the confrontation with the outlaws had been brutal, a stark reminder of the perils that shadowed their path. Yet, amidst the violence, an unspoken bond between them had begun to rekindle, a connection forged in the crucible of shared adversity.

As they navigated the winding trails, the terrain grew increasingly treacherous. Jagged rocks jutted from the earth, and the dense underbrush whispered with unseen dangers. The air was thick with tension, each rustle of leaves or snap of a twig setting their nerves on edge.

Suddenly, the unmistakable scent of smoke wafted through the air. Ellie signaled for McKenna to halt, her eyes narrowing as she scanned the horizon.

"Do you see that?" she murmured, pointing toward a

thin plume of smoke rising in the distance.

McKenna nodded, his expression grim. "Could be a campfire. Or something else."

Cautiously, they approached the source of the smoke, their hands hovering near their weapons. As they crested a hill, the scene below unfolded before them—a small settlement, or what remained of it. Charred ruins smoldered, and the acrid smell of burnt wood and flesh hung heavy in the air.

Ellie's heart clenched at the sight. "What happened here?"

McKenna dismounted, surveying the devastation. "Looks like an attack. Recent, too."

As they ventured deeper into the ruins, the full extent of the carnage became evident. Bodies lay strewn about, some bearing the telltale signs of gunshot wounds, others mutilated beyond recognition. The brutality was staggering, a chilling testament to the savagery that lurked in the frontier's shadows.

Among the debris, Ellie noticed something—a crude arrow, its shaft embedded in a fallen beam. She knelt, examining it closely. "This isn't like any arrow I've seen before."

McKenna joined her, his brow furrowing. "It's possible a local tribe was involved. But this level of violence... it's unusual."

Ellie looked around, her mind racing. "We need to find out who did this. And why."

As they prepared to leave, a faint sound reached Ellie's ears—a soft, pitiful whimper. She followed the noise to a collapsed structure, where a small child lay trapped beneath the rubble, their face streaked with soot and tears.

"McKenna! Over here!"

Together, they worked to free the child, carefully lifting the debris. The child, a young girl no older than six, clung to Ellie, her body trembling with fear.

"It's okay," Ellie whispered, holding the girl close. "You're safe now."

McKenna's eyes softened as he watched Ellie comfort the child. "We should get her out of here. Find somewhere safe."

Ellie nodded, her resolve hardening. "And then we find out who did this. They need to be stopped."

As they rode away from the desolate settlement, the weight of their mission pressed heavily upon them. The frontier was a land of untamed beauty, but beneath its majestic facade lay a darkness that threatened to consume all in its path. Ellie and McKenna knew that their journey would only grow more perilous, but together, they were determined to face whatever horrors awaited them.

# CHAPTER EIGHTEEN

The sun hung low in the sky as Ellie, McKenna, and the young girl they had rescued approached the outskirts of Redemption, a frontier town nestled amidst the rugged terrain. The journey had been arduous, with the child—whom they learned was named Sarah—remaining mostly silent, her wide eyes reflecting the trauma she had endured.

As they entered the town, the trio drew curious glances from the townsfolk. Redemption was a modest settlement, its main street lined with a handful of establishments: a general store, a saloon, a blacksmith, and a modest church. The air was thick with the mingling scents of horse sweat, dust, and the faint aroma of freshly baked bread.

Ellie guided Sarah toward the general store, hoping to find provisions and perhaps some information. McKenna, ever vigilant, scanned the surroundings, his hand never straying far from the revolver at his hip.

Inside the store, the atmosphere was dim, the wooden floor creaking underfoot. An elderly man stood behind the counter, his spectacles perched precariously on the bridge of his nose.

"Afternoon," Ellie greeted, offering a polite nod.

The old man looked up, his gaze shifting from Ellie to Sarah, and then to McKenna. "Afternoon. What can I do for you folks?"

"We're in need of supplies," Ellie replied. "And perhaps some information."

The man's eyes narrowed slightly. "Information, eh? What kind?"

Ellie hesitated, choosing her words carefully. "We came across a settlement a day's ride from here. It was... attacked. Do you know anything about it?"

The old man's expression darkened. "Heard some folks talkin' about it. Said it was the Black Creek settlement. Good people there. Shame what happened."

"Do you know who was responsible?" McKenna interjected.

The old man sighed, removing his spectacles and rubbing the bridge of his nose. "Rumors mostly. Some say it was renegade Indians. Others think it was outlaws lookin' to stir up trouble."

Ellie exchanged a glance with McKenna. "We're looking for a place to rest for the night. Is there an inn nearby?"

The old man nodded. "The Silver Spur down the street. Decent place. Tell Martha I sent you."

"Thank you," Ellie said, offering a small smile.

As they left the store, the sun had dipped below the

horizon, casting long shadows across the town. The Silver Spur was a modest establishment, its exterior weathered but welcoming. Inside, the common room was sparsely populated, a few patrons nursing drinks and engaging in muted conversations.

Martha, a stout woman with graying hair and a warm demeanor, greeted them. "Evenin'. Lookin' for a room?"

"Yes, please," Ellie replied. "And perhaps a meal, if it's not too much trouble."

Martha's eyes softened as she noticed Sarah clinging to Ellie's side. "Of course. Poor thing looks famished. I'll have somethin' brought up to your room."

Once settled in their modest quarters, Ellie and McKenna sat by the window, the weight of the day's events pressing heavily upon them.

"Do you think it was really Indians who attacked Black Creek?" Ellie asked, her voice barely above a whisper.

McKenna shook his head. "I don't know. But something doesn't sit right with me. The brutality... it seemed excessive, even for a raid."

Ellie nodded, her thoughts drifting. "We need to find out the truth. For Sarah's sake, and for all those who suffered."

McKenna reached out, his hand covering hers. "We'll get to the bottom of this. Together."

Their eyes met, and for a moment, the walls they'd built around their hearts began to crumble. The shared history between them, the unspoken feelings, all lingered in the space between their intertwined fingers.

The moment was interrupted by a soft knock on the door. Martha entered, carrying a tray laden with steaming bowls of stew and fresh bread.

"Thought you could use a good meal," she said with a smile.

"Thank you, Martha," Ellie replied warmly.

As they ate, Sarah finally spoke, her voice trembling. "Will the bad men come here too?"

Ellie leaned down, brushing a strand of hair from Sarah's face. "No, sweetheart. You're safe here. I promise."

But as the night deepened and the town of Redemption settled into an uneasy slumber, Ellie couldn't shake the feeling that the true danger was still lurking in the shadows, waiting to strike.

# CHAPTER NINETEEN

The first light of dawn crept through the thin curtains of their room at the Silver Spur, casting a pale glow over the weary faces of Ellie and McKenna. Sarah slept soundly between them, her small form a poignant reminder of the innocence lost amidst the frontier's brutality.

Ellie rose quietly, careful not to disturb the child. She glanced at McKenna, who met her gaze with a silent nod. The unspoken understanding between them had deepened, their shared experiences forging a bond that transcended words.

Stepping outside, the crisp morning air filled Ellie's lungs as she surveyed the awakening town of Redemption. The events of the previous days weighed heavily on her mind—the massacre at Black Creek, the enigmatic clues, and the pervasive sense of impending danger.

McKenna joined her, his expression mirroring her concern. "We need to find out more about what happened at Black Creek," he said, his voice low.

Ellie nodded. "Agreed. But we must be cautious. Trust is a scarce commodity here."

Their first stop was the town's modest church, a simple wooden structure that served as both a place of worship and a community gathering point. Inside, they found Reverend Samuel, a middle-aged man with graying hair and kind eyes, arranging hymnals.

"Good morning, Reverend," Ellie greeted.

He looked up, offering a warm smile. "Good morning. How can I assist you?"

"We're seeking information about the attack on Black Creek," McKenna said. "Anything you can tell us would be helpful."

The reverend's face grew somber. "A tragic event. Many good people lost their lives."

"Do you know who was responsible?" Ellie pressed.

Reverend Samuel sighed. "There are rumors, but nothing certain. Some say it was renegade natives; others believe it was outlaws exploiting the chaos."

Ellie and McKenna exchanged a glance. The ambiguity only deepened their unease.

As they left the church, a commotion drew their attention to the town square. A group of men had gathered, their voices raised in anger. At the center stood Sheriff Thompson, a burly man with a stern demeanor, attempting to maintain order.

"What's going on?" Ellie asked a bystander.

"Another settler found dead near the outskirts," the man replied grimly. "Folks are saying it's the natives again."

Ellie's heart sank. The cycle of violence seemed

unending.

Determined to uncover the truth, they approached the sheriff.

"Sheriff Thompson," McKenna began, "we heard about the attack. Can you tell us more?"

The sheriff eyed them warily. "Who are you folks?"

"Just concerned travelers," Ellie replied. "We want to help if we can."

He studied them for a moment before nodding. "Found the body this morning. Same as the others—mutilated, left as a warning."

"Do you believe it's the natives?" McKenna asked.

The sheriff shrugged. "Could be. But something feels off. Too calculated."

Ellie considered his words. "May we see the body?"

He hesitated but then gestured for them to follow. They were led to a small outbuilding where the victim lay. The sight was gruesome—deep lacerations, signs of a struggle, and a look of sheer terror frozen on the man's face.

Examining the wounds, McKenna frowned. "These injuries... they don't match typical native weapons."

Ellie nodded in agreement. "It's almost as if someone wants us to think it's the natives."

Their investigation was interrupted by a loud crash from outside. Rushing out, they saw a group of armed men mounting their horses.

"What's happening?" Ellie called out.

One of the men sneered. "We're gonna teach those savages a lesson."

Before they could react, the posse galloped off, leaving a cloud of dust in their wake.

Ellie turned to McKenna, her eyes filled with determination. "We have to stop them. Innocent lives are at stake."

McKenna nodded. "Let's ride."

As they mounted their horses and sped after the posse, the weight of their mission pressed upon them. The frontier was a land of untamed beauty, but beneath its surface lay a darkness fueled by fear, hatred, and betrayal. Ellie and McKenna were determined to shine a light into that darkness, no matter the cost.

# CHAPTER TWENTY

The relentless sun beat down upon the arid landscape as Ellie and McKenna urged their horses forward, the dust from the posse's trail still fresh. The weight of their mission pressed heavily upon them; they had to prevent the impending clash between the settlers and the native tribes, a confrontation that promised only bloodshed and sorrow.

As they navigated the rugged terrain, the oppressive heat seemed to intensify the tension that hung in the air. The distant cawing of crows echoed ominously, and the occasional rustle in the underbrush hinted at unseen predators lurking nearby. The frontier was a land of untamed beauty, but it was also a realm where danger was ever-present, both from nature and man.

Ellie glanced at McKenna, noting the determined set of his jaw and the steely resolve in his eyes. Their shared history, once a source of pain and regret, had transformed into a bond forged in the crucible of adversity. The unspoken feelings between them simmered beneath the surface, a silent acknowledgment of the connection that had never truly been severed.

As they crested a ridge, the scene below caused them to rein in their horses abruptly. The posse had converged upon a small encampment nestled beside a meandering creek. Tents fashioned from animal hides dotted the area, and the smoke from cooking fires spiraled lazily into the sky. Men, women, and children of the Tonkawa tribe went about their daily routines, unaware of the imminent threat.

The settlers, armed and agitated, formed a semicircle around the camp. Their leader, a burly man with a thick beard and a scar running down his cheek, stepped forward, brandishing a rifle.

"Step away from the camp!" Ellie shouted, spurring her horse down the slope, McKenna close behind.

The leader turned, his eyes narrowing as he took in the newcomers. "Who the hell are you?"

"People who don't want to see unnecessary bloodshed," McKenna replied evenly.

The man spat on the ground. "These savages attacked our settlements. We're here for justice."

"Do you have proof?" Ellie challenged. "Or are you just looking for someone to blame?"

Before the man could respond, a figure emerged from the largest tent—a tall, dignified Tonkawa elder with weathered skin and piercing eyes. He raised a hand, signaling his people to remain calm.

"We have no quarrel with you," the elder said in measured English. "We seek only to live in peace."

The leader of the posse sneered. "Peace? Tell that to the folks at Black Creek."

"Enough!" Ellie interjected. "This cycle of violence helps no one. We need to find the true culprits, not scapegoat innocent people."

A tense silence settled over the group, the weight of Ellie's words hanging in the air. The settlers shifted uneasily, the fire of their anger dimming as doubt crept in.

Suddenly, a blood-curdling howl pierced the air, sending a shiver down Ellie's spine. From the shadows of the surrounding woods, a pack of wolves emerged, their eyes gleaming with predatory intent. The horses whinnied in fear, and the settlers raised their weapons, panic evident in their movements.

"Hold your fire!" McKenna commanded. "You'll only provoke them."

The wolves advanced, their growls resonating like a death knell. Ellie dismounted slowly, her eyes never leaving the lead wolf—a massive creature with a coat as dark as midnight and scars that told tales of countless battles.

Drawing her knife, Ellie approached the wolf cautiously, her movements deliberate and unthreatening. The tension was palpable, every eye fixed on the unfolding confrontation.

The wolf bared its teeth, a low growl rumbling from its throat. Ellie paused, her heart pounding in her chest. She extended her hand, palm open, a gesture of trust and submission.

For a moment, time seemed to stand still. Then, with a huff, the wolf turned and retreated into the forest, the pack following suit. A collective sigh of relief swept through the group.

The elder stepped forward, his eyes filled with gratitude. "You have averted much suffering today. We are in your debt."

Ellie shook her head. "No debts. Just a shared desire for peace."

The leader of the posse lowered his rifle, shame coloring his features. "Maybe... maybe we were wrong."

McKenna placed a hand on the man's shoulder. "Understanding is the first step toward reconciliation."

As the sun dipped below the horizon, casting the land in hues of gold and crimson, Ellie and McKenna knew that their journey was far from over. But for the first time, hope glimmered on the horizon—a hope that, together, they could heal the wounds of the past and forge a new path forward.

# CHAPTER
# TWENTY-ONE

The sun dipped below the horizon, casting long shadows over the rugged terrain as Ellie and McKenna made their way back to Redemption. The day's events weighed heavily on them—the confrontation with the posse, the tense encounter with the Tonkawa tribe, and the narrow escape from the wolf pack. The frontier was an unforgiving land, where danger lurked in every shadow, and survival demanded constant vigilance.

As they rode side by side, the silence between them was filled with unspoken words. Their shared history, once a source of pain and regret, had resurfaced amidst the chaos, bringing with it a complex web of emotions.

Ellie stole a glance at McKenna, noting the hardened lines of his face softened by the fading light. Memories of their past flooded her mind—the stolen glances, the whispered promises, the dreams they once shared. But the years had changed them both, and the chasm between who they were and who they had become seemed insurmountable.

"Do you ever think about the old days?" McKenna's voice broke the silence, his tone laced with a vulnerability she hadn't heard in years.

Ellie hesitated, her heart pounding in her chest. "Sometimes," she admitted. "But the past is a dangerous place to dwell."

He nodded, his gaze fixed on the horizon. "I suppose it is. But it's hard to forget what we had."

The weight of his words hung between them, a fragile bridge connecting their fractured souls.

As they approached the outskirts of Redemption, the distant glow of lanterns flickered like beacons in the encroaching darkness. The town, with its rough-hewn buildings and dusty streets, was a stark reminder of the harsh realities of frontier life.

Suddenly, a blood-curdling scream pierced the night, sending a chill down Ellie's spine. They spurred their horses forward, racing toward the source of the sound.

In the dim light, they saw a figure stumbling toward them—a young woman, her dress torn and bloodied, her face a mask of terror.

"Help me!" she cried, collapsing into Ellie's arms.

Ellie held her close, her heart aching at the sight of the girl's injuries. "What happened?"

"They... they came out of nowhere," the girl sobbed. "Attacked our wagon... killed my family..."

McKenna scanned the darkness, his hand resting on the

hilt of his revolver. "Who did this?"

"I don't know," she whispered. "They were like ghosts... silent and deadly..."

Ellie exchanged a grim look with McKenna. The frontier was home to many dangers—outlaws, hostile tribes, wild animals—but this attack seemed different, more sinister.

"We need to get her to safety," McKenna said, his voice tense.

They helped the girl onto Ellie's horse and made their way to the Silver Spur. Martha, the innkeeper, gasped at the sight of the injured girl but quickly ushered them into a back room.

As they tended to her wounds, the girl introduced herself as Clara, a settler traveling west with her family in search of a new beginning. Her story was all too familiar—a tale of hope shattered by the brutal realities of the frontier.

"We were ambushed," Clara recounted, her voice trembling. "They killed my parents and took my brother. I managed to escape, but..."

Ellie squeezed her hand. "You're safe now. We'll find your brother, I promise."

McKenna's eyes met Ellie's, a silent agreement passing between them. They couldn't ignore this atrocity. The frontier was a land of lawlessness, but they would bring justice to those who preyed upon the innocent.

As the night deepened, Ellie sat by Clara's bedside, her thoughts a whirlwind of emotions. The attack had awakened something within her—a fierce determination to protect the vulnerable, to stand against the darkness that threatened to consume them all.

McKenna stood at the window, his silhouette outlined by the moonlight. "We'll need to be careful," he said quietly. "Whoever did this is still out there."

Ellie nodded, her resolve hardening. "We'll find them. And we'll make them pay."

The frontier was a harsh and unforgiving place, but Ellie and McKenna were no strangers to its perils. Together, they would face whatever dangers lay ahead, their shared past fueling their fight for justice in a land where survival was a daily battle.

# CHAPTER TWENTY-TWO

The first light of dawn crept through the thin curtains of the Silver Spur's modest room, casting a pale glow over Clara's sleeping form. Ellie sat nearby, her eyes heavy with fatigue but her mind racing with the horrors Clara had recounted. The frontier was a land of untamed beauty, but beneath its vast skies lay dangers that could shatter the human spirit.

McKenna entered quietly, a steaming cup of coffee in hand. "How is she?" he asked, his voice a low rumble.

"Resting," Ellie replied, accepting the cup with a grateful nod. "But her sleep is troubled. Nightmares, I suspect."

McKenna's jaw tightened. "We need to find her brother and bring those responsible to justice."

Ellie met his gaze, a flicker of their shared past passing between them. "Agreed. But we must tread carefully. The frontier is rife with dangers, both seen and unseen."

As they discussed their next steps, a commotion erupted outside. Peering through the window, they saw a group of townsfolk gathered around a wagon, their faces etched with fear and anger.

"Another attack," McKenna muttered, reaching for his hat.

They hurried outside to find Sheriff Thompson addressing the crowd.

"Found 'em at first light," the sheriff was saying. "Same as before—mutilated, no sign of who did it."

Ellie approached, her heart pounding. "Sheriff, who were they?"

"A family passing through," Thompson replied grimly. "No one from around here."

The crowd murmured, fear giving way to suspicion.

"It's the natives," someone shouted. "They're attacking settlers!"

"We should strike first!" another voice added.

Ellie raised her hands, trying to calm the crowd. "We don't know that. Jumping to conclusions will only lead to more bloodshed."

A man stepped forward, his face contorted with rage. "And who are you to tell us what to do? You're not from here!"

McKenna moved to Ellie's side, his presence imposing. "She's trying to prevent a massacre. We need to find out who's really behind these attacks."

The sheriff nodded. "They're right. We need to investigate before taking any action."

The crowd grumbled but began to disperse, the tension lingering in the air.

Ellie turned to McKenna. "We should examine the site. Maybe there's something the sheriff missed."

He nodded. "Let's go."

They rode out to the site of the attack, a secluded spot along a narrow trail. The scene was gruesome—bodies lay strewn about, their lifeless eyes staring into the void. Ellie swallowed hard, steeling herself against the horror.

McKenna dismounted, scanning the area. "These wounds... they're not consistent with native weapons."

Ellie crouched beside one of the bodies, noting the precision of the injuries. "You're right. This was done by someone with knowledge of anatomy."

As they searched the area, Ellie noticed a piece of fabric caught on a nearby branch. She examined it—a fragment of a uniform.

"McKenna, look at this."

He took the fabric, his brow furrowing. "Military issue. But what would soldiers be doing out here?"

Ellie's mind raced. "Maybe it's not soldiers. Could be deserters or imposters."

McKenna nodded. "Either way, it means someone is trying to incite a war between the settlers and the natives."

Ellie stood, determination hardening her features. "We need to find Clara's brother. He might have seen something."

As they mounted their horses, a distant howl echoed through the trees—a chilling reminder of the predators that roamed the frontier, both animal and human.

The trail ahead was fraught with danger, but Ellie and McKenna were resolute. They would uncover the truth, no matter the cost.

# CHAPTER TWENTY-THREE

The sun hung low in the sky, casting an amber glow over the rugged landscape as Ellie and McKenna rode deeper into the frontier. The weight of their mission pressed heavily upon them: to find Clara's brother and uncover the truth behind the brutal attacks plaguing the settlers.

The trail was treacherous, winding through dense forests and across rocky terrains. The air was thick with tension, every rustle in the underbrush setting their nerves on edge. The frontier was a land of untamed beauty, but it was also rife with dangers—both human and wild.

As they ventured further, the signs of civilization faded, replaced by the raw, unspoiled wilderness. The calls of distant wolves echoed through the trees, a haunting reminder of the predators that roamed these lands. Ellie tightened her grip on the reins, her eyes scanning the shadows for any sign of movement.

"We should make camp soon," McKenna suggested, his

voice breaking the silence.

Ellie nodded, her thoughts drifting to Clara and the horrors she had endured. The image of the young woman's tear-streaked face fueled her determination. They had to find her brother and put an end to the violence.

As dusk settled, they found a small clearing near a babbling brook. McKenna set about gathering firewood while Ellie tended to the horses. The routine tasks provided a semblance of normalcy amidst the uncertainty.

Once the fire was crackling, they sat in companionable silence, the flames casting flickering shadows on their faces. The unspoken tension between them was palpable, a complex web of shared history and unresolved feelings.

"Do you ever wonder how things might have been different?" McKenna asked suddenly, his gaze fixed on the fire.

Ellie looked at him, her heart aching with the weight of unspoken words. "Every day," she admitted softly.

He met her eyes, the flicker of the flames reflecting in his gaze. "Maybe once this is over, we can find a way to start anew."

Before Ellie could respond, a blood-curdling scream pierced the night, sending a chill down her spine. They sprang to their feet, weapons drawn, as the sound of rustling leaves and snapping branches grew closer.

From the darkness emerged a figure, stumbling and gasping for breath. It was a young boy, his clothes torn and bloodied, his face etched with terror.

"Help... please..." he managed to utter before collapsing at their feet.

Ellie knelt beside him, her heart pounding. "It's okay, you're safe now. What's your name?"

"Tommy," he whispered, his voice trembling.

McKenna scanned the surrounding darkness, his senses on high alert. "What happened, Tommy?"

"They... they took my sister," he sobbed. "Attacked our camp... killed everyone else..."

Ellie exchanged a grim look with McKenna. The pattern was disturbingly familiar.

"Who did this?" she asked gently.

Tommy shook his head, tears streaming down his face. "I don't know... they came out of nowhere... like ghosts..."

McKenna's jaw tightened. "We need to move. If they're still out there, we're all in danger."

They quickly doused the fire and gathered their belongings. Ellie helped Tommy onto her horse, his small frame trembling with fear.

As they rode through the night, the weight of their mission grew heavier. The frontier was a land of untamed beauty, but beneath its surface lurked dangers that threatened to consume them all.

Ellie glanced at McKenna, their shared past a silent presence between them. In this unforgiving land, they would need to rely on each other more than ever.

As dawn approached, they reached a ridge overlooking a sprawling valley. In the distance, smoke rose from a cluster of tents—an encampment.

"Could be them," McKenna murmured.

Ellie nodded, her resolve hardening. "Let's find out."

With Tommy's fate intertwined with their own, they descended into the valley, ready to face whatever dangers awaited them in the heart of the frontier.

# CHAPTER TWENTY-FOUR

As the first light of dawn crept over the horizon, Ellie, McKenna, and the rescued boy, Tommy, cautiously approached the encampment they had spotted the previous night. The air was thick with tension, each of them acutely aware of the dangers that lay ahead.

The camp was nestled in a secluded valley, hidden from prying eyes by dense foliage and rugged terrain. Smoke from smoldering fires mingled with the morning mist, creating an eerie atmosphere. The distant murmur of voices and the occasional clatter of metal indicated that the camp was occupied.

Ellie signaled for them to dismount and proceed on foot. They tethered their horses in a concealed grove and advanced silently, using the natural cover to their advantage. As they drew closer, the details of the encampment became clearer.

A cluster of makeshift tents and lean-tos formed a

haphazard circle around a central fire pit. Men milled about, some sharpening weapons, others tending to wounds. The air was thick with the scent of unwashed bodies and the metallic tang of blood.

McKenna's eyes narrowed as he took in the scene. "These aren't soldiers," he muttered. "Looks more like a band of outlaws."

Ellie nodded in agreement. "But what are they doing out here? And why attack innocent settlers?"

Tommy tugged at Ellie's sleeve, his eyes wide with fear. "That's them," he whispered. "The ones who took my sister."

Ellie's heart clenched at the boy's words. She placed a reassuring hand on his shoulder. "We'll get her back, Tommy. I promise."

They retreated to a safe distance to formulate a plan. McKenna spread a crude map on the ground, marking their position and the layout of the camp.

"We need to find where they're keeping the captives," he said. "And we need to do it without alerting the whole camp."

Ellie studied the map, her mind racing. "There," she said, pointing to a larger tent set apart from the others. "That looks like a holding area."

McKenna nodded. "Makes sense. We'll need a distraction to draw their attention away."

Tommy spoke up, his voice trembling but determined. "I can help. I know how to move quietly. I can create a diversion."

Ellie looked at the boy, admiration mingling with

concern. "It's dangerous, Tommy. Are you sure?"

He nodded vigorously. "I want to save my sister."

McKenna placed a hand on Tommy's shoulder. "Alright, son. Here's what we'll do..."

As the sun climbed higher, they put their plan into motion. Tommy circled around the camp, gathering stones and sticks. At the agreed-upon moment, he began creating noise, throwing stones into the underbrush and mimicking animal calls.

The camp erupted into chaos as the men scrambled to investigate the disturbance. Ellie and McKenna seized the opportunity, slipping into the camp undetected.

They reached the large tent and peered inside. A group of captives huddled together, their faces gaunt and eyes hollow with despair.

Ellie scanned the group and spotted a young girl clutching a tattered doll. "Tommy's sister," she whispered.

McKenna nodded. "Let's get them out of here."

They entered the tent, and Ellie knelt beside the girl. "We're here to help. Your brother sent us."

The girl's eyes widened with hope. "Tommy?"

Ellie smiled. "Yes. We're getting you out of here."

As they ushered the captives toward the edge of the camp, a shout rang out. They had been spotted.

"Go!" McKenna barked, drawing his revolver. "I'll hold them off."

Ellie hesitated, but McKenna's steely gaze brooked no

argument. She led the captives into the forest as gunshots echoed behind them.

They ran until their lungs burned and their legs threatened to give out. Finally, they reached the grove where the horses were hidden.

Tommy emerged from the trees, his face lighting up as he saw his sister. "Sarah!"

The siblings embraced, tears streaming down their faces.

Ellie scanned the forest anxiously, her heart pounding. Moments later, McKenna appeared, bloodied but alive.

"Let's move," he said grimly. "They'll be coming after us."

They mounted their horses, the captives riding double, and set off at a brisk pace. The frontier was a harsh and unforgiving land, but they had won a small victory today.

As they rode, Ellie glanced at McKenna, their shared past and the day's events forging a renewed bond between them. In this untamed wilderness, they would need each other more than ever.

# CHAPTER TWENTY-FIVE

The sun dipped below the horizon, casting long shadows over the rugged terrain as Ellie, McKenna, and their group of rescued captives pressed onward. The weight of their recent encounter hung heavily in the air, each member of the party lost in their own thoughts.

Ellie rode alongside Sarah, the young girl they had saved, who clung tightly to her brother Tommy. The siblings' reunion had been a brief moment of light in an otherwise dark journey. Ellie couldn't help but feel a pang of sorrow for the innocence lost in such a harsh land.

McKenna took the lead, his eyes scanning the horizon for any signs of pursuit. The frontier was an unforgiving place, teeming with dangers both human and wild. He knew all too well that their escape from the outlaw camp was only a temporary reprieve.

As night fell, they found a secluded grove to make camp. The group moved with practiced efficiency, setting up a small fire and arranging their sparse belongings. The flickering flames cast eerie shadows, and the distant howl of a wolf served as a haunting reminder of the predators that roamed the wilderness.

Ellie sat by the fire, her thoughts drifting to the past. The journey had rekindled memories of her and McKenna's shared history—a time when life seemed simpler, and the future was full of promise. But the frontier had a way of changing people, forging them into something harder, more resilient.

McKenna approached, his expression unreadable. "Mind if I join you?"

She offered a faint smile. "Of course."

He settled beside her, the silence between them filled with unspoken words.

"This land... it takes its toll," McKenna said quietly, his gaze fixed on the fire.

Ellie nodded. "It does. But it also reveals who we truly are."

He looked at her, his eyes reflecting the flickering flames. "And who are we, Ellie?"

She met his gaze, the weight of their past hanging between them. "Survivors."

Before McKenna could respond, a rustling in the bushes drew their attention. They sprang to their feet, weapons at the ready.

A figure emerged from the shadows—a man, disheveled and weary, his hands raised in a gesture of surrender.

"Please," he implored, his voice hoarse. "I mean no harm."

Ellie and McKenna exchanged a wary glance.

"Who are you?" McKenna demanded.

The man swallowed hard. "Name's Samuel. Samuel Harper. I was part of a wagon train heading west... we were attacked."

Ellie's heart tightened. "Attacked? By whom?"

"Outlaws," Samuel replied, his voice trembling. "They came out of nowhere... killed most of us. I managed to escape."

McKenna's jaw clenched. "Did you see where they went?"

Samuel nodded. "They took the survivors north, towards the canyon."

Ellie felt a surge of determination. "We have to help them."

McKenna placed a hand on her shoulder. "It's a trap, Ellie. They could be waiting for us."

She met his gaze, her eyes steely. "We can't abandon them."

He sighed, knowing she was right. "Alright. But we need a plan."

As they huddled to discuss their next move, the wind carried the distant howl of wolves—a chilling reminder of the predators that lurked in the darkness.

The frontier was a land of untamed beauty and relentless danger. But amidst the chaos, Ellie and McKenna found strength in their shared purpose, their bond forged anew in the crucible of the wild.

# CHAPTER TWENTY-SIX

The morning sun cast a pale light over the rugged landscape as Ellie, McKenna, Samuel, and the rescued captives prepared to continue their journey. The events of the previous days had left them weary, but determination burned in their eyes. The frontier was an unforgiving land, and they knew that danger lurked in every shadow.

As they broke camp, McKenna approached Ellie, his expression grave. "We need to move quickly. The outlaws will be on our trail, and this terrain offers little cover."

Ellie nodded, glancing at the group. The rescued captives, though grateful, were weak and frightened. Among them, Tommy and his sister Sarah clung to each other, their faces pale but resolute.

"We'll head north," Ellie suggested. "There's a settlement a few days' ride from here. We can find shelter and supplies."

Samuel, still recovering from his ordeal, stepped forward. "I know the area well. I can guide us through the safest paths."

With a plan in place, they set off, the horses' hooves crunching softly against the dry earth. The landscape was a mosaic of rolling hills, dense forests, and treacherous ravines. The beauty of the frontier was undeniable, but so was its peril.

As they rode, the group remained vigilant. The threat of outlaw pursuit was ever-present, but the wilderness itself posed its own dangers. Predators, both human and animal, roamed these lands, and the line between hunter and hunted was often blurred.

The sun climbed higher, and the heat became oppressive. They paused near a stream to rest and refill their canteens. Ellie knelt by the water's edge, splashing her face with the cool liquid. As she looked up, she noticed McKenna watching her, a distant look in his eyes.

"Penny for your thoughts?" she asked, offering a faint smile.

He sighed, glancing away. "Just thinking about the past... and the choices we've made."

Ellie felt a pang of nostalgia mixed with regret. "We did what we had to survive."

McKenna met her gaze, his eyes reflecting a depth of emotion that words couldn't capture. "And now? What are we surviving for?"

Before Ellie could respond, a sudden rustling in the bushes snapped their attention. McKenna drew his revolver, and Ellie reached for her rifle. The group tensed, eyes scanning the surrounding foliage.

From the underbrush emerged a massive grizzly bear, its fur matted and eyes gleaming with a predatory hunger. The beast let out a deafening roar, rising onto its hind legs, towering over them.

Panic surged through the group. The horses reared, sensing the imminent danger. Ellie took aim, her hands steady despite the adrenaline coursing through her veins.

"Stay calm!" McKenna barked, positioning himself between the bear and the others.

The grizzly charged, its powerful limbs propelling it forward with terrifying speed. Ellie fired, the bullet striking the bear's shoulder, but it only seemed to enrage the creature further.

McKenna fired two shots in quick succession, aiming for the beast's chest. The bear stumbled, blood oozing from its wounds, but it continued its relentless advance.

Just as the bear closed the distance, Samuel, wielding a makeshift spear, lunged forward, driving the sharpened point into the bear's side. The grizzly let out a pained roar, swiping its massive paw and sending Samuel sprawling to the ground.

Seizing the moment, McKenna fired a final shot, the bullet finding its mark between the bear's eyes. The beast collapsed with a heavy thud, the ground trembling beneath its weight.

Breathing heavily, Ellie rushed to Samuel's side. He was bruised and bleeding, but alive.

"That was a brave thing you did," she said, helping him to his feet.

He winced, offering a weak smile. "Couldn't let it have all the fun."

McKenna approached, his expression a mix of admiration and concern. "We need to keep moving. The gunshots will have drawn attention."

The group quickly gathered their belongings, casting wary glances at the fallen bear. The encounter had been a stark reminder of the brutal realities of the frontier.

As they continued their journey, the landscape grew more treacherous. The dense forests gave way to rocky outcrops and narrow passes. The air was thick with tension, every shadow seeming to conceal a potential threat.

As dusk approached, they reached a narrow canyon, its towering walls casting long shadows. Samuel, still leading the way, paused, his expression troubled.

"This is the quickest route," he said, "but it's also a known ambush spot for outlaws."

McKenna surveyed the canyon, his jaw set. "We don't have much choice. If we backtrack, we'll lose valuable time."

Ellie nodded in agreement. "We'll have to risk it. Stay alert, and keep close."

They entered the canyon, the walls pressing in around them. The silence was oppressive, broken only by the occasional clatter of loose stones under

# CHAPTER TWENTY-SEVEN

The narrow canyon walls loomed overhead, casting deep shadows that swallowed the dwindling light. Ellie, McKenna, Samuel, and the group of rescued captives advanced cautiously, the oppressive silence amplifying their unease. Every footfall seemed to echo, a stark reminder of their vulnerability in this confined passage.

McKenna, leading the procession, raised a hand to halt the group. His eyes scanned the rocky ledges above, searching for any sign of movement. The canyon was a notorious ambush site, and the weight of that knowledge pressed heavily upon them.

"Stay close and keep your eyes sharp," he whispered, his voice barely audible.

Ellie nodded, her grip tightening on her rifle. Beside her, young Tommy clung to his sister Sarah, their faces pale but determined. The rescued captives huddled together, their fear palpable.

As they pressed forward, a faint rustling echoed from above. McKenna's eyes darted upward, catching a fleeting glimpse of movement—a shadow shifting against the rock.

"Ambush!" he shouted, diving for cover.

Chaos erupted as gunfire rained down from the canyon rims. Ellie pulled Tommy and Sarah behind a boulder, shielding them from the onslaught. The captives scattered, seeking refuge wherever they could.

McKenna returned fire, his shots precise and measured. He spotted their assailants—Native warriors, their faces painted for battle, moving with lethal grace along the canyon's edge.

Ellie's heart pounded as she took aim, her mind racing. She had heard tales of such attacks, where Native tribes employed guerrilla tactics—concealment, surprise, and swift, devastating strikes. The reality was more harrowing than any story.

A warrior emerged from the shadows, charging toward their position with a blood-curdling yell. Ellie fired, the recoil jolting her shoulder as the attacker fell. But there was no time to dwell; another assailant was already closing in.

Samuel, wielding his makeshift spear, engaged the attacker in a desperate struggle. The two men grappled, the clash of metal and flesh echoing through the canyon. With a guttural cry, Samuel drove the spear into the warrior's chest, the lifeless body collapsing at his feet.

The battle raged on, the confined space amplifying the violence. Ellie and McKenna fought side by side, their movements synchronized in a deadly dance. The air was thick with gunpowder and the metallic scent of blood.

Amidst the chaos, a piercing scream cut through the din. Ellie's eyes darted toward the sound, her heart clenching as she saw Sarah being dragged away by a warrior.

"No!" Ellie screamed, abandoning her cover to pursue them.

McKenna reached out to stop her, but she was already gone, sprinting across the open ground. Bullets whizzed past her as she closed the distance, her focus solely on the terrified girl.

With a primal yell, Ellie tackled the warrior, the two of them tumbling to the ground. They grappled fiercely, the warrior's knife flashing in the dim light. Ellie fought with everything she had, her fingers clawing at his eyes, her knee driving into his abdomen.

Finally, she managed to wrest the knife from his grasp, plunging it into his chest. The warrior gasped, his body going limp beneath her.

Breathing heavily, Ellie scrambled to her feet, pulling Sarah into her arms. The girl's body trembled with sobs, her small hands clutching Ellie's shirt.

"It's okay, I've got you," Ellie whispered, her voice shaking.

The gunfire began to subside, the attackers retreating as quickly as they had appeared. McKenna approached, his face grim, a fresh wound bleeding on his arm.

"Is she alright?" he asked, concern etched in his features.

Ellie nodded, though her own body ached from the

confrontation. "She's safe."

They regrouped, assessing their losses. Two of the rescued captives lay dead, their bodies already growing cold. The rest were shaken but alive.

"We need to move," McKenna urged. "They'll be back with reinforcements."

Ellie agreed, helping Sarah to her feet. The group pressed on, the weight of their ordeal heavy upon them.

As they emerged from the canyon, the night sky stretched above them, a vast expanse of stars offering little comfort. The frontier was a harsh and unforgiving land, where danger lurked in every shadow.

But amidst the brutality, there was also resilience—a determination to survive, to protect one another, and to find hope in the darkest of times.

Ellie glanced at McKenna, their eyes meeting in a silent acknowledgment of their shared past and the uncertain future ahead. In this untamed wilderness, their bond was both a strength and a vulnerability, a reminder of what they had lost and what they still fought to preserve.

# CHAPTER TWENTY-EIGHT

The moon hung high, casting an ethereal glow over the rugged terrain as Ellie, McKenna, Samuel, and the remaining survivors pressed onward. The harrowing ambush in the canyon had left them battered, both physically and emotionally. Each step forward was a testament to their resilience, but the weight of loss and the omnipresent threat of danger loomed large.

Ellie glanced at the group, her eyes lingering on young Tommy and his sister Sarah. The siblings walked hand in hand, their faces etched with fatigue and fear. Ellie felt a surge of protectiveness; she had promised to keep them safe, and she intended to honor that vow.

McKenna, ever vigilant, scanned the horizon. His rugged features were hardened by years of frontier life, yet there was a softness in his gaze when it settled on Ellie. Their shared history was a complex tapestry of love, loss, and unspoken words.

As dawn approached, the group reached a dense forest. The towering pines offered a semblance of cover, but also concealed unknown perils. Samuel, their guide, paused at the forest's edge.

"We can take shelter here," he suggested, his voice hoarse. "But we must remain alert. These woods are known territory for predators—both animal and human."

Ellie nodded, appreciating Samuel's caution. "We'll set up a temporary camp. Everyone needs rest."

The group settled amidst the trees, the canopy above filtering the early morning light. Ellie and McKenna took turns keeping watch, their senses attuned to the forest's symphony of sounds.

As Ellie sat by the dimming campfire, memories of their past flooded her mind. She recalled stolen moments under starlit skies, whispered promises, and the painful choices that had driven them apart.

McKenna approached, his footsteps silent on the forest floor. "Penny for your thoughts?"

She offered a faint smile. "Just reminiscing. This land... it holds so many memories."

He sat beside her, the proximity stirring a familiar warmth. "We've been through hell and back, Ellie. But somehow, we always find our way to each other."

Their eyes met, the unspoken emotions passing between them like a palpable force. Before either could speak, a distant howl pierced the silence.

Ellie tensed, her hand instinctively reaching for her rifle. "Wolves."

McKenna nodded, his expression grim. "And they're close."

The group roused, fear evident in their eyes. The howls grew louder, more numerous—a haunting chorus that sent shivers down their spines.

Samuel tightened his grip on his weapon. "We need to move. Now."

Gathering their belongings, they hurried through the forest, the underbrush snagging at their clothes. The howls pursued them, a relentless reminder of the predators drawing near.

As they navigated the labyrinth of trees, Ellie spotted a rocky outcrop ahead. "There! We can take refuge on those rocks."

Scrambling up the incline, they reached the summit just as the first wolf emerged from the shadows. The creature's eyes gleamed with a predatory hunger, its fur a matted gray.

Ellie raised her rifle, aiming steadily. "Stay behind me," she instructed the others.

The wolf advanced, lips curled in a snarl. Ellie fired, the shot echoing through the forest. The bullet struck true, and the wolf collapsed.

But there was no time to celebrate. More wolves appeared, their numbers overwhelming.

McKenna and Samuel joined the defense, their weapons blazing. The air was thick with tension, the scent of gunpowder mingling with the earthy aroma of the forest.

Despite their efforts, the wolves pressed on, driven

by primal instinct. One lunged at Samuel, its jaws snapping inches from his face.

Ellie reacted swiftly, her rifle butt connecting with the wolf's skull, sending it sprawling.

The battle raged, each moment a fight for survival. The group's unity and determination were their only advantages against the relentless assault.

Finally, as the first rays of sunlight pierced the canopy, the remaining wolves retreated, melting back into the shadows from whence they came.

Breathless and bloodied, the group surveyed the aftermath. Several wolves lay dead, but miraculously, none of the humans had suffered fatal injuries.

Ellie wiped sweat from her brow, her hands trembling. "Is everyone alright?"

Nods and murmurs of affirmation followed, though exhaustion was evident.

McKenna approached Ellie, concern etched on his face. "You were incredible back there."

She managed a weary smile. "We all were."

As they regrouped, the gravity of their situation settled upon them. The frontier was an unforgiving land, where danger lurked at every turn.

Yet, amidst the brutality, there was a glimmer of hope —a testament to the human spirit's capacity to endure, to protect, and to find connection even in the darkest of times.

Ellie and McKenna shared a lingering glance, the unspoken bond between them reaffirmed. In this unforgiving land, their shared history and mutual respect became the bedrock upon which they built their resolve.

As the group prepared to move forward, Samuel approached Ellie, his expression a mix of gratitude and determination.

"We can't afford to linger," he advised. "The forest may have shielded us from the sun, but it also harbors other dangers. We need to find open ground and assess our next move."

Ellie nodded in agreement. "You're right. Let's gather everyone and push on. We need to find a safer place to rest and plan our next steps."

The survivors, though weary, rallied together, their collective will driving them forward. The encounter with the wolves had not only tested their physical endurance but had also strengthened their unity.

As they emerged from the forest's edge, the landscape before them unfolded into rolling plains bathed in the golden hues of dawn. The sight was both a relief and a reminder of the vastness of the frontier—a land of untamed beauty and relentless challenges.

Ellie took a deep breath, the fresh morning air filling her lungs. She glanced at McKenna, who offered a reassuring nod.

"We'll make it through this," he said quietly. "Together."

She smiled, a flicker of hope igniting within her. "Together."

With renewed determination, the group set forth into the unknown, each step a testament to their resilience and an unwavering commitment to one another.

The frontier held many secrets, and as they ventured deeper into its embrace, they knew that their journey was far from over. But with courage, unity, and the unbreakable bonds forged in adversity, they were ready to face whatever lay ahead.

# CHAPTER
# TWENTY-NINE

The sun climbed steadily, casting long shadows over the rolling plains as Ellie, McKenna, Samuel, and the remaining survivors pressed onward. The harrowing encounter with the wolves had left them weary, but their resolve remained unbroken. Each step forward was a testament to their determination to survive in the unforgiving frontier.

As they traversed the open landscape, the group remained vigilant, acutely aware of the myriad dangers that could emerge without warning. The vastness of the plains offered little cover, making them feel exposed under the expansive sky.

Ellie walked alongside McKenna, their silence filled with unspoken thoughts. The shared experiences of the past days had rekindled a connection between them, one forged in the crucible of adversity.

"Do you remember the last time we were in a place like

this?" McKenna asked, breaking the silence.

Ellie nodded, a faint smile tugging at her lips. "I do. It was before everything changed."

Their conversation was interrupted by Samuel's voice from the front of the group. "There's a river up ahead. We can refill our canteens and rest for a moment."

The prospect of fresh water lifted their spirits, and they quickened their pace. As they approached the riverbank, the gentle babble of the water provided a soothing backdrop, a stark contrast to the harshness of their journey.

While the others tended to their needs, Ellie wandered a short distance upstream, seeking a moment of solitude. The reflection of the sky on the water's surface mesmerized her, pulling her into memories long buried.

She recalled a time when the world seemed full of promise, when she and McKenna had dreamed of a future together. But the frontier had a way of reshaping dreams, turning hope into hardship.

Her reverie was broken by the sound of footsteps approaching. Turning, she found McKenna standing beside her, his expression mirroring the weight of their shared history.

"It's been a long road," he said softly.

"Longer than I ever imagined," Ellie replied, her voice tinged with melancholy.

McKenna reached out, gently taking her hand. "We've both made choices. Some we regret, others we cherish. But through it all, we've found our way back to each other."

Ellie looked into his eyes, seeing the sincerity and the unspoken apology. "Perhaps it's time we stop running from the past and start facing the future together."

Before McKenna could respond, a sudden commotion erupted from the direction of the group. Shouts and the unmistakable sound of gunfire shattered the tranquility.

Instinctively, Ellie and McKenna drew their weapons and sprinted back toward the others. As they neared, they saw Samuel and the rest of the survivors engaged in a desperate struggle against a band of attackers.

The assailants were a mix of rugged frontiersmen and Native warriors, their faces painted for battle. The alliance was an uneasy one, born out of mutual interest rather than trust.

Ellie took cover behind a fallen log, firing at an attacker who was advancing on Sarah and Tommy. The man fell, but more took his place, their numbers overwhelming.

McKenna fought beside Samuel, the two men forming a formidable defense. But it was clear they were outmatched, the attackers' ferocity threatening to overrun them.

In the chaos, Ellie spotted the leader of the attackers—a tall man with a scar running down the side of his face. His eyes locked onto hers, and a cruel smile spread across his lips.

With a sinking feeling, Ellie recognized him. It was Donovan, a man from her past she had hoped never to see again.

"Ellie," Donovan called out, his voice dripping with mockery. "Fancy meeting you here."

Ellie's grip tightened on her rifle. "What do you want, Donovan?"

He laughed, a sound devoid of humor. "Isn't it obvious? Everything."

Before she could respond, Donovan raised his hand, signaling his men to cease their attack. The sudden silence was deafening, the tension palpable.

"Let's not waste any more lives," Donovan said, his tone deceptively conciliatory. "Surrender now, and I might just let you live."

Ellie glanced at McKenna and Samuel, seeing the exhaustion and determination in their eyes. They had fought too hard to give up now.

Taking a deep breath, Ellie stepped forward, her voice steady. "We won't surrender. Not to you."

Donovan's expression hardened. "So be it."

With a swift motion, he drew his pistol and fired. The shot rang out, and Ellie felt a searing pain in her side. She staggered but remained standing, her vision blurring.

McKenna's roar of rage echoed in her ears as he charged at Donovan, tackling him to the ground. The two men grappled, each fighting for dominance.

Samuel and the others renewed their efforts, the battle descending into a brutal melee.

Ellie struggled to stay conscious, her hand pressed against the searing pain in her side where Donovan's bullet had struck. The world around her blurred, the cacophony of battle fading into a distant hum. She forced herself to focus, to remain present, knowing that succumbing to darkness could mean the end for her and her companions.

Through her wavering vision, she saw McKenna and Donovan locked in a brutal struggle, each man's face a mask of determination and fury. McKenna's fists flew with a primal ferocity, driven by a need to protect those he cared for. Donovan, equally relentless, countered with savage blows, his eyes gleaming with malice.

Samuel, meanwhile, rallied the remaining survivors, coordinating their defense against the attackers. His voice rang out, commanding and steady, instilling a semblance of order amidst the chaos. The settlers, though weary and outnumbered, fought with a tenacity born of desperation, their makeshift weapons clashing against those of their assailants.

Ellie knew she had to act. Gritting her teeth against the pain, she reached for her rifle, fingers trembling as they closed around the familiar grip. With great effort, she raised the weapon, taking aim at Donovan, who had gained the upper hand in his struggle with McKenna.

Just as Donovan drew a knife, poised to strike a fatal blow, Ellie fired. The bullet found its mark, striking Donovan in the shoulder. He cried out, the knife slipping from his grasp as he staggered backward.

McKenna seized the opportunity, delivering a powerful punch that sent Donovan crashing to the ground, unconscious. Breathing heavily, McKenna turned to Ellie, his expression a mixture of relief and concern.

"Ellie!" he shouted, rushing to her side. "You're hurt."

She managed a weak smile. "Just a scratch," she lied, her voice barely above a whisper.

McKenna tore a strip of cloth from his shirt, pressing it against her wound to staunch the bleeding. "Stay with me," he urged, his voice thick with emotion.

Around them, the tide of battle began to turn. With their leader incapacitated, the attackers' resolve wavered. Samuel and the settlers pressed their advantage, driving the remaining assailants into retreat.

As the last of the attackers fled into the wilderness, a heavy silence settled over the battlefield. The survivors gathered, tending to their wounded and mourning the fallen.

Ellie's vision dimmed, the edges of her consciousness fraying. She felt McKenna's hand clasping hers, his grip a lifeline anchoring her to the world.

"Don't you dare leave me," he whispered, his voice breaking.

Summoning the last of her strength, Ellie squeezed his hand. "I'm not going anywhere," she murmured before the darkness claimed her.

# CHAPTER THIRTY

The relentless sun dipped below the horizon, casting the rugged landscape in hues of amber and crimson. After days of arduous travel and harrowing encounters, Ellie, McKenna, Samuel, and the remaining survivors found themselves approaching a small frontier town nestled against the backdrop of towering mesas.

The town, though modest, bustled with the evening's activities. The clinking of glasses and murmur of conversations spilled from the saloon, while the distant sound of a piano played a jaunty tune. For the weary travelers, it was a beacon of normalcy amidst the chaos that had defined their journey.

Samuel reined in his horse and turned to the group. "We should rest here for the night. The horses need tending, and we could all use a decent meal and some sleep."

Ellie nodded in agreement, her eyes scanning the town. "Agreed. Let's find an inn and see about some provisions."

As they made their way down the main street, the townsfolk cast curious glances their way, noting the dust and fatigue that clung to them. Ellie couldn't help but feel a pang of self-consciousness, aware of the grime and weariness that marked their appearance.

They soon arrived at a modest inn, its wooden sign creaking gently in the evening breeze. A kindly woman greeted them at the door, her eyes crinkling with a warm smile.

"Welcome, travelers. You look like you've had quite the journey. Come in, come in."

Inside, the inn was cozy, with the comforting aroma of hearty stew wafting from the kitchen. The group secured rooms and arranged for baths—a luxury they hadn't enjoyed in far too long.

Ellie and McKenna were shown to adjacent rooms, each furnished with a simple bed and a basin for washing. A steaming tub was brought in shortly after, and Ellie sighed in relief at the prospect of cleansing away the layers of dirt and tension.

After her bath, Ellie donned a clean dress provided by the innkeeper and stepped out into the hallway, feeling more like herself than she had in days. As she moved toward the stairs, McKenna emerged from his room, his hair damp and his usual rugged appearance softened.

He offered her a smile, one that reached his eyes and conveyed a sense of shared understanding. "You clean up well," he teased gently.

She chuckled softly. "As do you. Shall we see about that meal?"

Downstairs, the inn's dining area was modest but inviting. They settled at a corner table, and soon, steaming bowls of stew and freshly baked bread were placed before them. The first bite was a revelation, the rich flavors a stark contrast to the meager rations they'd subsisted on.

As they ate, a comfortable silence settled between them, the unspoken bond forged through shared trials providing a sense of companionship that needed no words.

After the meal, McKenna leaned back, his gaze fixed on Ellie. "It's been a long road," he said quietly.

She met his eyes, the flickering candlelight casting shadows that danced across his features. "It has. But moments like this make it worthwhile."

He reached across the table, his hand covering hers. "Ellie, I've been thinking... About us. About the future."

Her heart skipped a beat, the vulnerability in his voice stirring emotions she'd kept guarded. "What are you saying, McKenna?"

He took a deep breath, his thumb gently tracing circles on the back of her hand. "We've faced death more times than I care to count. And through it all, the thought of losing you was more terrifying than any danger we've encountered. I don't want to waste any more time. I want to be with you, Ellie. Truly be with you."

Tears welled in her eyes, the weight of his words sinking deep into her soul. "Oh, McKenna... I've wanted the same. But the world we live in, the dangers we face..."

He squeezed her hand gently. "We'll face them together. No more running, no more hiding from what we feel. Life is too uncertain to deny ourselves the chance at happiness."

A tear slipped down her cheek, and she nodded, a smile

breaking through. "Together, then."

He stood, moving to her side of the table, and pulled her into a tender embrace. The world outside the inn's walls faded away, leaving just the two of them in a moment of profound connection.

As they held each other, the future remained uncertain, the challenges ahead daunting. But in that embrace, they found a sanctuary—a promise that, come what may, they would face it side by side.

# CHAPTER
# THIRTY-ONE

The morning sun cast a golden hue over the frontier town as Ellie, McKenna, Samuel, and the other survivors prepared to continue their journey. The brief respite had rejuvenated their spirits, but an undercurrent of tension remained palpable.

As they gathered their belongings, the innkeeper approached Ellie, her expression grave.

"Ma'am, I couldn't help but overhear your plans," she began cautiously. "There's been talk of increased hostilities in the territories you're heading into. Some say the Sioux are on the warpath again."

Ellie exchanged a concerned glance with McKenna. The Sioux Wars had been a series of brutal conflicts between the United States and various Sioux tribes, marked by fierce battles and significant casualties on both sides.

"Thank you for the warning," Ellie replied, her voice steady. "We'll be cautious."

As they mounted their horses and set out, the weight of the innkeeper's words hung over them. The open plains stretched endlessly ahead, a vast expanse that offered both freedom and peril.

Days passed with little incident, the monotony of travel broken only by the occasional sighting of wildlife or distant thunderheads rolling across the horizon. The group remained vigilant, acutely aware of the dangers that could emerge without warning.

One evening, as the sun dipped below the horizon, painting the sky in shades of crimson and gold, they made camp near a gently flowing river. The serene setting provided a false sense of security, masking the perils that lurked in the shadows.

As darkness settled, the group gathered around the campfire, the flickering flames casting dancing shadows on their weary faces. The conversation was subdued, each person lost in their thoughts.

Suddenly, a distant howl pierced the night, sending a chill through the camp. The horses shifted nervously, sensing the presence of predators nearby.

McKenna rose to his feet, his hand instinctively reaching for his rifle. "Wolves," he muttered, scanning the darkness beyond the firelight.

Ellie stood beside him, her eyes narrowing as she strained to see into the inky blackness. "They're close," she whispered.

The howls grew louder, more numerous, echoing off the surrounding hills. The pack was closing in, drawn by the scent of the camp and its occupants.

Samuel moved to the horses, attempting to calm them. "We need to keep them at bay," he said urgently. "If they spook the horses, we'll be stranded."

The group formed a defensive perimeter around the campfire, their weapons at the ready. The tension was palpable, each person acutely aware of the imminent threat.

Without warning, a pair of glowing eyes appeared at the edge of the firelight, followed by another, and then another. The wolves had arrived, their sleek forms barely visible in the darkness.

A low growl rumbled from the leader of the pack, a massive creature with a thick, matted coat and piercing yellow eyes. The beast bared its teeth, saliva dripping from its maw as it prepared to attack.

McKenna took aim and fired, the crack of the rifle echoing through the night. The bullet struck the wolf squarely in the chest, sending it sprawling to the ground.

The pack hesitated, momentarily thrown off by the loss of their leader. But hunger and instinct soon overrode caution, and they lunged forward as one, a snarling mass of fur and fangs.

Ellie fired her pistol, the muzzle flash illuminating the feral faces of the attackers. Beside her, Samuel swung a burning branch, attempting to ward off the encroaching predators.

The battle was chaotic, a blur of movement and sound. The wolves were relentless, their attacks driven by desperation. The group fought valiantly, but the sheer number of assailants threatened to overwhelm them.

In the midst of the fray, a wolf broke through the line, charging directly at Ellie. She raised her pistol, but the beast was too quick, knocking her to the ground.

McKenna saw her fall, a surge of adrenaline propelling him forward. He tackled the wolf, wrestling it away from Ellie. The two rolled across the ground, a tangle of limbs and fury.

With a grunt of effort, McKenna managed to draw his knife, plunging it into the wolf's side. The creature yelped and went limp, its lifeblood staining the earth.

Breathing heavily, McKenna rose to his feet, extending a hand to Ellie. "Are you alright?" he asked, concern etched across his features.

She nodded, accepting his hand and standing shakily. "Thanks to you," she replied, her voice trembling.

The remaining wolves, sensing the tide had turned, retreated into the night, their mournful howls echoing in the distance.

The group surveyed the aftermath, the ground littered with the bodies of the fallen predators. They had survived, but the encounter had left them shaken.

As they tended to their wounds and reinforced their defenses, Ellie couldn't shake the feeling that the attack had been more than a random encounter. The frontier was a harsh and unforgiving place, and dangers lurked around every corner.

But as she looked at her companions, their faces illuminated by the flickering firelight, she felt a renewed sense of determination. They had faced death and emerged victorious. Whatever challenges lay ahead, they would confront them together.

# CHAPTER
# THIRTY-TWO

The relentless sun beat down as Ellie and McKenna rode through the arid expanse, their horses kicking up clouds of dust with each weary step. The weight of their journey pressed heavily upon them, but an unspoken determination kept them moving forward.

As dusk approached, they reached a small settlement nestled beside a meandering river. The settlement was a modest cluster of wooden structures, with the distant sound of a blacksmith's hammer ringing through the air. The scent of fresh bread wafted from a nearby bakery, evoking memories of simpler times.

Dismounting, they led their horses to a trough outside the local inn. Ellie glanced at McKenna, her eyes reflecting a mixture of hope and apprehension.

"Do you think we'll find any leads here?" she asked, her voice tinged with fatigue.

McKenna placed a reassuring hand on her shoulder. "We

have to try. Every place we visit brings us one step closer to her."

Inside the inn, the atmosphere was warm and inviting. Patrons chatted amiably, and a fiddler played a lively tune in the corner. Approaching the bar, McKenna caught the attention of the innkeeper, a burly man with a thick beard and kind eyes.

"Evening," McKenna began. "We're looking for information about a group that might have passed through here some time ago. They... they took our daughter."

The innkeeper's expression softened. "I'm sorry to hear that. Many folks come and go, but I do recall a group traveling with a young girl not too long ago. They headed north, towards the mountains."

Ellie's heart quickened. "Did you see the girl? Was she... did she seem alright?"

He nodded slowly. "She seemed healthy, but scared. I'm sorry I can't tell you more."

Though the information was scant, it was the most promising lead they'd had in weeks. That night, as they settled into their room, Ellie sat by the window, gazing at the moonlit landscape.

"She's out there, McKenna," she whispered. "I can feel it."

He joined her, wrapping an arm around her shoulders. "And we'll find her, Ellie. No matter what it takes."

As they held each other, the vast wilderness stretched out before them, filled with unknown challenges. But for the first time in a long while, hope flickered in their hearts, guiding them toward the next chapter of their journey.

# CHAPTER THIRTY-THREE

**M**ercy McKenna's days had blurred into a relentless march of fear and exhaustion. The rugged terrain of the frontier was unforgiving, each step a battle against jagged rocks and thorny underbrush. Her captors, Jedediah "Jed" Crowe, Silas, and Buck, showed no mercy, driving her forward with curt commands and menacing glares.

One evening, as the sun dipped below the horizon, casting long shadows over their makeshift camp, Mercy was left momentarily unattended. Her wrists were raw from the coarse ropes, and hunger gnawed at her insides. Desperation clawed at her thoughts, urging her to act.

Summoning every ounce of courage, she began to work at the knots binding her wrists. The rough fibers bit into her skin, but she persisted, driven by the hope of escape. Just as the ropes began to loosen, a heavy boot slammed down beside her, sending a jolt of terror through her body.

"Thought you could slip away, did ya?" Silas sneered, yanking her to her feet. His grip was vice-like, fingers digging into her arm.

Before she could respond, Jed's imposing figure loomed over them. His cold eyes bore into hers, and without a word, he backhanded her across the face. Pain exploded in her cheek, and she crumpled to the ground, stars dancing in her vision.

"Let that be a lesson," Jed growled. "Next time, you won't get off so easy."

As the men settled around the campfire, Mercy lay on the cold ground, tears streaming down her face. The physical pain was excruciating, but it was the crushing weight of hopelessness that threatened to consume her.

Through the haze of despair, she overheard fragments of their conversation.

"We can't keep her forever," Buck muttered, his deep voice tinged with unease.

"We won't need to," Jed replied. "Once we get what we want, she's of no use to us."

Silas chuckled darkly. "And if we don't get it?"

Jed's silence was more ominous than any words.

As the fire crackled and the men lapsed into silence, Mercy's thoughts drifted to her parents. She could almost feel her mother's gentle touch, hear her father's reassuring voice. The memories were a balm to her wounded spirit, and she clung to them, drawing strength from the love they had shared.

In the days that followed, Mercy observed her captors

closely, searching for any weakness she could exploit. She noticed the way Silas's hands trembled when he handled his pistol, the way Buck avoided eye contact, as if ashamed. Even Jed, with his steely demeanor, had moments where his gaze would grow distant, haunted by unseen demons.

One night, as a storm raged overhead, Mercy was jolted awake by raised voices.

"This ain't right, Jed!" Buck shouted, his face contorted with anger. "She's just a kid!"

Jed's expression was a mask of fury. "You knew what you signed up for. There's no turning back now."

Silas stepped between them, his eyes darting nervously. "Calm down, both of you. We can't afford to be at each other's throats."

As the men argued, Mercy felt a flicker of hope. Their unity was fracturing, and she knew that if she was to escape, it would be through the cracks forming between them.

That night, as the storm's fury spent itself and the camp settled into uneasy silence, Mercy made a silent vow. She would survive this ordeal, not just for herself, but for her parents, who she knew were out there, searching for her. And when the time was right, she would seize her chance and break free from the shadows that sought to claim her.

# CHAPTER THIRTY-FOUR

The relentless sun beat down upon the desolate landscape, casting long shadows over the arid terrain. Mercy McKenna trudged forward, her body weakened by days of grueling travel and scant nourishment. Her once vibrant auburn hair hung in tangled strands, and her emerald eyes, now dulled by fatigue, scanned the horizon for any sign of reprieve.

Jedediah "Jed" Crowe led the procession, his imposing figure a constant reminder of her captivity. Beside him, Silas and Buck rode in silence, their expressions inscrutable. The oppressive heat seemed to sap the energy from all, but the men pressed on, driven by motives Mercy could only guess at.

As dusk approached, the group reached a narrow canyon, its towering walls offering a semblance of shelter. Jed signaled for a halt, and the men dismounted, setting up a rudimentary camp. Mercy was roughly shoved to the ground, her wrists bound tightly with coarse rope. The rough fibers bit into her skin, leaving angry red welts.

The men gathered around a small fire, the flickering flames casting eerie shadows on the canyon walls. Mercy's stomach churned with hunger, but she knew better than to expect any kindness from her captors. She curled into herself, seeking solace in the memories of her family, the warmth of her mother's embrace, and the strength of her father's reassuring presence.

The night was punctuated by the distant howls of coyotes, their mournful cries echoing through the canyon. Mercy's thoughts drifted to the tales she'd heard of the dangers lurking in the wilderness—predators both animal and human. The frontier was a harsh and unforgiving place, where survival was a daily battle against the elements and one's own fears.

As the firelight danced, casting grotesque shapes, Jed's gaze settled on Mercy. His eyes, cold and calculating, seemed to pierce through her, stripping away any semblance of hope. He rose and approached her, his boots crunching on the gravelly ground.

"You thinkin' of runnin' again?" he drawled, a sinister smile tugging at the corner of his mouth.

Mercy shook her head, her voice caught in her throat.

"Good," he continued, crouching down to her level. "Because out here, there's worse things than us. You wouldn't last a day."

He reached out, his rough hand gripping her chin, forcing her to meet his gaze. The smell of sweat and tobacco clung to him, making her stomach turn.

"Remember that," he whispered, his voice dripping with

menace.

Releasing her, he stood and returned to the fire, leaving Mercy trembling in the darkness. Tears welled in her eyes, but she blinked them away, refusing to give him the satisfaction.

The night wore on, the temperature plummeting as the stars wheeled overhead. Mercy shivered, the thin fabric of her dress offering little protection against the cold. Sleep was a distant dream, her mind racing with thoughts of escape and the dangers that lay beyond the canyon walls.

In the early hours before dawn, a rustling sound jolted her from her restless state. She strained her ears, trying to discern its source. The men were asleep, their snores echoing softly. The sound came again, closer this time—a soft, deliberate movement.

Her heart pounded in her chest as she scanned the darkness. A shadow detached itself from the canyon wall, moving with stealthy grace. As it drew nearer, the figure of a man emerged, his features obscured by the gloom.

Panic surged through her. Was this a new threat? Another predator drawn to her vulnerability?

The figure paused a few feet away, crouching low. A faint whisper reached her ears.

"Don't be afraid," the voice said, barely audible. "I'm here to help."

Hope and fear warred within her. Could she trust this stranger? What if it was a trap?

Before she could decide, the man moved closer, and in the dim light, she caught a glimpse of his face—weathered, with piercing eyes that held a glint of determination.

"I'm with the U.S. Marshal's service," he whispered urgently. "We've been tracking these men. I'm going to get you out of here."

Relief flooded through her, mingling with disbelief. Was this real? After days of despair, was salvation finally at hand?

The man produced a knife and swiftly cut her bonds, his movements efficient and silent.

"Can you walk?" he asked, concern evident in his tone.

She nodded, though her legs felt like lead.

"We need to move quickly," he said, helping her to her feet. "Stay close and keep quiet."

Together, they slipped into the shadows, leaving the camp and her captors behind. The canyon walls loomed around them, but for the first time since her ordeal began, Mercy felt a glimmer of hope.

As they navigated the treacherous terrain, the first light of dawn began to creep over the horizon, painting the sky in hues of pink and gold. The promise of a new day, and perhaps a new beginning, lay ahead.

# CHAPTER THIRTY-FIVE

The sun dipped below the horizon, casting the rugged landscape into a deep indigo. The chill of the desert night settled in, a stark contrast to the day's relentless heat. Mercy McKenna sat huddled near the campfire, its flickering flames offering scant warmth against the encroaching cold. The coarse rope binding her wrists had rubbed her skin raw, each movement eliciting a sharp sting.

Her captors—Jedediah "Jed" Crowe, Silas, and Buck—conversed in low tones, their faces obscured by the dancing shadows. Their voices, though muted, carried an undercurrent of tension that set Mercy's nerves on edge. She strained to catch snippets of their conversation, hoping for any clue that might aid her escape.

"We can't keep movin' like this," Silas muttered, his voice tinged with frustration.

Jed's response was a terse growl. "We do what we must. The girl's our leverage."

Mercy's heart pounded in her chest, each beat a drum signaling her dread. The vastness of the wilderness pressed in around her, amplifying her isolation. She longed for the familiar embrace of her mother's arms, the comforting murmur of her father's voice. The memories felt like lifetimes ago, slipping through her fingers like grains of sand.

As the night deepened, the campfire's glow cast eerie silhouettes on the canyon walls. The howls of distant coyotes echoed through the night, their mournful cries a haunting lullaby. Mercy shivered, not solely from the cold, but from the pervasive fear that gnawed at her insides.

In the quiet moments, when her captors' attention waned, Mercy lifted her gaze to the star-studded sky. The constellations sprawled above, indifferent to her plight. She whispered a silent prayer, her lips barely moving.

"Please, Ma, Pa... find me," she implored, her voice a fragile thread in the vast expanse. "Guide me home."

Tears welled in her eyes, but she blinked them away, unwilling to show weakness. She couldn't afford despair; she needed to stay strong, to believe that rescue would come.

The night wore on, each passing minute stretching into an eternity. Mercy's thoughts churned, a tumultuous sea of fear and hope. She replayed the events leading to her capture, searching for any detail she might have missed, any opportunity she could exploit.

Her captors' voices occasionally pierced the silence, their words a stark reminder of her predicament.

"We should've left her," Buck grumbled. "She's more trouble than she's worth."

Jed's retort was sharp. "She's our ticket. Don't forget that."

Mercy clenched her fists, the rough rope digging into her flesh. She refused to be a pawn in their game. Determination flared within her, a spark in the darkness. She would find a way to escape, to return to her family.

As the first light of dawn tinged the horizon, Mercy made a silent vow. No matter the cost, she would survive. She would not let fear consume her. She would fight, with every ounce of strength she possessed, until she was free.

# CHAPTER
# THIRTY-SIX

The relentless sun beat down upon the barren landscape, casting distorted shadows over the cracked earth. Mercy McKenna stumbled forward, her legs trembling with exhaustion. Each step was a monumental effort, her body screaming for rest, but the harsh prodding of Jedediah "Jed" Crowe's rifle butt forced her onward.

The group had been traversing the unforgiving desert for days, the monotony of the terrain broken only by the occasional skeletal remains of creatures that had succumbed to its merciless embrace. Mercy's throat was parched, her lips cracked and bleeding. The canteen she had been grudgingly offered contained water that tasted of rust and despair, doing little to quench her thirst.

As the sun dipped below the horizon, painting the sky in hues of crimson and gold, the group halted near a cluster of jagged rocks. The men busied themselves setting up a makeshift camp, their movements mechanical and devoid of conversation. Mercy was shoved to the ground, her wrists bound tightly with coarse rope that bit into her flesh.

The night air grew cold, a stark contrast to the day's oppressive heat. Mercy shivered, drawing her knees to her chest in a futile attempt to conserve warmth. The flickering flames of the campfire cast eerie shadows, illuminating the hardened faces of her captors.

Silas, his gaunt features accentuated by the firelight, rummaged through a worn leather satchel, producing a piece of dried meat. He tore into it with a ferocity that spoke of suppressed rage. Buck sat silently, his eyes vacant as he stared into the flames, lost in thoughts unknown.

Jed approached Mercy, a sinister smile playing on his lips. He crouched beside her, the stench of sweat and tobacco assaulting her senses.

"Hungry?" he sneered, holding a piece of the dried meat just out of her reach.

Mercy's stomach churned with hunger, but she refused to meet his gaze, focusing instead on a distant point beyond the firelight.

"Suit yourself," Jed shrugged, tossing the meat into the dirt at her feet before rising to join the others.

Tears welled in Mercy's eyes, but she blinked them away, unwilling to show weakness. The vastness of the desert mirrored the emptiness she felt inside, a void left by the absence of hope.

As the night deepened, the men settled into a restless sleep, their snores mingling with the distant howls of coyotes. Mercy lay awake, her mind a whirlwind of fear and despair. She thought of her parents, the warmth of her mother's embrace, the strength of her father's reassuring presence. Were they searching for her? Did they hold onto hope, or had they resigned themselves to the possibility of her loss?

The stars above seemed indifferent to her plight, their cold light offering no comfort. Mercy closed her eyes, whispering a silent prayer into the void.

"Please, if there's anyone listening, help me. Give me strength."

The wind carried her plea into the darkness, a fragile thread of hope in an otherwise desolate world.

As exhaustion finally claimed her, Mercy drifted into a fitful sleep, her dreams haunted by faceless figures and endless expanses of sand. The line between reality and nightmare blurred, each as unforgiving as the other.

Morning came too soon, the harsh light of dawn banishing the fleeting respite of sleep. The men roused themselves, their movements sluggish and irritable. Jed kicked at Mercy's feet, jolting her awake.

"Time to move," he barked, yanking her to her feet.

Mercy's legs wobbled beneath her, but she forced herself to stand, swallowing down the bile that rose in her throat. The journey continued, each step a testament to her dwindling strength.

As the sun climbed higher, the heat became oppressive, waves of it distorting the horizon. Mercy's vision blurred, black spots dancing at the edges. She stumbled, her knees hitting the ground hard.

"Get up!" Jed snarled, but his voice seemed distant,

echoing as if from a great chasm.

Mercy tried to rise, but her body betrayed her, collapsing into the dust. Darkness encroached upon her vision, the world narrowing to a single point before consuming her entirely.

In the depths of unconsciousness, Mercy floated, free from pain and fear. But even here, the shadows of her captors loomed, a constant reminder that escape was but a fleeting illusion.

# CHAPTER THIRTY-SEVEN

Mercy McKenna's consciousness wavered between the oppressive heat of the day and the biting cold of the desert night. Her body, battered and bruised, lay motionless on the unforgiving ground. The world around her was a blur of indistinct shapes and muted sounds, as if she were trapped in a suffocating fog.

The voices of her captors—Jedediah "Jed" Crowe, Silas, and Buck—drifted through the haze, their words a jumbled cacophony that she struggled to comprehend.

"She ain't gonna make it," Silas muttered, his tone laced with irritation.

"We need her alive," Jed snapped back. "She's our bargaining chip."

Mercy felt a rough hand grip her shoulder, shaking her violently. Her eyes fluttered open, the harsh light of the campfire stabbing into her retinas. Jed's face loomed above her, his features twisted into a mask of frustration.

"Wake up, girl," he growled. "We ain't got time for your fainting spells."

Pain radiated through her body as she was hauled to a sitting position. Her wrists, still bound by the coarse rope, throbbed with each heartbeat. The taste of blood lingered in her mouth, a metallic reminder of her earlier collapse.

"Drink," Buck said gruffly, thrusting a dented canteen toward her lips.

The water was lukewarm and brackish, but Mercy gulped it down greedily, her parched throat burning with each swallow. As the liquid coursed through her, a semblance of clarity returned to her mind.

The desert stretched out around them, an endless expanse of sand and rock bathed in the eerie glow of the moon. The vastness of it all pressed down on Mercy, amplifying her sense of isolation and despair.

"We move at first light," Jed announced, his voice brooking no argument. "Get some rest."

The men settled around the campfire, their silhouettes flickering against the canyon walls. Mercy curled into herself, seeking warmth and comfort that the cold earth refused to provide.

As the stars wheeled overhead, she closed her eyes and whispered a silent prayer.

"Ma, Pa... if you can hear me, please... help me."

Tears slipped down her cheeks, carving paths through the grime that coated her skin. The weight of her captivity pressed heavily upon her, threatening to crush the last vestiges of hope she clung to.

In the depths of her despair, a thought surfaced—a flicker of defiance amidst the darkness. She would not let them break her. She would endure, for herself and for the family she prayed was searching for her.

With renewed determination, Mercy vowed to seize any opportunity that presented itself. She would watch, wait, and when the moment was right, she would fight for her freedom.

As the first light of dawn crept over the horizon, painting the sky in hues of pink and gold, Mercy steeled herself for the trials ahead. The road to liberation would be fraught with peril, but she was resolved to traverse it, no matter the cost.

# CHAPTER THIRTY-EIGHT

**M**ercy McKenna's world had shrunk to a relentless cycle of torment and fleeting moments of fitful rest. The days bled into nights, each indistinguishable from the last, marked only by the shifting hues of the sky and the unyielding brutality of her captors.

As the sun dipped below the horizon, casting long shadows over the desolate landscape, the group halted to make camp. The air was thick with the scent of sagebrush and the distant cry of a lone coyote, a haunting melody that mirrored Mercy's own desolation.

Jedediah "Jed" Crowe, ever the vigilant leader, barked orders at Silas and Buck, his gravelly voice cutting through the stillness. Mercy was roughly shoved to the ground, her wrists bound tightly with coarse rope that chafed her already raw skin. The cold seeped into her bones, and she curled into herself, seeking warmth and solace that the barren earth refused to provide.

The flickering flames of the campfire cast eerie shadows, illuminating the harsh lines etched into the men's faces. Their laughter, coarse and devoid of mirth, grated on Mercy's ears, a cruel reminder of her helplessness. She closed her eyes, willing herself to disappear, to become one with the darkness that enveloped her.

In the quiet moments between their jeers, Mercy's thoughts turned inward, a desperate attempt to escape the grim reality of her situation. She thought of her parents, their faces a blur in her memory, and wondered if they were searching for her, if they held onto hope as tenuously as she did.

A sudden movement jolted her from her reverie. Jed loomed over her, his eyes glinting with a predatory gleam. He knelt beside her, his breath hot against her ear.

"You thinkin' of runnin', girl?" he whispered, his voice dripping with menace.

Mercy shook her head, fear constricting her throat.

"Good," he sneered, his hand gripping her chin with bruising force. "Because there's nowhere to run. Out here, you're mine."

He released her with a shove, and she fell back onto the hard ground, tears stinging her eyes. The weight of his words settled over her like a shroud, suffocating any flicker of hope that dared to ignite within her.

As the night deepened, the temperature plummeted, and Mercy's body trembled uncontrollably. The men had fallen into a restless sleep, their snores a discordant symphony that filled the air. She stared up at the vast expanse of the night sky, the stars cold and indifferent to her suffering.

A shooting star streaked across the heavens, a brief flash of light in the darkness. With a trembling breath, Mercy closed her eyes and whispered a silent prayer.

"Please," she implored, her voice barely audible. "Help me. Give me strength."

The wind carried her plea into the void, and she wondered if anyone—or anything—was listening. The enormity of her isolation pressed down upon her, and for a moment, she teetered on the edge of despair.

But deep within her, a spark flickered—a stubborn ember of defiance that refused to be extinguished. She would endure. She would survive. And when the opportunity arose, she would fight for her freedom, no matter the cost.

With renewed resolve, Mercy closed her eyes, allowing the exhaustion to pull her into a restless sleep, her mind clinging to the fragile hope that tomorrow might bring a chance for escape.

# CHAPTER THIRTY-NINE

The relentless sun had finally dipped below the horizon, casting the vast desert into a canvas of deep purples and blues. Mercy McKenna sat huddled near the meager campfire, its flickering flames offering little warmth against the encroaching chill of the night. Her wrists, raw and bleeding from the coarse ropes, throbbed in rhythm with her heartbeat. Every muscle in her body ached from the day's forced march, but it was the gnawing fear that truly exhausted her.

Jedediah "Jed" Crowe, Silas, and Buck busied themselves with their evening routines, their gruff voices and occasional laughter piercing the stillness. Mercy kept her gaze lowered, avoiding their eyes, praying to remain invisible. The weight of her captivity pressed heavily upon her, each day eroding a bit more of her spirit.

As the night deepened, the distant howl of a wolf echoed through the canyon, a haunting melody that sent shivers down Mercy's spine. She glanced toward the sound, her imagination conjuring images of gleaming eyes and sharp fangs lurking just beyond the firelight. The wilderness was as much a captor as the men who held her, its myriad dangers a constant reminder of her vulnerability.

The men seemed unfazed by the nocturnal calls, but Mercy's senses were heightened, every rustle of the wind or crackle of the fire magnified in her mind. She thought of her parents, wondering if they were searching for her, if they held onto hope as she tried to do. Tears welled in her eyes, but she blinked them away, unwilling to show any sign of weakness.

Suddenly, a series of guttural growls erupted from the darkness, followed by the unmistakable sounds of a struggle. The men sprang to their feet, hands reaching for their weapons.

"What in tarnation?" Buck muttered, peering into the shadows.

From the gloom emerged a pack of wolves, their eyes glowing with predatory intent. They circled the camp, drawn by the scent of food and the vulnerability of the lone human separated from the group—Mercy.

Jed raised his rifle, aiming at the nearest wolf. "Stay back!" he shouted, firing a warning shot into the air.

The wolves hesitated, their formation wavering, but hunger drove them forward. One lunged toward Mercy, its teeth bared.

A shot rang out, and the wolf yelped, collapsing mere feet from her. Silas lowered his smoking gun, his expression grim.

The pack, sensing the danger, retreated into the night, their mournful howls echoing long after they had vanished.

Mercy's heart raced, the adrenaline coursing through her veins leaving her trembling. She had been moments away from a brutal end, and the realization left her both terrified and oddly emboldened.

Jed approached her, his face a mask of anger. "You almost got yourself killed," he spat. "Stay close to the fire and don't move unless we tell you."

She nodded mutely, the words catching in her throat.

As the camp settled back into an uneasy calm, Mercy's mind raced. The encounter with the wolves had ignited a spark within her—a realization that the wilderness, with all its perils, could also be her ally. If she could navigate its dangers, perhaps she could find a way to escape her human captors.

The night wore on, and while the men slept fitfully, Mercy remained awake, her thoughts consumed with plans of escape. She knew the risks were immense, but the alternative —remaining a prisoner, subject to their whims—was a fate she could no longer endure.

As the first light of dawn crept over the horizon, painting the sky in shades of pink and gold, Mercy made a silent vow. She would seize the first opportunity to flee, to embrace the wild unknown rather than the cruel certainty of her captors. Her journey would be fraught with danger, but freedom, no matter how perilous, was a prize worth any risk.

# CHAPTER FORTY

The relentless sun had begun its descent, casting elongated shadows over the rugged terrain. Mercy McKenna trudged alongside her captors, her body aching from days of relentless travel. The once-overwhelming fear had settled into a numb resignation, yet a flicker of hope remained—a hope that she might find a way to escape or that her parents were searching for her.

Jedediah "Jed" Crowe led the group, his silhouette sharp against the dusky sky. He was a man hardened by life, his exterior as unyielding as the rocks they traversed. Yet, unbeknownst to Mercy, cracks had begun to form in his hardened demeanor.

As night fell, the group made camp near a secluded grove. The air was thick with the scent of pine and damp earth, a welcome change from the arid plains. Silas and Buck busied themselves with the fire, while Jed approached Mercy, who sat apart, her hands bound and eyes distant.

"Here," Jed grunted, tossing a worn blanket at her feet. "Nights get cold in these parts."

Startled, Mercy looked up, meeting his gaze. There was an unfamiliar softness in his eyes, a glimmer of something she couldn't quite place. She nodded in silent gratitude, pulling the blanket around her shoulders.

The fire crackled, casting dancing shadows on the surrounding trees. The men ate in silence, the weight of their journey pressing down on them. Mercy nibbled on the stale bread she was given, her mind racing with thoughts of escape.

Later, as the others slept, Mercy remained awake, staring into the dying embers. A rustling sound broke the silence, and she turned to see Jed approaching. He sat down beside her, his presence both intimidating and oddly comforting.

"Can't sleep?" he asked, his voice low.

She shook her head, unsure of what to say.

Jed sighed, rubbing a hand over his face. "This life... it ain't what I wanted."

Surprised by his candor, Mercy glanced at him, curiosity piqued.

"Had dreams once," he continued, staring into the darkness. "But the world has a way of crushing 'em."

For a moment, the gap between captor and captive seemed to narrow. Mercy saw not a ruthless outlaw, but a man burdened by regrets and lost aspirations.

"Why are you telling me this?" she whispered.

Jed met her gaze, his eyes reflecting the flickering flames. "Maybe 'cause you remind me of someone I lost. Someone I failed to protect."

A heavy silence settled between them, broken only by the distant call of a night bird. In that moment, an unspoken understanding passed between them—a fragile bond forged in the crucible of shared suffering.

As the first light of dawn crept over the horizon, painting the sky in hues of pink and gold, Mercy felt a glimmer of something she hadn't felt in days: compassion. Perhaps, within the heart of her captor, there was a flicker of humanity—a flicker that might be her salvation.

# CHAPTER
# FORTY-ONE

The desert night had settled into a profound silence, broken only by the occasional crackle of the campfire and the distant call of nocturnal creatures. Mercy McKenna sat apart from her captors, her thoughts a turbulent sea of fear, hope, and confusion. The days of captivity had begun to blur together, each one an arduous test of her endurance.

Jedediah "Jed" Crowe observed her from across the fire, his brow furrowed in contemplation. The hardened outlaw had noticed a change in Mercy—a resilience that both intrigued and unsettled him. He found himself grappling with unfamiliar feelings of protectiveness, a sentiment he hadn't anticipated.

As the firelight danced on the rugged faces of the men, Silas leaned in, his voice a low murmur.

"Jed, we need to talk," he said, casting a wary glance toward Mercy.

Jed nodded, rising to his feet. "Buck, keep an eye on the girl," he ordered, before stepping away with Silas into the shadows.

Once they were out of earshot, Silas turned to Jed, his expression grim.

"Jed, I've been thinkin'. What if we got the wrong girl?"

Jed's eyes narrowed. "What are you gettin' at?"

Silas sighed, rubbing the back of his neck. "I mean, what if this ain't the McKenna girl we were after? We never got a good look at her before the snatch, and folks say there's another girl in town 'bout her age."

Jed's jaw tightened as he considered Silas's words. The possibility of a mistaken identity hadn't crossed his mind, and the realization sent a chill down his spine.

"If that's true," Jed muttered, "we're in deeper trouble than we thought."

Back at the campfire, Mercy sensed the tension among her captors. She couldn't hear their conversation, but their furtive glances and hushed tones spoke volumes. A seed of doubt took root in her mind—did they realize they had taken the wrong person?

As the night wore on, Jed returned to the campfire, his face a mask of conflicting emotions. He approached Mercy, his gaze searching hers.

"Girl," he began, his voice softer than she'd ever heard it, "I need to ask you somethin'. What's your full name?"

Mercy hesitated, her heart pounding. "It's Mercy," she replied cautiously.

Jed nodded slowly, a troubled look in his eyes. "Mercy, do you have any kin by the name of McKenna?"

She shook her head. "No, sir. My pa's name was Thompson."

A heavy silence settled between them as Jed absorbed this revelation. The weight of their mistake pressed down on him, and he felt a pang of guilt—a foreign sensation for a man of his disposition.

"I see," he murmured, more to himself than to her.

Mercy watched him, a flicker of hope igniting within her. Perhaps this mistake could be her salvation.

As the first light of dawn crept over the horizon, painting the sky in hues of pink and gold, the camp stirred. Jed gathered the men, his demeanor somber.

"We've made a grave error," he confessed, his voice heavy with regret. "This ain't the girl we were after."

Silas and Buck exchanged uneasy glances, the gravity of their situation sinking in.

"What do we do now?" Buck asked, his voice tinged with fear.

Jed looked over at Mercy, who sat quietly, her eyes reflecting a mixture of apprehension and hope. He took a deep breath, the weight of leadership pressing upon him.

"We can't undo what's been done," he said slowly. "But maybe... maybe we can make it right."

The men nodded reluctantly, understanding the unspoken decision. Their journey had taken an unexpected turn, and the path ahead was uncertain.

As they prepared to break camp, Jed approached Mercy once more.

"I'm sorry," he said quietly, the sincerity in his voice surprising them both.

Mercy looked up at him, her expression unreadable. "What happens now?" she asked softly.

Jed sighed, glancing toward the horizon. "Now, we find a way to set things right."

And with that, the unlikely group set off into the unknown, each step a testament to the fragile bonds formed under the vast desert sky.

# CHAPTER FORTY-TWO

The first light of dawn crept over the horizon, casting a pale glow on the rugged landscape. Mercy McKenna stirred from a restless sleep, her body aching from the harsh conditions of captivity. The revelation of her mistaken identity had introduced a tense uncertainty among her captors, and she sensed that the dynamics within the group were shifting.

Jedediah "Jed" Crowe stood apart from the camp, his gaze fixed on the distant mountains. The weight of their error pressed heavily upon him, and he grappled with the moral implications of their actions. His thoughts were interrupted by a distant, rhythmic sound—a low rumble that seemed to resonate through the earth.

Silas approached, his expression tense. "Jed, you hear that?"

Jed nodded, his eyes narrowing. "Sounds like horses. A lot of 'em."

The men quickly roused themselves, scanning the horizon for the source of the sound. As the sun climbed higher, a plume of dust became visible, accompanied by the unmistakable silhouettes of mounted riders.

"Indians," Buck muttered, his hand instinctively reaching for his rifle.

Jed raised a hand, signaling for caution. "Hold on. Let's not jump to conclusions."

As the riders drew nearer, it became clear that they were indeed a group of Native American warriors, their faces painted and expressions stern. The leader, a tall man with a feathered headdress, raised his hand in a gesture of greeting.

Jed stepped forward, his hands open to show he meant no harm. "We come in peace," he called out.

The leader regarded him silently for a moment before speaking in halting English. "Why are you here?"

Jed chose his words carefully. "We're passing through, heading west. We mean no trouble."

The leader's gaze shifted to Mercy, who stood behind Jed, her hands still bound. "Why is the woman tied?"

Jed hesitated, aware of how their situation might appear. "There was a misunderstanding. We're trying to make it right."

The leader's eyes narrowed. "Release her."

Jed glanced back at Mercy, then nodded to Silas, who reluctantly cut her bonds. Mercy rubbed her wrists, looking between Jed and the leader with a mix of fear and hope.

The leader dismounted, approaching Mercy. "Are you

harmed?"

She shook her head, her voice barely above a whisper. "No."

The leader turned back to Jed. "You will leave this land. Now."

Jed nodded. "We will. Thank you."

As the warriors mounted their horses and rode away, the tension in the camp began to dissipate. Jed turned to his men. "Pack up. We're moving out."

As they prepared to leave, Mercy approached Jed. "Thank you," she said softly.

Jed met her gaze, a flicker of something unspoken passing between them. "Let's get moving," he replied gruffly.

As they continued their journey, the encounter with the Native American warriors lingered in their minds, a stark reminder of the complexities of the land they traversed and the fragile nature of their own humanity.

# CHAPTER FORTY-THREE

The sun hung low in the sky, casting an amber glow over the desolate landscape. Mercy McKenna trudged alongside her captors, the weight of her predicament pressing heavily upon her. The revelation of her mistaken identity had introduced a palpable tension among the group, each member grappling with the moral implications of their actions.

Jedediah "Jed" Crowe led the procession, his gaze fixed on the horizon. The rugged terrain stretched endlessly before them, a testament to the unforgiving nature of the frontier. The silence was broken only by the rhythmic crunch of boots against gravel and the distant cawing of ravens circling overhead.

As dusk settled, the group made camp near a cluster of jagged rocks that offered minimal shelter from the elements. The air was thick with the scent of impending rain, and dark clouds loomed ominously on the horizon. The men worked in terse silence, their movements mechanical and devoid of the camaraderie that once defined their interactions.

Mercy sat apart from the others, her wrists still bearing the raw imprints of the ropes that had bound her. She watched as Silas and Buck gathered firewood, their faces etched with fatigue and something else—perhaps regret. Jed approached her, his expression unreadable.

"Storm's comin'," he remarked, his voice a gravelly murmur.

Mercy nodded, her eyes scanning the darkening sky. "Looks like a bad one."

Jed crouched beside her, his gaze intense. "We need to talk. About what happens next."

Before Mercy could respond, a deafening crack of thunder reverberated through the air, followed by a blinding flash of lightning. The heavens opened, unleashing a torrential downpour that drenched them within moments.

"Get under the rocks!" Jed shouted, his voice barely audible over the roar of the storm.

The group scrambled for cover, huddling beneath the overhang as the storm raged around them. The wind howled like a wounded beast, and the rain fell in sheets, turning the ground into a treacherous mire.

As the tempest intensified, a new sound emerged—a distant rumble that grew steadily louder. Jed's eyes widened in realization.

"Flash flood!" he bellowed. "We need to move, now!"

Panic surged through the group as they scrambled to

gather their belongings. The ground trembled beneath their feet, and the rumble grew to a roar as a wall of water surged toward them, carrying debris and uprooted trees in its wake.

Mercy felt a strong hand grasp her arm, pulling her to her feet. It was Jed, his face set in grim determination.

"This way!" he shouted, leading her toward higher ground.

The group fought their way through the deluge, the water rising rapidly around them. Silas stumbled, his foot caught in the mire, and let out a strangled cry as the floodwaters swept him off his feet.

"Silas!" Buck yelled, reaching out a hand, but it was too late. Silas disappeared beneath the churning waters, his scream swallowed by the storm.

Mercy felt a surge of horror, but there was no time to process the loss. Jed urged her forward, his grip unyielding as they climbed toward a rocky outcrop that offered a precarious refuge from the raging flood.

They reached the outcrop, collapsing onto the slick stone as the waters surged below. The storm showed no signs of abating, and the night was filled with the relentless fury of nature unleashed.

Hours passed before the rain subsided and the floodwaters began to recede. The landscape was unrecognizable, transformed into a muddy wasteland strewn with debris.

The survivors sat in stunned silence, the weight of their ordeal pressing heavily upon them. The loss of Silas hung over them like a shroud, a stark reminder of the fragility of life on the frontier.

Jed finally broke the silence, his voice hoarse. "We need to keep moving. Find shelter and regroup."

Buck nodded numbly, his eyes hollow. Mercy glanced at Jed, a question in her eyes.

"What now?" she asked softly.

Jed met her gaze, his expression hardening. "Now, we survive."

As they gathered their meager belongings and set off into the uncertain dawn, Mercy couldn't shake the feeling that their greatest challenges still lay ahead. The storm had tested their physical endurance, but the true tempest was brewing within—their moral compasses spinning wildly as they navigated the treacherous terrain of guilt, redemption, and the unrelenting quest for survival.

# CHAPTER FORTY-FOUR

The storm had passed, leaving behind a transformed and treacherous landscape. The once-familiar terrain was now a chaotic expanse of mud, debris, and uprooted vegetation. The air was thick with the scent of damp earth and the lingering tension of survival.

Mercy McKenna, Jedediah "Jed" Crowe, and Buck stood in somber silence, the weight of Silas's loss pressing heavily upon them. The flash flood had not only claimed their companion but had also stripped them of essential supplies, leaving them vulnerable in the unforgiving wilderness.

"We need to find shelter," Jed said, his voice rough from exhaustion. "And figure out our next move."

Buck nodded, his usual bravado subdued. "Ain't much left of our gear. We're gonna have to make do."

Mercy remained silent, her mind a whirlwind of emotions. The harrowing experience had forged an unspoken bond between her and her captors, blurring the lines between enemy and ally.

As they navigated the altered landscape, the group stumbled upon a narrow cave entrance, partially concealed by fallen rocks. The interior was dark and uninviting, but it offered a semblance of safety from the elements.

"This'll have to do for now," Jed muttered, leading the way inside.

The cave was cool and damp, the walls glistening with moisture. They settled in, using what remained of their belongings to create makeshift bedding. The silence was heavy, each person lost in their thoughts.

As night fell, the temperature dropped, and the cave grew colder. Mercy shivered, pulling her tattered shawl tighter around her shoulders. Noticing her discomfort, Jed removed his coat and draped it over her without a word.

"Thank you," she whispered, her voice barely audible.

Jed nodded, his expression unreadable. "Get some rest. We'll need our strength come morning."

Sleep came fitfully, haunted by the memories of the flood and the uncertainty of what lay ahead. The howling wind outside served as a constant reminder of nature's unpredictable fury.

In the early hours before dawn, Mercy awoke to the sound of hushed voices. She remained still, straining to hear the conversation between Jed and Buck.

"We can't keep goin' like this," Buck was saying, his tone edged with desperation. "We're low on supplies, and the girl's slowin' us down."

Jed's response was measured. "Leavin' her ain't an option. We took her, and it's our responsibility to see this through."

Buck scoffed. "Responsibility? Since when did you grow a conscience, Jed?"

There was a tense pause before Jed replied, his voice firm. "Since now. We do this right, or not at all."

Mercy felt a surge of gratitude toward Jed, mingled with a profound sense of guilt. Their predicament was a direct result of her abduction, and the realization weighed heavily on her conscience.

As dawn broke, casting a pale light into the cave, the group prepared to move on. The journey ahead was fraught with uncertainty, but an unspoken resolve had settled among them. They were bound together by circumstance, each person's fate intertwined with the others.

Emerging from the cave, they were greeted by a transformed world. The storm had carved new paths through the landscape, creating obstacles and challenges they could not have anticipated.

"Stay close," Jed instructed, his eyes scanning the horizon. "We don't know what we're walkin' into."

The group moved cautiously, the weight of their situation pressing down upon them. The line between captor and captive had blurred, leaving them as equals in the face of the wilderness's relentless trials.

As they pressed on, the true test lay not in the external challenges they faced, but in the internal struggles that threatened to tear them apart. Trust had to be earned, and redemption sought, in a land where survival was the only law.

# CHAPTER
# FORTY-FIVE

The relentless sun beat down upon the trio as they trudged through the arid expanse, the aftermath of the storm leaving the land both parched and treacherous. Mercy McKenna's feet ached with each step, her body weary from the unending journey. Beside her, Jedediah "Jed" Crowe maintained a stoic silence, his gaze fixed on the horizon, while Buck lagged behind, his demeanor growing increasingly sullen.

As dusk approached, they stumbled upon the remnants of an abandoned homestead—a dilapidated cabin, its roof partially caved in, surrounded by overgrown weeds. The sight offered a glimmer of hope for respite.

"We'll camp here tonight," Jed announced, his voice breaking the silence.

Buck grunted in agreement, dropping his pack unceremoniously by the cabin's entrance. Mercy followed suit, her eyes scanning the decaying structure.

Inside, the air was musty, filled with the scent of aged wood and neglect. A broken table lay overturned, and remnants of a life once lived were scattered across the floor—rusted utensils, a torn quilt, a child's wooden toy.

As night fell, they managed to kindle a small fire using scraps of wood, its flickering light casting dancing shadows on the cabin walls. The crackling flames provided a semblance of comfort amidst the desolation.

After a meager meal, Buck retreated to a corner, muttering about taking the first watch. Jed and Mercy sat across from each other, the silence between them thick with unspoken words.

Finally, Jed cleared his throat, his gaze distant. "This place... reminds me of home," he began, his voice tinged with a rare vulnerability.

Mercy looked up, curiosity piqued. "Where was home for you?"

"A small farm, not too different from this," he replied, gesturing around the cabin. "Had a wife, a daughter..."

He paused, the weight of his memories evident. "She was about your age. Bright, full of life. But then..."

He swallowed hard, his voice faltering. "Cholera swept through our town. Took her from us in a matter of days."

Mercy's heart ached at his confession. "I'm so sorry, Jed."

He nodded, a bitter smile tugging at his lips. "After that, nothing mattered. I left, took up with the wrong crowd. Figured if the world could be so cruel, why shouldn't I?"

The revelation hung heavy in the air, offering Mercy a

glimpse into the man behind the outlaw's facade.

"People make choices," she said softly. "But it's never too late to make different ones."

Jed met her gaze, a flicker of hope in his eyes. "Maybe you're right."

Their conversation was interrupted by a sudden noise outside—a rustling, followed by hushed voices. Jed's hand instinctively went to his revolver, and Buck was instantly alert, weapon drawn.

"Who's out there?" Jed called, his voice firm.

A tense silence followed before a figure stepped into the doorway—a man, disheveled and weary, hands raised in a gesture of peace.

"Please," the stranger implored. "I mean no harm. Just seeking shelter."

Behind him, two more figures emerged—a woman clutching a small child, both looking equally haggard.

Jed exchanged a glance with Buck, who shrugged indifferently. Mercy, however, felt a pang of empathy.

"Let them in," she urged. "They need help."

After a moment's hesitation, Jed nodded. "Alright. But no funny business."

The family entered cautiously, gratitude evident in their eyes. As they settled by the fire, the man introduced himself as Samuel, his wife as Clara, and their daughter as Emily.

"We've been on the road for weeks," Samuel explained. "Lost our home in the storm. Been trying to find a safe place ever since."

As the night wore on, stories were exchanged, and a fragile sense of camaraderie developed. Yet, beneath the surface, tensions simmered—resources were scarce, and trust was a luxury none could afford.

Unbeknownst to them all, in the shadows beyond the cabin, unseen eyes watched their every move, plotting the next challenge that fate would throw their way.

# CHAPTER FORTY-SIX

The morning sun cast a pale light over the dilapidated cabin, its rays filtering through the gaps in the weathered wood. Mercy McKenna stirred from a restless sleep, the weight of the previous day's revelations heavy on her mind. The presence of Samuel, Clara, and their daughter Emily had introduced a fragile sense of normalcy, but beneath the surface, tensions simmered.

As the group gathered around the remnants of the fire, the air was thick with unspoken concerns. Supplies were dwindling, and the uncertainty of their journey loomed large.

"We need to discuss our next steps," Jedediah "Jed" Crowe began, his tone authoritative yet measured. "Our provisions won't last much longer, and we can't afford to stay here."

Samuel nodded in agreement. "There's a trading post a few days' journey from here. We might find what we need there."

Buck, who had been silently sharpening his knife, looked up with a scowl. "And how do we know we can trust them?"

"We don't," Jed replied evenly. "But we don't have many options."

Mercy observed the exchange, noting the growing friction between Jed and Buck. The loss of Silas had altered the group's dynamics, and the introduction of the new family had only added to the complexity.

As they prepared to set out, Clara approached Mercy, her expression a mix of gratitude and concern.

"Thank you for convincing them to let us stay," Clara said softly. "I don't know what we would have done otherwise."

Mercy offered a reassuring smile. "We're all in this together now."

The journey was arduous, the terrain unforgiving. The sun beat down mercilessly, and the scarcity of water became an ever-present concern. Emily, the youngest among them, struggled to keep pace, her small frame wilting under the harsh conditions.

As dusk approached, they made camp near a sparse grove of trees, the first semblance of shelter they'd encountered in hours. The mood was somber, each member of the group lost in their own thoughts.

After a meager meal, Jed motioned for Mercy to join him a short distance from the camp. She followed, curiosity piqued.

"I need to tell you something," Jed began, his voice low. "About why we took you."

Mercy's heart quickened. This was the moment she'd been dreading, yet desperately needed to understand.

"It was supposed to be a simple job," Jed continued. "Grab the girl, deliver her to the buyer, and collect the payment."

"But why me?" Mercy asked, her voice trembling. "My family has no money. There's no ransom to be had."

Jed sighed, running a hand through his hair. "It wasn't about ransom. The buyer wanted a girl of a certain age, certain appearance. You fit the description."

"So it was a mistake?" Mercy pressed.

"In a way," Jed admitted. "But once we had you, there was no turning back."

The revelation left Mercy reeling. She had been taken not for who she was, but for what she represented—a commodity to be traded.

"Who is this buyer?" she demanded.

Jed shook his head. "I don't know. The arrangements were made through intermediaries. All I know is that the payment was substantial."

Mercy felt a surge of anger and despair. Her life had been uprooted, her future thrown into uncertainty, all for the sake of someone else's profit.

As they returned to the camp, the weight of the revelation hung heavy between them. The path ahead was fraught with danger, and the true nature of their predicament was only beginning to unfold.

# CHAPTER FORTY-SEVEN

The oppressive heat of the day had given way to a stifling night, the air thick with humidity and the distant rumble of an approaching storm. Mercy McKenna sat by the dwindling campfire, her thoughts a tangled web of fear and uncertainty. The revelation of her abduction's true nature had left her reeling, and the path ahead seemed more treacherous than ever.

Jedediah "Jed" Crowe stood at the edge of the camp, his silhouette illuminated by sporadic flashes of lightning. His gaze was fixed on the horizon, where dark clouds gathered ominously. Beside him, Buck paced restlessly, his agitation palpable.

"We need to find shelter," Jed announced, turning to face the group. "That storm's rolling in fast."

Samuel, cradling a sleeping Emily in his arms, nodded in agreement. "There's a cave system not far from here," he suggested. "We might find refuge there."

Clara, her face etched with worry, glanced at Mercy. "Can you manage?" she asked softly.

Mercy mustered a weak smile. "I'll be fine," she replied, though her body ached with exhaustion.

The group hastily gathered their meager belongings and set off into the encroaching darkness, the wind picking up and carrying with it the scent of rain. The terrain was rugged, and the first droplets began to fall as they reached the mouth of the cave—a yawning chasm that seemed to swallow the light.

Inside, the air was cool and damp, the walls glistening with moisture. The sound of dripping water echoed through the cavern, creating an eerie symphony. They ventured deeper, seeking a dry spot to wait out the storm.

As they settled in, the full fury of the tempest unleashed outside. Thunder roared, and the cave entrance was illuminated by blinding flashes of lightning. The ground trembled with each clap, and the howling wind carried the scent of ozone and wet earth.

"We should be safe here," Jed assured the group, though his eyes betrayed a hint of unease.

Hours passed, the storm showing no sign of abating. The group huddled together for warmth, the darkness pressing in around them. Mercy found herself seated beside Jed, the proximity offering a strange comfort.

"You ever been in a storm like this?" she asked, her voice barely audible over the din.

Jed shook his head. "Not in a long time," he replied. "Nature has a way of reminding us how small we are."

A sudden noise from deeper within the cave—a

low, guttural growl—sent a chill down Mercy's spine. She exchanged a fearful glance with Jed, who immediately reached for his revolver.

"Stay close," he whispered, rising to his feet.

The growl sounded again, closer this time. The group tensed, eyes straining to pierce the darkness. Suddenly, a pair of glowing eyes appeared in the blackness, followed by another, and another.

"Wolves," Buck hissed, his hand tightening around his rifle.

The pack emerged from the shadows, their sleek forms moving with predatory grace. The lead wolf, larger than the rest, bared its teeth, a low snarl rumbling from its throat.

"Don't make any sudden moves," Jed cautioned, his voice steady. "They're likely seeking shelter from the storm, same as us."

The two groups faced each other, the tension palpable. The wolves' eyes gleamed in the dim light, their breath visible in the cool air. For a moment, time seemed to stand still.

Then, as if reaching a silent agreement, the lead wolf turned and retreated into the depths of the cave, the rest of the pack following suit. The group exhaled collectively, the danger seemingly passed.

"That was too close," Clara murmured, clutching Emily tightly.

Jed nodded, his expression grim. "We need to stay alert. There could be other dangers lurking."

As the storm raged on outside, the group remained

vigilant, the encounter with the wolves a stark reminder of the perils they faced—not just from the elements, but from the wild creatures that called this land home.

In the heart of the cave, surrounded by darkness and the relentless fury of the storm, Mercy couldn't shake the feeling that their ordeal was far from over. The wilderness was a harsh and unforgiving place, and survival would demand every ounce of their strength and resolve.

# CHAPTER FORTY-EIGHT

The storm had finally abated, leaving the landscape drenched and the air thick with the scent of wet earth. As dawn broke, the group emerged cautiously from the cave that had served as their refuge. The sky was a canvas of muted grays, with the sun struggling to pierce through the lingering clouds.

Mercy McKenna stretched her stiff limbs, the events of the previous night still vivid in her mind. The encounter with the wolf pack had been a stark reminder of the dangers that lurked in the wilderness. She cast a glance at Jedediah "Jed" Crowe, who was already surveying their surroundings, his expression inscrutable.

"We should get moving," Jed announced, his voice cutting through the morning stillness. "The trading post isn't far, but we need to stay vigilant."

Buck grunted in agreement, though his eyes held a glint of impatience. The tension between him and Jed had been simmering, an unspoken conflict that Mercy sensed but couldn't fully understand.

Samuel and Clara gathered their belongings, with little Emily clutching a worn doll to her chest. The family had been a silent addition to their group, their presence both a comfort and a complication.

As they set off, the terrain proved challenging. The recent downpour had transformed the dirt paths into treacherous mud, slowing their progress. The dense foliage dripped with residual moisture, and the air was thick with humidity.

Hours passed in arduous travel, the group's energy waning. The forest around them was alive with the sounds of unseen creatures, the rustling of leaves, and the distant calls of birds. The oppressive atmosphere weighed heavily on their spirits.

As they navigated a narrow trail flanked by towering trees, a sudden movement caught Mercy's eye. Before she could react, a figure emerged from the underbrush—a man, disheveled and wild-eyed, brandishing a rusted knife.

"Hand over your supplies!" the stranger demanded, his voice a frantic rasp.

Jed stepped forward, his hand hovering near his holstered revolver. "We don't want any trouble," he said evenly. "But we can't afford to lose what little we have."

The man's eyes darted between the members of the group, his desperation palpable. "I haven't eaten in days," he pleaded. "Please... just a bit of food."

Mercy felt a pang of sympathy, but before she could

speak, Buck interjected. "We don't owe you anything," he snarled. "Get lost before I make you."

The stranger's grip tightened on his knife, and for a tense moment, it seemed violence was inevitable. But then, with a defeated sigh, he lowered his weapon and slunk back into the forest, disappearing as suddenly as he had appeared.

The encounter left the group shaken, a stark reminder of the desperation that pervaded the frontier. They resumed their journey, the weight of their circumstances pressing heavily upon them.

As dusk approached, they reached a clearing where the remnants of an old campsite lay abandoned. A dilapidated wagon rested on its side, its wheels broken and its contents scattered.

"We'll camp here for the night," Jed declared, though the unease in his voice was evident.

As they settled in, Clara approached Mercy, her expression troubled. "I couldn't help but notice," she began hesitantly, "the way those men look at you. Is everything... alright?"

Mercy forced a smile, though her heart raced. "I'm fine," she lied. "Just tired from the journey."

Clara seemed unconvinced but nodded, retreating to tend to Emily. Mercy watched her go, the burden of her secret growing heavier with each passing day.

As night fell, the group huddled around a modest fire, the flickering flames casting long shadows. The forest around them was alive with nocturnal sounds—the hoot of an owl, the rustle of leaves, the distant howl of a wolf.

Sleep came fitfully, each member of the group wrestling with their own fears and uncertainties. The challenges of the journey had taken their toll, and the path ahead remained fraught with peril.

Unbeknownst to them, hidden eyes watched from the darkness, and the true extent of the dangers they faced had yet to be revealed.

# CHAPTER FORTY-NINE

The morning sun cast a pale light over the makeshift campsite, its rays filtering through the dense canopy of trees. Mercy McKenna awoke to the sounds of the wilderness—a symphony of chirping birds and rustling leaves. The events of the previous days weighed heavily on her mind, but there was little time for reflection.

Jedediah "Jed" Crowe was already up, his eyes scanning the horizon with a wary intensity. Buck sat a short distance away, sharpening his knife with deliberate strokes, his demeanor as tense as ever. Samuel and Clara tended to their daughter, Emily, who clung to her mother with a mixture of fatigue and fear.

"We need to keep moving," Jed announced, breaking the morning silence. "The trading post is still a day's journey ahead, and we can't afford any delays."

The group nodded in agreement, quickly gathering their belongings. The path ahead was fraught with uncertainty, and each step seemed heavier than the last.

As they ventured deeper into the forest, the terrain became increasingly treacherous. The recent rains had turned the trails into a quagmire, making progress slow and arduous. The dense foliage closed in around them, casting eerie shadows that danced with each gust of wind.

Hours passed in weary silence, the only sounds being the squelch of mud underfoot and the occasional call of distant wildlife. The oppressive humidity clung to them, sapping their strength and dampening their spirits.

As the sun reached its zenith, they came upon a wide river, its waters swollen and swift from the recent storms. The remnants of a crude wooden bridge jutted from the banks, half-submerged and broken.

"We'll need to find a way across," Jed stated, his brow furrowing as he assessed the situation.

Buck scoffed, his impatience evident. "We don't have time for this. Let's just ford the river and be done with it."

"The current's too strong," Samuel interjected, concern etched on his face. "We could be swept away."

A tense debate ensued, with tempers flaring and anxiety mounting. Mercy watched the exchange, her own fears bubbling beneath the surface.

Finally, Jed raised a hand, silencing the argument. "We'll follow the riverbank upstream," he decided. "There might be a safer crossing point."

Reluctantly, the group complied, trudging along the muddy banks as the sun dipped lower in the sky. The journey was grueling, each step a battle against the sucking mire and the relentless pull of exhaustion.

As dusk approached, they stumbled upon a narrow section of the river where a fallen tree spanned the rushing waters—a natural bridge, slick with moss and precarious.

"This is our chance," Jed declared, though his tone carried a note of caution. "But we need to be careful."

One by one, they inched across the slippery log, hearts pounding with each tentative step. The roar of the river filled their ears, and the spray of cold water misted their faces.

Mercy was halfway across when her foot slipped, sending her sprawling onto the log. A gasp escaped her lips as she clung desperately to the rough bark, her legs dangling over the churning abyss.

"Hold on!" Jed shouted, rushing to her aid. With a firm grip, he hauled her back onto the log, his eyes locking onto hers with an intensity that sent a shiver down her spine.

"Thank you," she whispered, her voice trembling.

He nodded, his expression unreadable. "Let's keep moving."

Once safely across, they continued their journey, the incident leaving them shaken but resolute. The forest seemed to close in around them as night fell, the darkness thick and impenetrable.

They made camp in a small clearing, the flickering flames of their fire casting long shadows that danced among the trees. The atmosphere was somber, each member of the group lost in their own thoughts.

As Mercy sat by the fire, she couldn't shake the feeling of

being watched. The hairs on the back of her neck prickled, and a sense of unease settled over her like a shroud.

Suddenly, a rustling in the underbrush snapped her attention to the edge of the clearing. Her breath caught in her throat as a pair of glowing eyes emerged from the darkness—a large, hulking figure stepping into the light.

A massive grizzly bear stood before them, its fur matted and its eyes gleaming with a predatory hunger. The beast let out a deafening roar, its jaws snapping as it advanced toward the group.

Panic erupted as everyone scrambled to their feet, weapons drawn and hearts racing. Jed fired a shot, the bullet grazing the bear's shoulder and eliciting an enraged bellow.

"Stay back!" Jed shouted, positioning himself between the bear and the others.

The bear charged, its massive form barreling toward them with terrifying speed. In the chaos, Buck lunged forward, brandishing his knife, but the bear swatted him aside with a powerful swipe, sending him crashing into a tree.

Samuel grabbed a burning log from the fire and thrust it toward the bear, the flames licking at its face, causing the beast to rear back with a furious snarl. The firelight glowed in its wild eyes, momentarily halting its advance. Mercy scrambled backward, clutching at the damp earth beneath her fingers as her heart thundered in her chest. The ground seemed to tilt beneath her as she watched the confrontation unfold—Jed, rifle steady, eyes locked onto the beast, and Samuel, gripping the flaming log with shaking hands. Clara clung to Emily, shielding the child as best she could, whispering a desperate prayer under her breath.

Buck groaned from where he lay sprawled against the base of the tree, dazed but alive. Blood dripped from a gash across his forehead, the crimson stark against his pallid skin. He struggled to sit up, his movements sluggish, his knife lying uselessly in the dirt several feet away. The bear, momentarily deterred by the fire, shook its head and let out another guttural roar, its massive paws churning up the earth as it paced in agitation.

"We can't kill it," Samuel hissed, his grip on the burning branch tightening. "A wounded bear is twice as dangerous."

Jed didn't lower his rifle. His jaw was clenched so tightly that the muscle in his cheek twitched, his mind racing through the possibilities. They were cornered, outmatched by the sheer brute strength of the beast, and yet—if they ran, if they turned their backs on it, they would not stand a chance.

Mercy's gaze darted around the clearing, her breath shallow. Then, she saw it. A cluster of deadfall—old, dried branches tangled together in the underbrush just beyond the campfire. If they could lure the bear closer, they might be able to trap it long enough to escape.

"Jed!" she gasped, pointing toward the thicket. "The branches—we can set them alight!"

He followed her gaze, understanding sparking in his eyes. Without hesitation, he nodded. "Samuel, get ready to throw that torch," he ordered. "Mercy, grab more wood—fast."

Mercy didn't hesitate. Her fingers trembled as she reached for the scattered kindling near the fire, her legs propelling her toward the deadwood pile. Every second counted. She could hear the heavy breaths of the bear, the rustle of its fur as it shifted, the sharp inhale of the others as they braced for its next charge.

"Now, Samuel!" Jed bellowed.

Samuel heaved the burning log toward the pile, the flames licking greedily at the brittle wood. The fire ignited instantly, crackling to life as smoke billowed into the night air. The bear let out a startled grunt, rearing back on its hind legs as the heat and light overwhelmed its senses. Its black eyes darted between the growing fire and the humans, weighing the threat.

For a tense moment, the world stood still.

Then, with a snort of frustration, the beast turned and lumbered back into the shadows, its hulking form melting into the darkness of the trees. The flames crackled, the smoke curling skyward, a silent testament to their narrow escape.

For several long seconds, no one moved. No one breathed. The only sound was the steady pounding of rain-soaked leaves and the distant rush of the river beyond the trees.

Buck groaned, breaking the silence. "Damn thing nearly tore me in half," he muttered, clutching his bleeding temple.

Jed turned toward him, his eyes cold, assessing. "Next time, don't rush a bear with a damn knife," he said flatly.

Buck scowled, but he said nothing. His pride had taken just as much of a beating as his body.

Mercy exhaled slowly, her hands still trembling. "We should move," she whispered. "That fire won't burn for long."

Jed nodded. "She's right. We're not safe here."

The others gathered what little they had, and within

minutes, they were moving again, their bodies weary but their minds sharpened by the night's terror. Mercy walked beside Jed, her breaths still uneven.

"You think it'll come back?" she asked.

He glanced down at her, his expression unreadable. "No," he said after a pause. "But something else might."

And with that ominous truth hanging between them, they pressed deeper into the wilderness, their footsteps swallowed by the vast, indifferent frontier.

# CHAPTER FIFTY

The grizzly's roar reverberated through the clearing, a primal sound that froze the group in their tracks. Mercy McKenna's heart pounded in her chest as she watched the massive creature advance, its eyes gleaming with predatory intent.

Jedediah "Jed" Crowe stood his ground, his revolver trained on the bear. He fired again, the shot echoing through the forest, but the bullet only grazed the beast's thick hide, further enraging it.

Samuel, clutching a burning log from the fire, attempted to ward off the grizzly, but the bear swatted the makeshift weapon aside with a powerful swipe of its paw. Clara shielded Emily behind her, her eyes wide with terror.

Buck, recovering from the bear's initial attack, staggered to his feet, blood trickling from a gash on his forehead. With a guttural yell, he lunged at the grizzly with his knife, aiming for its throat.

The bear reared up on its hind legs, towering over Buck, and brought its massive claws down in a devastating arc. Buck was thrown backward, his knife clattering to the ground as he landed in a crumpled heap, unmoving.

"Buck!" Mercy screamed, but there was no response.

Jed seized the momentary distraction to reload his revolver, his hands moving with practiced precision. He took aim, his jaw set with grim determination, and fired a shot that struck the bear squarely between the eyes.

The grizzly let out a final, pained roar before collapsing to the ground, its massive body stirring up a cloud of dust as it fell. The clearing fell silent, save for the ragged breaths of the survivors.

Mercy rushed to Buck's side, her hands trembling as she checked for a pulse. To her relief, he was still alive, though unconscious and badly injured.

"We need to tend to his wounds," Samuel said, kneeling beside her. "Clara, bring me the medical kit."

Clara hurried to comply, her face pale but composed. Emily clung to her mother's skirts, her eyes wide with fear and confusion.

As Samuel worked to stabilize Buck, Jed approached Mercy, his expression unreadable.

"Are you hurt?" he asked, his voice gruff.

Mercy shook her head, though her body ached from the night's ordeals. "I'm fine," she replied, her voice barely above a whisper.

Jed nodded, his gaze lingering on her for a moment before he turned his attention to the fallen bear. "We'll need to move camp," he said. "The smell of blood will attract other predators."

The group worked quickly, gathering their belongings and fashioning a makeshift stretcher to carry Buck. The forest seemed to close in around them as they moved through the darkness, the weight of their situation pressing heavily upon them.

As dawn broke, they found a new campsite near a babbling brook, the sound of the water providing a semblance of tranquility. They set up camp, exhaustion evident in every movement.

Samuel tended to Buck's wounds, his expression grim. "He's lost a lot of blood," he said quietly. "We need to get him to a doctor as soon as possible."

Jed nodded, his brow furrowed in thought. "The trading post should have a physician," he said. "We'll make for it at first light."

As the others settled in for a restless sleep, Mercy found herself unable to rest. She wandered to the edge of the brook, the cool water soothing her frayed nerves.

Jed approached her, his footsteps silent on the soft earth. "You should try to get some rest," he said, his tone softer than she'd ever heard it.

"I can't," she admitted, her voice trembling. "Every time I close my eyes, I see that bear... and Buck..."

Jed was silent for a moment, his gaze fixed on the flowing water. "This land is unforgiving," he said finally. "It tests us in ways we can't always be prepared for."

Mercy looked at him, searching his face for any hint of the man beneath the hardened exterior. "Why are you doing this?" she asked suddenly. "Why did you take me?"

Jed's jaw tightened, and for a moment, she thought he wouldn't answer. But then he sighed, a weary sound that seemed to carry the weight of the world.

"It was a mistake," he said quietly. "You weren't the one we were supposed to take. But once it was done... there was no going back."

Mercy felt a surge of anger and despair. "So I'm just collateral damage?" she demanded, her voice rising.

Jed met her gaze, his eyes reflecting a depth of emotion she hadn't expected. "I never wanted this," he said, his voice barely above a whisper. "But now... I have to see it through."

Before she could respond, he turned and walked away, leaving her alone with her thoughts and the gentle murmur of the brook.

As the first rays of dawn crept over the horizon, Mercy remained by the brook, her mind a storm of emotions. Jed's confession echoed in her ears—You weren't the one we were supposed to take. But once it was done... there was no going back.

There was something in his voice that unsettled her— not quite regret, not quite justification. Just a raw, unspoken weight he carried. She didn't know whether to hate him for his part in all this or acknowledge that something within him was shifting. Either way, none of it changed the fact that she was still a prisoner, bound for a fate she couldn't control.

Behind her, the camp stirred to life. Samuel was tending to Buck, his face grim with worry. Buck was still unconscious, his breathing shallow. Clara wiped his brow with a damp cloth, whispering quiet reassurances to Emily, who was curled up beside her mother, still too young to understand the full gravity of their situation.

Jed stood a few feet away, his rifle slung over his shoulder, staring into the distance. His posture was tense, shoulders rigid as if bracing for another storm.

Mercy turned away from the brook and approached the fire where Samuel and Clara sat.

"How is he?" she asked softly, glancing at Buck.

Samuel shook his head. "He's alive, but barely. That bear did a number on him. If we don't get him to a doctor soon, he won't make it."

Mercy swallowed the lump in her throat. She wasn't sure how she felt about Buck—he had been cruel, dismissive, and eager to see her sold to the highest bidder. But now, lying there, pale and motionless, he didn't seem like the menacing outlaw she had feared. He looked... human. Fragile. Mortal.

Clara glanced at Mercy, hesitating before she spoke. "Last night... I heard you and Jed talking."

Mercy's stomach tightened. "And?"

Clara met her eyes with quiet intensity. "You're not with them by choice, are you?"

The words hit like a punch to the gut. Mercy didn't answer, but the silence spoke for itself.

Samuel let out a slow breath, his jaw tightening. "Damn it," he muttered under his breath. "I knew something was off about this whole situation."

Mercy opened her mouth to respond, but before she

could, a rustling noise from the nearby brush set everyone on edge.

Jed turned sharply, his revolver already drawn.

"Stay down," he ordered in a low voice, scanning the tree line.

The rustling grew louder, followed by the unmistakable sound of hooves trampling through the undergrowth.

Samuel quickly reached for his rifle, positioning himself protectively in front of Clara and Emily. Mercy felt her pulse hammering in her throat as she dropped low, pressing herself into the damp earth.

Then, out of the shadows, several men emerged on horseback, their faces obscured by wide-brimmed hats and dust-covered scarves. Their presence sent a shiver of unease through the camp.

Jed stepped forward, his expression unreadable, though Mercy saw the tension in his jaw.

The leader of the riders—a burly man with a thick scar running down his left cheek—tilted his head, surveying the group with an amused smirk.

"Well, well," he drawled. "Ain't this an interesting sight?"

Jed's grip on his revolver tightened. "What do you want?"

The man dismounted his horse with an easy arrogance, taking his time as he walked forward. He cast a glance toward Mercy, then at Buck's unconscious form.

"We've been lookin' for you, Crowe," the man continued,

his voice dripping with amusement. "Seems like you and your crew have been makin' quite a mess of things lately. My boss ain't too happy about that."

Jed's expression darkened. "Tell your boss I don't answer to him anymore."

The man chuckled, shaking his head. "See, that's the thing, Crowe. You don't get to just walk away. You owe him, and he intends to collect."

Mercy felt the shift in the air—something dangerous, something that could explode at any second.

"Who are they?" she whispered to Samuel.

"Outlaws," Samuel murmured back. "But not like Jed and Buck. These ones... they answer to someone bigger. Someone worse."

A sinking feeling settled in Mercy's stomach. The pieces were falling into place. These men weren't just looking for Jed. They were here for her.

The leader of the gang turned his attention back to Mercy, his smirk widening. "Ain't she a pretty little thing?" he mused. "I reckon she's worth quite a bit to the right people."

Jed took a step closer, his voice low and sharp. "She's not part of this."

The leader raised an eyebrow. "Oh, but she is, Crowe. You think we don't know about the deal? About the girl?"

He let out a bark of laughter. "Hell, your buyer's been real anxious. Word is, he ain't too happy that you've been takin' your sweet time. See, that girl there? She ain't just some random pickup. She's special. And the man who wants her ain't the kind you keep waitin'.'"

Mercy felt her blood turn cold.

Jed didn't flinch, but something in his posture shifted—something lethal, something barely restrained.

"You tell your boss he'll get his money," Jed said. "But not from her."

The leader's grin faltered for just a second, before twisting into something darker.

"That so?" he mused, his fingers hovering over the hilt of his gun.

Silence stretched between them, heavy with the weight of imminent violence.

Then, in a blink, the leader drew his gun.

Jed moved faster.

The gunshot rang out like thunder, splitting the morning air.

Chaos erupted.

Samuel pulled Clara and Emily down behind the wagon, shielding them from the flying bullets. Mercy scrambled for cover, her breath coming in ragged gasps as the gunfight exploded around her.

Jed fired again, his bullet striking one of the riders, who crumpled to the ground with a grunt. Buck, still barely conscious, groaned as the gunfire roared in his ears.

The outlaws returned fire, bullets whizzing past as the group fought for survival.

And through it all, one thought pulsed in Mercy's mind

—

Who is this buyer?

And why is she so valuable?

The answer was out there. And she feared it was something far worse than she had ever imagined.

# CHAPTER FIFTY-ONE

The sun dipped below the horizon, casting long shadows over the dense forest. The air was thick with tension as the echoes of the recent gunfight faded into an unsettling silence. Mercy McKenna crouched behind a fallen log, her heart pounding in her chest, each beat a reminder of her precarious situation.

The clearing was littered with the aftermath of the skirmish. Several of the assailants lay motionless, their lifeless forms a stark testament to the violence that had erupted moments before. Jedediah "Jed" Crowe stood amidst the chaos, his revolver still smoking, eyes scanning the perimeter for any lingering threats.

Samuel and Clara huddled together, shielding young Emily from the gruesome scene. Their faces were pale, etched with a mixture of fear and disbelief. Buck, though grievously injured from the earlier bear attack, had managed to fire a few shots before collapsing once more, his condition now critical.

As the adrenaline began to wane, the gravity of their situation settled over the group like a suffocating blanket. The realization that they had been ambushed by men connected to Jed's past dealings was a chilling reminder of the dangers that lurked in these untamed lands.

Jed approached Mercy, his expression a mask of stoic resolve. "We need to move," he said tersely. "There could be more of them."

Mercy nodded, swallowing her fear. "What about Buck?"

Jed's gaze flickered to his fallen comrade, a shadow of conflict passing over his features. "We'll do what we can for him, but we can't stay here."

Samuel stepped forward, his voice trembling but determined. "There's a settlement not far from here. They might have a doctor."

Clara glanced at her husband, concern evident in her eyes. "Can we make it there before nightfall?"

Jed considered this, then nodded. "It's our best chance. Let's move."

The group gathered their belongings, fashioning a makeshift stretcher to carry Buck. The journey was arduous, the forest growing denser as darkness enveloped them. Every rustle of leaves, every snap of a twig, set their nerves on edge.

As they trudged through the underbrush, Mercy couldn't shake the feeling of being watched. The events of the past days had left her weary, but a newfound resolve burned within her. She was determined to survive, to uncover the truth behind her abduction, and to find a way back to her family.

Hours passed, the forest seemingly endless, until finally, the faint glow of lanterns pierced the darkness. A small settlement emerged before them, a cluster of modest cabins nestled amidst the trees.

The inhabitants, alerted by the approach of strangers, emerged cautiously. An elderly man stepped forward, his weathered face illuminated by the flickering light.

"What brings you folks out here at this hour?" he inquired, his tone wary but not unkind.

Samuel spoke up. "Our friend is gravely injured. We were told there might be a doctor here."

The old man nodded. "Doc Harris lives yonder. We'll take you to him."

As they followed the villagers to the doctor's cabin, Mercy couldn't help but notice the curious glances cast her way. Whispers followed in their wake, fragments of conversations reaching her ears.

"Isn't that the girl from the posters?"

"Could it really be her?"

A sense of unease settled over her. Posters? What were they talking about?

Upon reaching the doctor's abode, a middle-aged man with spectacles perched on his nose greeted them. He quickly assessed Buck's condition and ushered them inside.

As Doc Harris tended to Buck, Mercy took the opportunity to explore the small cabin. Her eyes fell upon a stack of papers on a nearby table. Curiosity getting the better of her, she picked one up.

Her blood ran cold. Staring back at her was a crude sketch of her own face, beneath which bold letters proclaimed:

WANTED: MERCY MCKENNA

FOR KIDNAPPING AND MURDER

A reward was offered for her capture.

The room seemed to spin as she grappled with the revelation. How could this be? She was the victim, not the perpetrator.

Jed entered the room, noticing the paper in her trembling hands. His eyes narrowed.

"Where did you find that?" he demanded.

"It's not true," Mercy whispered, her voice shaking. "I didn't do any of this."

Jed's expression softened slightly, but his guard remained up. "I know," he said quietly. "But someone wants you to take the fall."

Tears welled in Mercy's eyes as the weight of the situation pressed down upon her. She was not only a captive, not only a pawn in someone else's dangerous game—she was now wanted for a crime she had never committed.

A bounty. A price on her head.

She could barely breathe as she turned to Jed, her voice breaking. "Who did this? Who put this out?"

Jed took the paper from her hands and examined it, his jaw tightening. His expression, already guarded, darkened further. "This isn't just any bounty."

Samuel and Clara, who had been standing nearby, now moved closer. Samuel's eyes scanned the poster, and his face paled. "Kidnapping and murder?" He looked at Mercy, searching her face. "Is this true?"

"No! Of course not!" Mercy exclaimed, shaking her head violently. "I—I don't even know what this is!"

Clara pulled Emily closer protectively, her gaze wary.

Jed exhaled slowly, rubbing a hand across his jaw. "Somebody's trying to pin something on you." His voice was low, thoughtful. "And if they're willing to put up a bounty this high... it means you're a bigger piece in this game than I thought."

Mercy's stomach twisted. "What game, Jed? What the hell is going on?"

Jed remained silent for a moment, then gestured for her to follow him outside. "We need to talk. Now."

Mercy hesitated but followed, stepping into the cool night air. The settlement was eerily quiet, the only sounds being the distant murmur of voices from inside the doctor's cabin and the chirping of crickets beyond the tree line.

Jed turned to face her, his hands on his hips, his posture tense. "I need you to listen real carefully, Mercy. This bounty? This isn't just about getting you back. This is about making sure you don't come back at all."

She swallowed hard. "You mean..."

"Yeah," he said grimly. "Somebody doesn't want you alive. They want you silenced."

Mercy's breath hitched. "But why?"

Jed let out a humorless chuckle. "Hell if I know. But someone went to a lot of trouble to make sure anyone who sees you doesn't ask too many questions. They want you dead and buried before you can figure out why."

Mercy felt the world spin beneath her feet. "Does this mean the buyer isn't just looking to own me? They're looking to kill me?"

Jed's silence was answer enough.

She turned away, gripping her arms, trying to keep her breath steady. This wasn't just about money, about trafficking, about being sold like cattle. This was deeper. Darker.

And the worst part?

She had no idea why.

Behind her, Jed sighed, running a hand through his hair. "We need to be real careful from here on out," he muttered. "If people in this town recognize you, there's a good chance someone will try to turn you in. Or worse."

Mercy spun to face him. "We can't stay here, Jed. We have to leave—tonight."

Jed nodded slowly. "I know."

"What about Buck?" she asked hesitantly. "He—he might not make it through the night."

Jed's lips pressed into a thin line. "Then we'll leave him here with Samuel and Clara. If he wakes up, they can decide what to do with him."

Mercy's chest tightened. Despite all the horrible things Buck had done—despite the way he had treated her—she still hated the idea of abandoning someone to die alone. But she also knew that staying here was a risk she couldn't afford to take.

"What about you?" she whispered. "Are you—are you coming with me?"

Jed's gaze met hers, something unreadable flickering in his eyes. "I'm the only thing standing between you and whoever wants you dead," he said quietly. "You think I'm just gonna let you run off alone?"

Mercy exhaled shakily. She didn't trust him—not completely. But in this moment, he was all she had.

"Alright," she murmured. "Then let's go."

Jed gave her a sharp nod and turned toward the settlement, eyes scanning the darkened cabins. "We'll take two of the horses from the corral out back," he said. "Pack light, take only what we need. If we ride hard, we'll be long gone before anyone knows we left."

Mercy glanced over her shoulder at the doctor's cabin, her heart clenching. Samuel and Clara had risked a lot by taking them in, and now she was leaving them with a half-dead outlaw and the mess she'd unknowingly dragged them into.

She didn't have time for goodbyes.

Jed moved fast, leading her behind the cabins where the corral stood, its wooden fencing slick with evening dew. Two horses—sturdy mustangs, strong enough for a long ride—stood tethered.

Jed worked quickly, saddling one and passing her the reins. "Can you ride?"

Mercy hesitated. "I—I've ridden before, but not like this."

He smirked slightly. "Guess you're about to learn real fast."

She swallowed hard and swung herself onto the horse, her hands gripping the reins tightly. Jed mounted beside her, his revolver already resting in his lap, his gaze sharp as he scanned the darkness.

Then, without another word, they kicked their horses into motion, disappearing into the night like ghosts.

# CHAPTER FIFTY-TWO

The moon hung high, casting a silvery glow over the rugged terrain as Mercy and Jed urged their horses forward. The rhythmic pounding of hooves against the earth was the only sound accompanying their escape into the night. The weight of the wanted poster burned in Mercy's mind, each mile deepening the chasm of fear and uncertainty within her.

They rode hard, the landscape transforming from dense forests to open plains, the cool night air biting at their skin. Jed's silhouette was a constant ahead of her, a silent guide through the labyrinth of the wilderness. Despite the urgency, he maintained a pace that her limited riding experience could match, a small mercy in their relentless flight.

As the first hues of dawn began to streak the horizon, Jed signaled a halt near a secluded grove. The horses, lathered and panting, gratefully slowed to a stop. Mercy dismounted clumsily, her legs trembling from the prolonged ride.

"We need to rest the horses," Jed muttered, his eyes scanning their surroundings. "And you need to eat."

Mercy nodded, too exhausted to argue. They led the horses into the cover of the trees, tying them loosely to allow grazing. Jed handed her a piece of dried meat and a canteen. She accepted them silently, her mind still reeling from the revelations of the night before.

As she chewed mechanically, she watched Jed. His face was a mask of stoic determination, but there was a tension in his posture, a rigidity that spoke of unease. The man who had once been her captor was now her only ally, a reality she struggled to reconcile.

"Jed," she began hesitantly, breaking the silence.

He glanced at her, his expression unreadable.

"Why did you take me?" The question had been gnawing at her, a festering wound in her consciousness.

Jed sighed, running a hand through his disheveled hair. "It was a mistake," he admitted. "You weren't the intended target."

"Then who was?"

He hesitated, as if weighing the consequences of his words. "A girl, about your age, from a wealthy family. Someone wanted leverage against her father."

Mercy felt a chill that had nothing to do with the morning air. "And now they're after me because...?"

"Because you can expose them," Jed said bluntly. "And because they don't like loose ends."

The gravity of his words settled over her like a shroud. She was a pawn in a game she didn't understand, hunted for reasons beyond her control.

"What do we do now?" she asked, her voice barely above a whisper.

Jed's gaze hardened. "We keep moving. Stay ahead of them. Find a way to clear your name."

"And how do we do that?"

He looked away, his jaw clenched. "I don't know yet."

The admission hung in the air between them, a stark reminder of their precarious situation. But in that moment, a fragile bond formed—a shared determination to survive against the odds.

After a brief rest, they mounted their horses once more, the rising sun casting long shadows across the landscape. With each passing mile, Mercy felt a steely resolve harden within her. She would not be a victim. She would uncover the truth, no matter the cost.

As they disappeared into the vast expanse of the frontier, the first tendrils of hope began to unfurl in her heart. The journey ahead was fraught with danger, but she was no longer alone. And together, they would face whatever perils lay ahead.

# CHAPTER FIFTY-THREE

The sun climbed higher, casting a harsh light over the sprawling plains as Mercy and Jed pressed onward. The vast expanse seemed endless, a sea of tall grasses swaying in the breeze, offering little in the way of cover or comfort. The events of the past days weighed heavily on them, but the relentless pursuit left no room for rest.

As the day wore on, the oppressive heat took its toll. Mercy's throat was parched, her lips cracked and dry. She glanced at Jed, noting the determined set of his jaw, the way his eyes constantly scanned the horizon. Despite his stoic exterior, she could see the strain etched on his features.

"We need water," she managed to croak, her voice barely audible over the rustling of the grass.

Jed nodded, his gaze shifting to the distant line of trees that marked the edge of the plains. "There's a river ahead," he said. "We can refill our canteens and rest the horses."

The promise of water spurred them on, and as they

approached the tree line, the faint sound of flowing water reached their ears. The sight of the river—a shimmering ribbon cutting through the landscape—brought a surge of relief.

They dismounted, leading their weary horses to the water's edge. Mercy knelt beside the river, cupping her hands to drink deeply, the cool liquid soothing her parched throat. Jed refilled their canteens, his eyes never ceasing their vigilant sweep of the surroundings.

As they rested, the tranquility of the moment was shattered by a distant rumble. Jed's head snapped up, his expression alert.

"What is it?" Mercy asked, her heart pounding.

"Stampede," Jed replied tersely, rising to his feet. "We need to move. Now."

They scrambled to mount their horses, the ground beneath them beginning to tremble as the sound grew louder. As they urged their mounts away from the river, a massive herd of bison emerged from the plains, a living tide of muscle and horn charging toward the water.

The sheer power of the stampede was awe-inspiring, the air thick with dust and the thunder of hooves. Mercy clung to her horse, her eyes wide with fear and fascination.

Jed led them to a rise overlooking the river, where they watched the herd surge forward, the bison plunging into the water with reckless abandon. The spectacle was both terrifying and mesmerizing, a stark reminder of the untamed wilderness they traversed.

As the last of the herd crossed the river, the dust began

to settle, leaving an eerie silence in its wake. Jed turned to Mercy, his expression grim.

"We need to keep moving," he said. "The noise could have drawn attention."

Mercy nodded, her body still trembling from the adrenaline. They urged their horses onward, leaving the river and the remnants of the stampede behind.

As dusk approached, they came upon the remnants of a wagon train, the charred frames of the wagons silhouetted against the darkening sky. The scene was hauntingly silent, the air heavy with the scent of smoke and decay.

"What happened here?" Mercy whispered, her eyes scanning the desolate site.

Jed dismounted, his expression somber. "Could be bandits," he said. "Or..."

He didn't finish the sentence, but Mercy understood. The threat of Indian attacks was a constant fear on the frontier, tensions between settlers and native tribes often erupting into violence.

As they cautiously explored the site, a faint sound reached Mercy's ears—a soft, pitiful whimper. She followed the noise to a partially collapsed wagon, where she found a young boy, no more than six years old, huddled beneath the wreckage.

"Jed!" she called, beckoning him over. "There's a child here."

Jed approached, his expression softening as he saw the boy. "Hey there, little fella," he said gently. "You're safe now."

The boy looked up, his eyes wide with fear and

confusion. "Mama... Papa..." he murmured, his voice trembling.

Mercy's heart ached for the child. She reached out, offering her hand. "We'll take care of you," she said softly. "What's your name?"

"Tommy," the boy replied, his small hand clutching hers.

As they led Tommy away from the wreckage, Mercy couldn't help but feel a deepening sense of dread. The dangers of the frontier were all too real, and their journey was fraught with perils both seen and unseen.

But in the midst of the darkness, there was a glimmer of hope—a reminder of the resilience of the human spirit, and the bonds that could form even in the most harrowing of circumstances.

As night fell, they set up a makeshift camp, the flickering fire casting long shadows as they huddled together for warmth. The vast expanse of the frontier stretched out around them, a wild and untamed land that held both danger and promise.

Mercy sat close to the fire, her arms wrapped around herself as she watched Tommy, the boy they had rescued, curl up near the flames. He clung to the woolen blanket Jed had given him, his small frame trembling in exhaustion.

"He won't survive on his own," Mercy murmured, her voice quiet but firm.

Jed, who had been tending to the horses, sat down beside her, stretching out his legs with a sigh. "No, he won't."

Mercy glanced at him. "Then what do we do? We can't just leave him behind."

Jed rubbed his jaw, staring into the flames. "We take him with us. For now." His voice was cautious, as if reluctant to take on yet another burden. "But the second we find a settlement that can take him in, we leave him there."

Mercy looked down at Tommy, his small face peaceful in sleep. "What if he has family out there somewhere?"

Jed exhaled sharply. "Then they're either dead, or they'll be looking for him. But we can't afford to go searchin'. The second we hit any town, bounty hunters, lawmen, or the bastards who want you dead might be waiting for us."

Mercy swallowed hard, nodding. It was the truth. The wanted posters were out there, and every mile they traveled increased the chances of someone recognizing her.

She pulled her blanket tighter around her shoulders and turned to Jed. "If that's the case, we can't stay in towns for long, can we?"

Jed shook his head. "No. And if we do, you can't be seen."

A knot tightened in Mercy's stomach. She was growing accustomed to the constant running, the secrecy, the fear of being caught. But this wasn't just about her anymore—Tommy was now caught in the middle of it, too.

Jed must have sensed her unease, because his tone softened just a little. "We'll figure it out. One step at a time."

Mercy nodded, but deep down, she wasn't sure if they could figure it out. She wasn't just running from bounty hunters or a buyer anymore. She was running from something much bigger—something she didn't yet understand.

She turned her gaze back to the fire, watching as the flames flickered against the cold night air. The wilderness stretched out beyond them, dark and endless. Somewhere out there, the people who had ordered her capture—who had framed her for kidnapping and murder—were still waiting.

And sooner or later, they were going to find her.

Mercy closed her eyes, exhaustion finally claiming her.

For now, she had to focus on surviving the next sunrise.

# CHAPTER FIFTY-FOUR

The morning sun bathed the vast frontier in a golden glow, casting elongated shadows across the rugged landscape as Mercy, Jed, and young Tommy pressed onward. Their journey had been relentless, a continuous push for survival against the dangers that lurked in the wilderness. Yet, with each passing day, a fragile thread of hope wove itself into their resolve—hope for sanctuary, for a future beyond the relentless pursuit that shadowed them.

They navigated through a dense thicket, the earthy scent of damp leaves and pine filling their lungs. The air was crisp, the remnants of the previous night's chill lingering in the underbrush. As they pressed forward, the faint but unmistakable sound of rushing water reached their ears. Jed raised a hand, signaling for them to halt, his keen eyes scanning the landscape.

"There's a stream ahead," he murmured, his voice laced with caution. "We can refill our canteens and let the horses rest."

Mercy exhaled, nodding as she glanced down at Tommy, whose small hands clutched the reins with weary determination. The boy had endured more hardship than any child should, yet his spirit remained unbroken, though exhaustion had begun to carve itself into his delicate features.

As they approached the stream, the gurgling water provided a stark contrast to the tension that had become their ever-present companion. The horses lowered their heads, drinking deeply as Mercy knelt beside the stream, cupping her hands to splash the cool liquid over her face. It was a fleeting moment of reprieve, one that reminded her how long it had been since she had felt anything resembling comfort.

Her gaze wandered across the clearing, drawn to the rough bark of a towering oak tree. Faint etchings scarred its surface, weathered by time but still discernible. She rose to her feet and moved closer, tracing the grooves with her fingertips. The symbols, though unfamiliar, stirred something deep within her—a recognition she couldn't quite place.

Jed joined her, his expression darkening as he studied the carvings. "These are old," he muttered. "Could be from a native tribe, or maybe settlers who passed through long before us."

Mercy frowned, her mind racing with unease. "Do you think it means something? A warning?"

Jed didn't answer immediately. Instead, he scanned the surrounding trees, the unease in his eyes mirroring her own. "Hard to say," he admitted. "But we should stay alert."

The moment was shattered by the distant, rhythmic

thud of hooves against the earth. Jed stiffened, his hand instinctively reaching for his revolver. The sound grew louder, closer. Whoever was approaching was riding hard.

"Riders," he said tersely, his eyes locking onto hers. "We need to move. Now."

Mercy didn't hesitate. She lifted Tommy onto his horse before swinging into her own saddle, her pulse quickening. With a sharp command, Jed spurred his mount forward, leading them away from the stream and deeper into the wild expanse of the frontier. The landscape shifted as they rode, the open plains giving way to rocky outcrops and gnarled clusters of trees, their skeletal branches clawing at the sky.

As the sun dipped lower, painting the horizon in hues of amber and crimson, they stumbled upon the remnants of an old settlement. The skeletal remains of dilapidated cabins stood like silent sentinels, their wooden frames weathered and splintered, bearing witness to a past long forgotten. A ghost town, abandoned and left to decay.

Jed reined in his horse, surveying the desolate scene. "We'll take shelter here for the night."

Mercy swallowed against the unease creeping up her spine. There was something unsettling about the place, something that whispered of lives lost and stories left unfinished. Yet, they had no choice. The alternative was to keep riding through the darkness, a risk they could ill afford.

As they settled within the crumbling remains of what had once been a general store, the night stretched on, thick with silence. The wind carried with it an eerie melody, rustling through broken windows and gaps in the rotting walls. Mercy wrapped her arms around herself, staring into the flickering fire as shadows danced along the floorboards.

"Jed," she murmured, her voice barely above a whisper. "Do you think we're retracing the steps of those who came before us?"

Jed exhaled slowly, his gaze fixed on the flames. "The frontier is full of stories, Mercy. Some are better left forgotten."

She nodded, though the unease in her chest remained. This land held echoes of the past—whispers of lives once lived, dreams once dreamt. And as she lay down beside Tommy, listening to the wind weave its mournful song through the ruins, she couldn't help but feel as though they had become a part of its story, entangled in a fate not yet fully written.

# CHAPTER FIFTY-FIVE

The morning sun cast long shadows over the desolate ghost town as Mercy, Jed, and young Tommy prepared to continue their journey. The eerie silence of the abandoned settlement weighed heavily on them, a stark reminder of the relentless dangers that lurked in the untamed frontier.

As they mounted their horses, the distant rumble of thunder echoed across the plains. Jed glanced toward the horizon, where dark, menacing clouds gathered, threatening an impending storm.

"We need to find shelter," he said, his voice tense. "A storm's coming, and it looks like a bad one."

Mercy nodded, her eyes scanning the surrounding landscape. The open plains offered little protection against the elements, and the prospect of facing a violent storm in such exposed terrain filled her with dread.

"There's a line of hills to the west," she suggested, pointing toward a distant ridge. "Maybe we can find a cave or some overhangs there."

Jed considered this for a moment before nodding. "It's our best bet. Let's move."

They urged their horses into a brisk trot, the wind picking up around them as the storm approached. The sky darkened ominously, and the first fat droplets of rain began to fall, splattering against the dry earth.

As they reached the base of the hills, the rain intensified, transforming into a torrential downpour. The wind howled, whipping the rain into their faces and making it difficult to see.

"Over there!" Jed shouted over the roar of the storm, pointing toward a dark opening in the hillside—a cave.

They dismounted and led their horses toward the shelter, the ground turning to mud beneath their feet. Inside, the cave was dry and offered a respite from the fury of the storm outside.

Mercy helped Tommy settle against the cave wall, wrapping a blanket around his small, shivering form. The boy's eyes were wide with fear, and he clung to her tightly.

"It's alright, Tommy," she murmured soothingly. "We're safe here."

Jed tended to the horses, ensuring they were secure and as comfortable as possible in the confined space. The cave was spacious enough to accommodate them, but the close quarters added to the tension that hung in the air.

As the storm raged outside, the flickering light from their small fire cast dancing shadows on the cave walls. The sound of the rain pounding against the earth and the occasional crash of thunder created a cacophony that made conversation difficult.

Mercy sat beside Tommy, her thoughts drifting to their precarious situation. The frontier was unforgiving, and each day brought new challenges that tested their resolve.

Jed joined them, his expression grim. "We can't stay here long," he said, his voice low. "Once the storm passes, we need to keep moving."

Mercy nodded, understanding the unspoken implications. The storm provided temporary cover, but it also hindered their progress. Their pursuers would not be deterred by a little rain, and every moment they remained in one place increased the risk of discovery.

As the hours passed and the storm began to subside, a tense silence settled over the group. The fire crackled softly, and the occasional drip of water from the cave ceiling was the only sound that punctuated the stillness.

Tommy had fallen asleep, his head resting on Mercy's lap. She gently stroked his hair, her mind racing with thoughts of their next move.

Jed stood at the cave entrance, peering out into the fading storm. "We should leave before dawn," he said quietly. "The ground will be muddy, but we can make up for lost time once it dries."

Mercy agreed, though the prospect of traveling through the treacherous terrain was daunting. They had no choice but to press on, driven by the hope of finding safety and the determination to survive.

As the first light of dawn crept into the cave, they prepared to continue their journey. The storm had passed, leaving the air crisp and the landscape glistening with moisture.

With Tommy securely mounted in front of Mercy, they set out once more into the vast, untamed wilderness. Each step forward was a testament to their resilience, a defiant stand against the myriad dangers that lay ahead.

The frontier was a land of unrelenting challenges, but it was also a place of untold beauty and boundless possibilities. As they ventured into the unknown, they carried with them the hope of a brighter future and the unbreakable bond forged through shared adversity.

# CHAPTER FIFTY-SIX

As Mercy, Jed, and young Tommy approached the settlement, the distant plume of smoke guided them like a beacon through the rugged terrain. The journey had been arduous, and the prospect of respite filled them with cautious hope.

Nestled within a sheltered valley, the settlement emerged—a modest cluster of log cabins and tents, encircled by a sturdy wooden palisade. The scent of woodsmoke and the murmur of voices hinted at a semblance of normalcy, a stark contrast to the perils they had faced.

At the entrance, a weathered man stood guard, his eyes narrowing as the trio approached. Jed raised a hand in greeting, his posture non-threatening.

"Evenin'," Jed called out. "We're travelers seeking shelter."

The guard scrutinized them for a moment before nodding. "Name's Elias," he replied. "We don't get many visitors. What's your business here?"

"Just lookin' for a place to rest," Jed said. "Been on the

trail a long while."

Elias glanced at Mercy and Tommy, noting their weary expressions. "You got any trouble followin' you?"

"No trouble," Jed assured. "Just need a safe place for the boy."

After a tense pause, Elias stepped aside. "Alright. But mind yourselves. We don't tolerate no nonsense here."

As they entered the settlement, the inhabitants cast curious glances their way. A woman tending a communal fire offered a tentative smile, while children peeked from behind doorways, their eyes wide with curiosity.

An elderly man approached, leaning heavily on a cane. "Welcome," he greeted, his voice raspy yet warm. "I'm Samuel, the elder here. You look like you've been through the wringer."

"We have," Mercy replied softly. "We're grateful for your hospitality."

Samuel nodded. "You're welcome to stay as long as you need. We've got a spare cabin yonder. It's humble, but it'll keep the weather off."

"Thank you," Jed said, inclining his head. "We won't be a burden."

Over the following days, the trio settled into the rhythm of the settlement. The cabin, though modest, provided a comfort they had long been denied. Mercy took to helping in the communal kitchen, her presence met with appreciation by the settlers.

Tommy, initially withdrawn, began to open up, playing with the other children and finding moments of joy amidst the simplicity of their new life. The shadows that had haunted his young eyes seemed to recede, replaced by the glimmers of a childhood rekindled.

Jed lent his skills to fortifying the settlement's defenses, working alongside the men to reinforce the palisade and ensure the safety of their newfound refuge. His demeanor, once guarded, softened in the face of the community's camaraderie.

As weeks turned into months, a sense of normalcy enveloped them. The specter of pursuit faded into a distant memory, and for the first time in what felt like an eternity, they allowed themselves to breathe freely.

One evening, as the sun dipped below the horizon, casting a golden hue over the valley, Mercy and Jed sat outside their cabin, watching Tommy chase fireflies with the other children.

"He's come a long way," Jed observed, a hint of a smile tugging at his lips.

"We all have," Mercy replied, her gaze distant. "It's almost hard to believe we've found a place like this."

Jed nodded, his expression contemplative. "It's a good place. Good people."

A comfortable silence settled between them, the weight of unspoken thoughts hanging in the air.

"Do you ever think about what's next?" Mercy asked softly.

Jed sighed, running a hand through his hair. "I try not to. Livin' day by day seems to be workin' so far."

Mercy nodded, though a flicker of uncertainty crossed her features. "I can't help but wonder if it's truly over. If we're really safe."

Jed placed a reassuring hand on her shoulder. "We've found somethin' good here. Let's not borrow trouble from tomorrow."

As the days continued to pass, the settlement became more than just a refuge; it became home. The bonds they formed with the settlers deepened, and the wounds of their past began to heal.

Yet, beneath the surface of their newfound tranquility, a subtle tension lingered—a silent acknowledgment that the world beyond the valley remained fraught with dangers unseen.

For now, however, they embraced the peace they had discovered, cherishing each moment of respite in the sanctuary they had come to call their own.

# CHAPTER FIFTY-SEVEN

In the months that followed their arrival, the settlement transformed from a mere refuge into a cherished home for Mercy, Jed, and young Tommy. The once unfamiliar faces of the settlers became those of friends and confidants, and the trio found themselves woven into the fabric of the community.

Jed, embracing a paternal role, took it upon himself to mentor Tommy in the ways of frontier life. Together, they embarked on daily adventures, exploring the surrounding woods and learning the skills essential for survival.

One crisp morning, as the first light of dawn painted the sky in hues of pink and gold, Jed roused Tommy from slumber.

"Time to rise, little man," Jed whispered, a gentle smile creasing his weathered face.

Tommy blinked sleepily, rubbing his eyes. "Where are we going, Jed?"

"Gonna teach you how to track deer," Jed replied, his voice filled with quiet enthusiasm. "It's a skill every frontiersman should know."

As they ventured into the forest, the air was alive with the sounds of nature—the chirping of birds, the rustle of leaves, and the distant babble of a brook. Jed knelt beside a patch of soft earth, pointing to a series of hoofprints.

"See here, Tommy," he said, his tone instructive. "These tracks are fresh. A deer passed through not long ago."

Tommy crouched beside him, his eyes wide with curiosity. "How can you tell?"

Jed chuckled softly. "It's all in the details. The depth of the print, the moisture in the soil. Takes practice, but you'll get the hang of it."

As they followed the trail, Jed shared stories of his own youth, imparting wisdom and life lessons. The bond between them deepened, resembling that of a father and son—a relationship built on trust, respect, and shared experiences.

Meanwhile, Mercy found solace in the company of the settlement's women. She assisted with daily chores, learning the arts of weaving, candle making, and herbal medicine. The camaraderie provided her with a sense of belonging she had long yearned for.

One afternoon, as the women gathered to quilt beneath the shade of a sprawling oak tree, Mercy listened intently to their conversations, absorbing the knowledge and traditions passed down through generations.

"You've got a knack for this, Mercy," remarked Clara, a matronly woman with kind eyes, as she observed Mercy's

215

meticulous stitching.

Mercy smiled, a flush of pride coloring her cheeks. "Thank you, Clara. I've had good teachers."

As the days turned into weeks, the trio became integral members of the community. They participated in communal gatherings, shared in the joys and sorrows of their neighbors, and contributed to the settlement's prosperity.

One evening, the settlement organized a barn dance— a rare but cherished occasion that brought everyone together in celebration. The barn was adorned with lanterns casting a warm glow, and the lively tunes of a fiddle filled the air.

Mercy, dressed in a simple yet elegant dress borrowed from Clara, felt a sense of normalcy she hadn't experienced in years. She laughed and danced with the other settlers, her worries momentarily forgotten.

Jed watched from the sidelines, a contented smile on his face as he observed Mercy's joy. Tommy tugged at his sleeve, his eyes alight with excitement.

"Come on, Jed! Dance with us!"

Jed chuckled, allowing himself to be pulled onto the dance floor. The three of them joined hands, spinning in carefree circles, their laughter echoing through the night.

In these moments, the hardships of their past seemed like distant memories. They had found a sanctuary, a place where they could heal and rebuild their lives.

As the dance drew to a close and the settlers began to disperse, Mercy, Jed, and Tommy sat beneath the stars, the cool night air wrapping around them like a comforting blanket.

"I never thought we'd find a place like this," Mercy mused, her voice soft.

"It's more than I ever hoped for," Jed agreed, his gaze fixed on the twinkling sky.

Tommy nestled between them, his eyelids heavy with sleep. "We're a family now, aren't we?"

Mercy and Jed exchanged a glance, their hearts swelling with affection.

"Yes, Tommy," Mercy whispered, placing a gentle kiss on his forehead. "We're a family."

In the tranquil days that followed, the trio continued to thrive, their bonds strengthening with each passing moment. They had discovered not only a safe haven but also the profound connection of a chosen family—a testament to the resilience of the human spirit and the enduring power of love.

# CHAPTER FIFTY-EIGHT

The settlement buzzed with excitement as the barn dance approached. For weeks, preparations had been underway—lanterns strung from wooden beams, tables set with fresh bread and roasted meat, and the sound of a well-tuned fiddle warming up for the night ahead.

For Mercy, Jed, and Tommy, it was the first real celebration they'd had in a long time. After months of survival, danger, and hardship, they finally had a night to just be like everyone else.

As the sun dipped below the horizon, the settlers gathered in the barn, their laughter and chatter filling the air. The scent of fresh cider and fire-roasted apples mixed with the warm aroma of woodsmoke.

Mercy had been reluctant at first, feeling out of place in the borrowed dress given to her by Maggie, a kind-hearted woman who had taken her under her wing. The fabric was soft, a deep blue that reminded Mercy of the sky before dusk. It felt odd to be dressed so nicely after so long on the road, but for once, she didn't feel like an outsider.

"Look, Mercy!" Tommy tugged on her sleeve, pointing toward the dance floor where couples spun in time to the lively tune of the fiddle. "Everyone's dancing!"

She smiled down at him, ruffling his hair. "You want to dance, Tommy?"

He nodded eagerly. "Will you show me how?"

With a laugh, Mercy took his small hands and led him onto the dance floor. He stumbled a little at first, stepping on her toes, but his face was alight with pure joy. The settlers around them clapped in rhythm, cheering on the little boy.

From the sidelines, Jed watched them, a small smile pulling at the corners of his mouth. Mercy had come so far from the scared girl he'd first kidnapped in the dead of night. She was strong, resilient, and—against all odds—still full of warmth.

The music changed to a slower waltz, and some of the couples paired off for the next dance. Mercy turned toward Jed, eyes shining.

"Your turn," she teased, holding out a hand.

Jed shook his head, chuckling. "I ain't much of a dancer, Mercy."

"It's not about being good at it," she said, nudging him playfully. "It's just about enjoying the night. Come on, old man."

Jed snorted. "Old man, huh?" But he took her hand anyway.

The moment was easy, natural—nothing like the hardened outlaw and the kidnapped girl they had once been. Instead, it felt like a father dancing with his daughter at a family gathering.

As they moved in slow steps, Jed glanced down at her and exhaled. "I never thought I'd have nights like this again," he admitted.

Mercy looked up, sensing the weight in his voice. "Because of your daughter?" she asked softly.

Jed nodded. "Yeah. You and Tommy... You remind me of what I lost. But in a way, you also remind me of what I still have."

Mercy squeezed his hand. "You're family now, Jed."

His throat tightened, and he gave a small nod. "Reckon I feel the same way, kid."

They danced in comfortable silence, moving in slow circles under the soft glow of the lanterns. Jed knew the moment wouldn't last forever—danger always had a way of finding them—but tonight, none of that mattered.

By the time the dance wound down, Mercy and Tommy were both laughing as they collapsed onto a bench beside Jed.

Tommy, his head resting against Jed's shoulder, yawned sleepily. "That was the best night ever," he murmured.

Mercy tucked the blanket around Tommy's small frame, smiling as she looked at the boy. "It really was, wasn't it?"

Jed wrapped an arm around Tommy's shoulders, ruffling his hair. "We'll have more nights like this, son. I promise."

And for the first time in a long while, Mercy truly believed him.

# CHAPTER FIFTY-NINE

In the days following the barn dance, the settlement settled back into its routine, but the warmth of the evening lingered in the hearts of Mercy, Jed, and Tommy. The dance had been a welcome respite, a momentary escape from the shadows that had long trailed them.

As winter's chill began to wane, the promise of spring brought renewed energy to the community. Fields needed tending, repairs awaited, and life pressed forward with its relentless rhythm.

One crisp morning, as the sun cast a golden hue over the frost-kissed ground, Jed approached Mercy with a thoughtful expression.

"Mercy," he began, "I've been thinkin'. You've got a knack for learnin' and helpin' folks. Maybe it's time you considered spendin' some time with Doc Harris. He could use an extra hand, and you'd pick up some valuable skills."

Mercy looked up, surprised. "You really think so?"

Jed nodded. "I do. It's clear you've got a good head on your shoulders. Could be a real help to the doc and the folks 'round here."

Touched by his confidence in her, Mercy agreed. The following day, she found herself in Doc Harris's modest clinic, a small cabin lined with shelves of jars and medical instruments.

Doc Harris, a grizzled man with kind eyes, welcomed her warmly. "Jed tells me you're interested in lendin' a hand. I could certainly use the help, especially with spring ailments on the rise."

Under his guidance, Mercy learned to mix herbal remedies, tend to minor wounds, and comfort the ailing. She discovered a sense of purpose in the work, a way to give back to the community that had embraced them.

Meanwhile, Tommy thrived under Jed's mentorship. The boy's initial shyness gave way to a burgeoning confidence as he learned to fish, track, and handle basic tools. Jed took pride in the boy's progress, seeing in him the promise of a bright future.

One afternoon, as they repaired a section of fencing, Tommy paused, wiping sweat from his brow. "Jed, do you think we'll stay here forever?"

Jed leaned on his hammer, considering the question. "I reckon that's up to us, Tommy. This place has been good to us, and we've made a home here. But life's full of twists and turns. Whatever comes, we'll face it together."

Tommy nodded, a determined look in his eyes. "As long as we're together, I'm not afraid."

As the days lengthened and the first blossoms appeared, the trio found a semblance of normalcy. They shared meals, laughter, and the simple joys of daily life. For the first time in a long while, the future seemed less daunting, the past's shadows held at bay by the light of newfound hope.

# CHAPTER SIXTY

The tranquility of the settlement had become a comforting routine for Mercy, Jed, and Tommy. Days were filled with communal work, shared meals, and the simple pleasures of frontier life. Yet, beneath the surface of this newfound peace, the shadows of their past lingered, waiting for an opportune moment to resurface.

One late afternoon, as the sun dipped toward the horizon, casting long shadows across the settlement, a distant rumble echoed through the valley. The settlers paused, exchanging uneasy glances. The sound was faint but unmistakable—the thunder of hooves approaching at a gallop.

Jed's instincts, honed by years of navigating danger, immediately went on high alert. He exchanged a knowing look with Mercy, who tightened her grip on Tommy's hand.

"Stay close," Jed murmured, his voice low and steady.

The settlers gathered near the center of the settlement, eyes fixed on the direction of the approaching sound. Moments later, a lone rider emerged from the tree line, his horse lathered in sweat, nostrils flaring. The man reined in his mount sharply, dismounting with a sense of urgency.

"Riders comin' hard from the east!" he called out, his voice tinged with panic. "Lookin' like a posse, and they ain't slowin' down!"

A murmur of concern rippled through the crowd. Jed stepped forward, his expression grim.

"How many?" he asked tersely.

"At least a dozen," the rider replied. "Heavily armed."

Jed's mind raced. The peaceful days they'd enjoyed had made him almost forget the dangers that lurked beyond the settlement's borders. But now, it seemed, their past had caught up with them.

"We need to prepare," Jed said, turning to the settlers. "Gather the women and children, get 'em to safety. The rest of you, arm yourselves. We don't know their intentions, but we can't take any chances."

As the settlers sprang into action, Mercy pulled Tommy close, her heart pounding. "Jed, what do we do?"

He placed a reassuring hand on her shoulder. "You and Tommy stay with the others. I'll see what's what. If things go south, you know where to go."

Mercy nodded, swallowing her fear. She knew the drill —if danger threatened, they had a predetermined hiding spot in the nearby woods, a place they'd scouted shortly after arriving at the settlement.

The sound of approaching riders grew louder, the ground vibrating with the force of their advance. Jed took a deep breath, steeling himself for the confrontation ahead.

Moments later, the posse thundered into view, a cloud of dust trailing behind them. They reined in their horses at the edge of the settlement, a tense standoff ensuing as the settlers faced them, weapons at the ready.

A man who appeared to be the leader of the posse stepped forward, his eyes scanning the assembled settlers. He was a burly figure, with a thick beard and a scar running down the side of his face.

"We're lookin' for a girl," he announced, his voice carrying an authoritative tone. "About yay high, brown hair, blue eyes. Goes by the name of Mercy. Anyone seen her?"

A chill ran down Mercy's spine. She tightened her grip on Tommy's hand, willing herself to remain calm.

Jed stepped forward, his expression neutral. "What's your business with this girl?"

The leader's eyes narrowed. "That's none of your concern. Just tell me if you've seen her."

Jed's mind raced. Revealing Mercy's presence could put the entire settlement at risk, but denying it might provoke the posse. He needed to buy time.

"Ain't seen anyone by that description," Jed lied smoothly. "This here's a peaceful settlement. We don't want no trouble."

The leader studied Jed for a moment, as if weighing the truth of his words. Finally, he grunted.

"If you do see her, you'd best let us know," he warned. "There's a bounty on her head, and harborin' a fugitive ain't somethin' you want to be caught doin'."

With that, he signaled to his men, and the posse wheeled their horses around, galloping back the way they had come.

As the dust settled, the settlers breathed a collective sigh of relief. Jed turned to Mercy and Tommy, his expression serious.

"We need to leave," he said quietly. "It's not safe here anymore."

Mercy nodded, her heart heavy. The settlement had been a haven, a place where they'd found a semblance of normalcy. But now, it seemed, their past had caught up with them, and the shadows they had tried to outrun had returned.

As they gathered their belongings and prepared to depart under the cover of night, Mercy cast one last look at the settlement—the place that had been their home, however briefly. She felt a pang of sorrow deep in her chest.

This had been the first place where she, Tommy, and Jed had felt truly safe. For the first time since she had been taken, she had known kindness, peace, and even laughter. But peace was not meant for them—not yet.

Jed tightened the straps on his saddlebags, his movements swift and efficient. "We leave now, before that posse decides to double back and check again."

Maggie, the kind woman who had taken Mercy under her wing, approached with a bundle wrapped in cloth. "Take this," she whispered. "Food, warm blankets, and some medicine. I wish there was more we could do."

Mercy took the bundle, feeling tears prick her eyes. "Thank you," she said, voice thick with emotion.

Maggie squeezed her arm. "You've been good for this place. We'll pray you find your way."

Jed nodded at the settlers who had gathered in the darkness, watching their quiet departure. Some looked worried, others resigned. They all knew the world outside these walls was unforgiving.

"Where will you go?" Elias, the settlement's leader, asked, his tone low but urgent.

Jed adjusted his hat, glancing at the night sky. "Northwest, towards the mountains. We'll stay off the main trails."

Elias gave a slow nod. "You'll always have a place here— if you can ever return."

Jed held his gaze for a long moment before mounting his horse. "Appreciate that."

Mercy helped Tommy onto his small pony, ensuring he was secure before swinging onto her own horse. She looked around, trying to commit every detail of this place to memory —the warm glow of lanterns, the scent of woodsmoke in the air, the kindness of people who had no reason to help them.

Then, with a sharp tug of the reins, they rode out into the night.

The moon was high, casting silver light across the open land. The rhythmic pounding of hooves was the only sound as they pushed forward, leaving behind the closest thing to a home they had known.

Tommy, wrapped tightly in his blanket, was quiet, but Mercy could feel the weight of his small body leaning against her. He was exhausted. They all were.

Jed rode slightly ahead, his silhouette dark against the starlit sky. "We'll ride for a few hours, then find a place to camp," he said over his shoulder. "We need to put some distance between us and that posse."

Mercy nodded, though she wasn't sure he could see her. Her mind raced with everything that had happened. Who were these men hunting her? Why was her face on a wanted poster?

She still didn't have answers, only the chilling truth—whoever had sent them wouldn't stop looking.

For the next few hours, they rode in silence, covering as much ground as they could. The air grew colder, and the wind howled across the open plains.

It wasn't until they reached the outskirts of a dense forest that Jed finally signaled for them to stop.

"This'll do for now," he murmured, dismounting. "We'll keep the fire low, just enough to stay warm."

Mercy slid off her horse, her muscles aching from the ride. Tommy, barely awake, leaned into her side.

"I got him," Jed said, lifting Tommy gently and setting him down on a bedroll. He tucked the boy's blanket around him tightly before sitting back against a fallen log, his gun across his lap.

Mercy sat beside him, rubbing her arms against the chill. "Jed," she said after a long moment, her voice quiet. "Do you think they'll find us again?"

Jed exhaled through his nose, staring into the fire's embers. "I don't know," he admitted. "But I do know one thing —we ain't gonna let 'em take you."

Mercy swallowed, staring at the flames. She wanted to believe him. But deep down, she knew this wasn't over. Not even close.

As the wind howled through the trees, she wrapped her arms around herself and silently prayed that, somehow, they would find a way to escape the shadows of the past before they closed in for good.

# CHAPTER SIXTY-ONE

The trio had been on the move for days, navigating through dense forests and treacherous terrain to stay ahead of their pursuers. The initial adrenaline that fueled their escape had waned, replaced by exhaustion and the gnawing uncertainty of their plight.

One evening, as the sun dipped below the horizon, casting long shadows through the towering pines, Jed signaled for them to halt. They had reached a secluded clearing beside a bubbling brook—a seemingly perfect spot to rest.

"We'll camp here tonight," Jed announced, his voice tinged with weariness. "Tommy, gather some firewood. Mercy, help me set up the shelter."

As they busied themselves with their tasks, an eerie silence settled over the forest, broken only by the occasional rustle of leaves and the distant call of a night bird. Unbeknownst to them, a pair of watchful eyes observed their every move from the shadows.

Later, as they sat around the crackling fire, sharing a meager meal, Mercy couldn't shake the feeling of being watched. She glanced around nervously, her eyes scanning the darkened tree line.

"Something wrong?" Jed asked, noticing her unease.

"I... I don't know," Mercy replied, her voice barely above a whisper. "I just have this feeling..."

Jed's expression hardened. "Stay close to the fire. I'll take first watch."

As the night deepened, Tommy drifted into a fitful sleep, while Mercy sat quietly, her senses on high alert. Jed stood at the edge of the clearing, his rifle cradled in his arms, eyes scanning the darkness.

Hours passed with no sign of danger, and Mercy's eyelids grew heavy. Just as she was about to succumb to sleep, a sudden movement caught her eye—a shadow darting between the trees.

"Jed!" she hissed, her heart pounding.

Before Jed could react, a figure lunged from the darkness, tackling him to the ground. Mercy screamed, scrambling to her feet as more assailants emerged, their faces obscured by masks.

Chaos erupted. Jed fought valiantly, but the attackers were numerous and well-prepared. One of them seized Mercy, dragging her away from the campsite.

"Let me go!" she cried, struggling against her captor's iron grip.

"Quiet, girl," the man growled, his voice muffled by the mask. "You're worth a lot of money."

Panic surged through Mercy as she realized the gravity

of their situation. These men were bounty hunters, and they had finally caught up to them.

As she was dragged deeper into the forest, the sounds of the struggle faded, leaving her isolated and terrified. Her mind raced, searching for a way to escape.

Summoning her courage, Mercy feigned a stumble, causing her captor to momentarily lose his balance. Seizing the opportunity, she twisted free and bolted into the darkness, branches whipping against her face as she ran.

Behind her, the man cursed loudly. "Get back here, you little—"

Ignoring his shouts, Mercy pushed herself harder, her breath coming in ragged gasps. She could hear the heavy footfalls of her pursuer closing in.

Just as her strength began to wane, she burst into another clearing and skidded to a halt. Before her lay a steep ravine, its depths shrouded in darkness.

Trapped, she turned to face her pursuer, who emerged from the trees with a triumphant sneer.

"Nowhere left to run, girl," he taunted, advancing slowly.

Desperation clawed at Mercy's chest. She glanced back at the ravine, then at the man approaching her.

In a split-second decision, she took a step back and let herself fall into the abyss.

The world became a blur of motion as she tumbled down the slope, branches and rocks tearing at her clothes and skin. Pain exploded through her body, and then—

Darkness.

# CHAPTER SIXTY-TWO

**M**ercy awoke to a world of pain. Every breath was a struggle, each movement sending sharp jolts through her battered body. The fall had left her disoriented, her surroundings a blur of darkness and indistinct shapes.

As her senses gradually sharpened, she became aware of the cold, damp earth beneath her and the faint, musty scent of decaying leaves. The canopy above was dense, allowing only slivers of moonlight to pierce through, casting eerie patterns on the forest floor.

Gritting her teeth, Mercy attempted to sit up, a groan escaping her lips as pain radiated from her left arm. Gingerly, she touched the area, her fingers brushing against a jagged tear in her sleeve and the warm, sticky sensation of blood. A deep gash marred her forearm, the wound oozing steadily.

Panic threatened to overtake her, but she forced herself to remain calm. She tore a strip from the hem of her dress, wrapping it tightly around the injury to stem the bleeding. The makeshift bandage was crude, but it would have to suffice.

Her head throbbed, and when she reached up to touch her temple, her fingers came away slick with blood. A probable concussion, she surmised, noting the dizziness that accompanied any sudden movement.

Surveying her surroundings, Mercy realized she had landed in a narrow ravine, its steep walls rising ominously on either side. The fall had been significant, and it was a miracle she was still alive. She recalled stories of people surviving great falls, their lives spared by sheer luck or the cushioning effect of foliage. Perhaps the dense underbrush had broken her descent, saving her from a fatal impact.

The forest was silent, the usual nocturnal chorus absent, as if the very woods were holding their breath. A shiver ran down her spine, not solely from the cold. She was alone, injured, and vulnerable in an unforgiving wilderness.

Memories of the attack flooded back—the masked men, the struggle, the terror. Jed and Tommy. Were they safe? Had they managed to escape? The thought of them captured or worse was unbearable.

Determination flared within her. She couldn't afford to succumb to despair. She needed to move, to find shelter and tend to her injuries properly. Staying in the ravine was not an option; it was a trap, a place where she could easily be cornered.

With great effort, Mercy rose to her feet, leaning against the rough bark of a tree for support. Her legs trembled, but she willed them to hold. She scanned the ravine, searching for a way out.

A narrow path caught her eye, a precarious trail that wound its way up the side of the ravine. It was steep and littered with loose stones, but it offered a potential escape.

Taking a deep breath, she began her ascent, each step a test of her resolve. The climb was arduous, her injuries sapping her strength, but she pressed on, driven by the need to survive.

Halfway up, her foot slipped on a loose rock, sending her sprawling onto her injured arm. A cry of pain escaped her, echoing through the silent forest. Tears blurred her vision, but she forced herself to continue, clawing her way upward.

After what felt like an eternity, Mercy reached the top, collapsing onto the forest floor, her chest heaving with exertion. She lay there for a moment, staring up at the canopy, the stars barely visible through the dense foliage.

The forest above the ravine was different—darker, more foreboding. The trees were ancient, their gnarled branches twisting like skeletal fingers. An oppressive silence hung in the air, broken only by the occasional rustle of unseen creatures.

Pushing herself to her feet, Mercy knew she couldn't remain exposed. She needed to find shelter, a place to rest and gather her strength. She stumbled forward, each step a battle against the pain that wracked her body.

As she moved deeper into the forest, she spotted a cluster of large rocks, their formation creating a small overhang. It wasn't much, but it would provide some protection from the elements.

Crawling beneath the overhang, Mercy curled into herself, the cold seeping into her bones. She closed her eyes, willing sleep to come, but her mind raced with fear and uncertainty.

Somewhere out there, Jed and Tommy were either searching for her or in need of help themselves. She had to find them, but first, she needed to survive the night.

As exhaustion finally claimed her, Mercy's last conscious thought was a silent plea: Please, let them be safe.

# CHAPTER SIXTY-THREE

The forest was a labyrinth of shadows and whispers as the masked man, known among his peers as Rourke, navigated the underbrush with predatory precision. His quarry, the girl named Mercy, had eluded him with a desperate plunge into the ravine. Now, under the cloak of night, he intended to reclaim his prize.

Rourke paused at the edge of the ravine, his cold eyes scanning the descent. The moonlight revealed broken branches and disturbed foliage—a clear indication of her fall. A lesser pursuer might have assumed her dead, but Rourke knew better. The hunted often possessed a tenacity that defied logic.

With calculated movements, he began his descent, boots finding purchase on the treacherous slope. The air was thick with the scent of damp earth and decaying leaves, muffling the sounds of his approach. As he reached the ravine's floor, he crouched, examining the impressions in the soft ground.

A smear of blood on a jagged rock caught his attention. He touched it, rubbing the crimson between his fingers. Still fresh. His lips curled into a predatory smile.

He moved silently, following the subtle trail—crushed grass, a fragment of torn fabric, droplets of blood glistening like dark jewels in the moonlight. Each sign told a story of her struggle, her determination to survive. But Rourke was patient; the forest was his domain, and he had all the time he needed.

As he advanced, the terrain began to change. The ravine walls closed in, and the canopy above thickened, casting deeper shadows. The air grew colder, and a faint mist clung to the ground, swirling around his ankles.

Rourke's senses were heightened, attuned to the slightest disturbance. A distant rustle drew his gaze—a deer, startled by his presence, bounded away, its white tail flashing in the darkness. He paid it no mind; his focus was unyielding.

Hours passed, the night deepening. Rourke's persistence was unwavering, his movements methodical. He knew she was injured, her pace hindered by pain and fatigue. It was only a matter of time before he closed the distance.

Then, he saw it—a faint impression in the mud, the outline of a small hand. Nearby, a patch of disturbed earth suggested she had rested here, perhaps seeking refuge. He crouched, studying the area, envisioning her movements.

A broken branch overhead indicated a recent passage. He reached up, feeling the rough edge where it had snapped. His eyes narrowed, calculating.

Rourke continued, his path leading him to a cluster

of large rocks forming a natural shelter. He approached cautiously, the silence pressing in around him. As he rounded the largest boulder, his gaze fell upon a small, crumpled figure nestled beneath the overhang.

Mercy lay unconscious, her face pale, a makeshift bandage wrapped around her arm. Her breathing was shallow, each exhale a faint mist in the cold air.

For a moment, Rourke stood over her, his expression inscrutable. Then, with deliberate care, he reached into his pack, retrieving a length of coarse rope. He worked swiftly, binding her wrists and ankles, ensuring there was no chance of escape.

As he secured the final knot, Mercy stirred, a soft moan escaping her lips. Her eyes fluttered open, confusion giving way to terror as she recognized her captor.

"No... please..." she whispered, her voice trembling.

Rourke's smile was devoid of warmth. "Hush now," he murmured, his tone almost gentle. "Struggle will only make this more difficult."

Tears welled in Mercy's eyes, her body trembling. She was too weak to resist, the fight drained from her by injury and exhaustion.

Rourke hoisted Mercy over his shoulder with ease, her slight frame offering little burden. He began the arduous climb out of the ravine, each step measured, his breathing steady. The damp earth shifted beneath his boots, but his grip was sure—he was a hunter by trade, and carrying an injured captive was nothing new to him.

Mercy, however, was not just any captive.

She stirred weakly, a soft whimper escaping her cracked lips. Every part of her ached, her body screaming in protest at the rough handling, but she was conscious enough to recognize her dire situation. The last thing she remembered was tumbling down the ravine, her escape attempt turning into a near-fatal disaster. Now, she was back in the hands of the very men she had fought so hard to escape.

Her wrists and ankles were bound so tightly the coarse rope bit into her skin. She could barely feel her hands. A sick sense of dread settled in her stomach—there would be no easy escape this time.

By the time Rourke reached the top of the ravine, the first streaks of dawn had begun to creep across the sky, washing the forest in a pale, eerie light. The morning mist clung to the ground in thick patches, making the world look even more dreamlike.

He set Mercy down against a gnarled tree trunk, adjusting her bindings before uncorking a canteen and pressing it against her lips.

"Drink," he ordered.

She hesitated, staring at him through dazed, fearful eyes.

"Unless you want to pass out again, you'd best take the water," he added.

Mercy wasn't in a position to refuse. Her lips were dry, her throat raw, and her entire body screamed for relief. She allowed a few gulps, the cool liquid shocking her parched throat. When she had her fill, Rourke pulled the canteen away and wiped his gloved hand across his jaw.

She knew she needed to keep him talking. If she could figure out why they were after her, she might stand a chance.

"Why... why are you doing this?" she croaked, her voice barely above a whisper.

Rourke gave her a long, appraising look, as if debating whether to answer. Then, with a slight shrug, he muttered, "Orders."

Mercy blinked. "Orders? From who?"

He smirked. "Now, that ain't your concern, girl."

Her stomach twisted. Someone wanted her—badly enough to send out bounty hunters and keep chasing her through hell and back. She had thought this was a case of mistaken identity, but now she wasn't sure.

"There's no money in this," she pressed, her voice desperate. "I'm no one special. Why are you still after me?"

Rourke didn't answer. His expression darkened for just a fraction of a second—just long enough for her to see something buried there. But he quickly masked it, his smirk returning as he pushed himself up and adjusted his coat.

"Doesn't matter. We're moving," he said gruffly.

He reached down and grabbed the back of her dress, hauling her up like a sack of grain. Mercy bit back a cry as her injuries flared with renewed pain.

They began moving through the forest, the underbrush crunching beneath their boots. Mercy tried to keep track of their direction, but her head throbbed too much, her thoughts sluggish.

The other masked men were nowhere to be seen. Were

they still searching for Jed and Tommy? Or had something happened to them?

The possibility sent a fresh wave of panic through her.

She had to get away.

Jed & Tommy—On the Hunt

Miles away, Jed and Tommy crouched behind a fallen log, their breath misting in the cold morning air.

Jed's face was set in a murderous scowl, his jaw clenched so tight it looked like he might crack a tooth. He had woken to find Mercy gone—and he knew what that meant.

"They took her," he growled, scanning the forest floor. "Bastards must've caught up to her after she fell."

Tommy, still shaken from the attack, was pale but resolute. "We gotta find her, Jed."

"We will," Jed muttered. "Ain't no way in hell I'm lettin' them keep her."

The two of them had been tracking since dawn, following the faint trail of footprints and bloodstains Mercy had left behind. Jed could tell she was hurt bad, and that knowledge made his blood boil.

They reached a patch of disturbed earth where it looked like someone had fallen—then been dragged away. Jed crouched, running his fingers along the prints.

"They're takin' her east," he muttered. "That means one thing—they're headin' to whoever put the bounty on her."

Tommy swallowed hard. "Who do you think it is?"

Jed shook his head. "Dunno. But I got a feelin' we're

about to find out."

He cocked his rifle, his expression grim.

Mercy was out there—and he was bringing her home.

# CHAPTER SIXTY-FOUR

Pain throbbed through Mercy's skull, dull and unrelenting. She had lost track of how long she had been slung over Rourke's shoulder, her body limp and exhausted from the struggle. She barely had the strength to keep her head from lolling forward, her eyes slipping in and out of focus.

The morning mist was starting to burn off, replaced by the harsh light of day filtering through the towering pines. The trees blurred past as Rourke carried her deeper into the wilderness, moving with the sure-footedness of a man who knew every inch of the land.

Her arms and legs were still tightly bound, the rope biting into her raw skin. She had tried to wiggle her fingers earlier, but they had gone numb from the lack of circulation.

She wanted to scream, to thrash, to do anything—but her body wouldn't obey.

Instead, she focused on her breathing. Stay calm. Stay

awake. If she lost consciousness again, she might not wake up next time.

Finally, after what felt like forever, Rourke came to a stop. He shifted her weight and dropped her unceremoniously onto the ground. The impact sent a shockwave of pain through her ribs, forcing a cry from her lips.

"Quit yer whimpering," Rourke muttered as he knelt to untie the ropes around her ankles. "You're lucky I ain't got orders to kill you outright."

Lucky? Mercy clenched her jaw, biting back a retort. She didn't feel lucky.

Rourke lifted his head, scanning the surroundings. The clearing they were in was different from the thick, tangled woods they had been moving through. Ahead, nestled at the base of a rocky hill, stood a cabin.

It wasn't abandoned.

Mercy could see a thin plume of smoke curling from the chimney, and the faint glint of a metal latch on the door. Someone was inside.

Her pulse spiked. Was this who he was delivering her to?

She shifted slightly, trying to turn her head. The cabin looked old, weather-worn, but sturdy. It was built from thick logs, the kind settlers used when they planned to stay in one place for a long time. Whoever lived here had been here a while.

Her stomach turned.

If she was handed off to whoever lived in that cabin, she

might never be seen again.

Rourke grabbed her by the arm, jerking her upright. "No more games, girl. Walk, or I'll make you."

Mercy stumbled forward, her legs barely holding her weight. She had no idea how far they had traveled, but she knew one thing: Jed and Tommy were too far away to save her now.

She had to save herself.

As they reached the front steps of the cabin, Rourke banged on the door three times.

For a long moment, nothing happened. Then, the sound of a heavy bolt sliding free echoed through the trees.

The door swung open.

A man stood in the doorway.

Mercy froze.

He wasn't what she had expected. She had imagined some ruthless bounty hunter, maybe someone scarred and ragged from years of chasing down men for money.

But this man was refined.

His clothes were clean, his boots polished, and his hair neatly combed back. He had a gold ring on his finger and a thin scar running from his temple to his jaw. His eyes—sharp and calculating—locked onto Mercy the way a merchant examines cattle before a sale.

"You brought her?" the man asked, voice smooth, like a politician's.

"Had to chase her through half the damn frontier,"

Rourke grunted. "But yeah, she's yours now. Just like we agreed."

Mercy's breath hitched.

Yours now?

She turned sharply to Rourke. "You—you sold me?"

The man in the doorway smirked. "Not quite, little one. You were never yours to begin with."

Something cold curled in Mercy's gut.

Before she could react, the man reached out, grabbed her chin between his gloved fingers, and forced her to look at him.

"Now," he murmured, his gaze studying her like she was a puzzle piece finally falling into place. "Let's find out if you're really who I think you are."

# CHAPTER SIXTY-FIVE

**M**ercy's heart raced as the man placed the photograph before her—a girl who looked strikingly similar, yet was undeniably someone else. The weight of his words settled heavily upon her:

"I just need everyone else to believe that you are."

She swallowed hard, her mind whirling with questions. Who was this girl? Why did he want to pass her off as someone else? And what would happen if she refused?

The man observed her intently, as if reading her thoughts. "You must have many questions," he said, his tone almost sympathetic. "Allow me to provide some clarity."

He settled into a chair opposite her, the flickering fire casting shadows across his face. "The girl in this photograph is Annabelle Sinclair, the sole heir to the Sinclair fortune—a vast empire of land, railroads, and enterprises that stretch across this territory."

Mercy listened, her brow furrowing. The name meant nothing to her.

"Several months ago," he continued, "Annabelle disappeared under mysterious circumstances. Despite exhaustive searches and substantial rewards offered, she was never found."

He leaned closer, his eyes gleaming with a predatory intensity. "You, my dear, bear an uncanny resemblance to Annabelle. With the right grooming and education, you could easily be passed off as her."

Mercy's stomach churned. "Why would you want to do that?"

A cold smile tugged at his lips. "Control of the Sinclair fortune would grant immense power and influence. By presenting you as the returned heiress, I can access that wealth and the opportunities it brings."

She recoiled at the implication. "And what if I refuse?"

His expression hardened. "Refusal is not an option. You will cooperate, or there will be... consequences."

Fear clutched at her, but beneath it simmered a spark of defiance. She couldn't let this man use her for his nefarious schemes.

Sensing her resistance, he sighed. "I had hoped we could do this the easy way. But if persuasion fails, there are other methods to ensure your compliance."

He stood, signaling to someone outside the room. A moment later, two imposing figures entered, their expressions devoid of empathy.

"Take her to the preparation room," he ordered. "Begin the conditioning process."

As the men advanced toward her, Mercy's mind raced. She had to find a way out, to escape before she was ensnared in this sinister plot.

But for now, resistance was futile. She would have to bide her time, gather her strength, and wait for the right moment to make her move.

As they led her away, the man's voice echoed behind her. "Remember, Mercy, the role you are to play is not just an opportunity—it's your only chance at survival."

The weight of his words settled upon her, but deep within, a resolve began to form. She would not be a pawn in his game. She would find a way to reclaim her freedom and uncover the truth behind this twisted masquerade.

# CHAPTER SIXTY-SIX

Mercy's stomach twisted as the two men dragged her down a dimly lit hallway. The scent of damp wood and old tobacco filled the air, and each step echoed against the cold stone floor. The deeper they went into the cabin, the clearer it became—this was no ordinary hideout.

She was led into a small, windowless room with only a chair, a table, and a single oil lamp. The men shoved her into the chair, securing her wrists behind it.

"You sit tight," one of them muttered before stepping outside.

The door shut with a loud click. Locked.

Mercy exhaled slowly, her mind racing. The photograph of Annabelle Sinclair still burned in her memory. She had never met this girl before. She didn't know why she looked like her, but one thing was clear—the man in charge wanted to use her as a pawn.

Her thoughts were interrupted when the door opened again.

The smooth-talking villain stepped inside, adjusting the cuffs of his finely tailored coat.

Mercy squared her shoulders, willing herself not to show fear. "You took the wrong person," she said, her voice steadier than she felt.

The man smiled slightly as he leaned against the table. "That depends on how you look at it," he mused. "You may not be Annabelle Sinclair, but you are far from insignificant."

Mercy frowned. "What do you mean?"

He studied her carefully, his gaze almost... curious. "You really don't know, do you?"

She shook her head, frustration bubbling beneath her fear. "Know what?"

The man tilted his head. "Tell me, Mercy McKenna—what do you know about the Sinclair family?"

Mercy hesitated. She had heard the name before. Even out in the frontier, people whispered about the Sinclairs—a powerful family, their wealth built on land, railroads, and cattle empires. But she had never had anything to do with them.

"Nothing," she admitted.

The man's expression darkened. "Then it seems I must enlighten you."

He walked to a cabinet, retrieved a folded piece of parchment, and tossed it onto the table before her. "Annabelle Sinclair wasn't just the only daughter of Franklin and Marianne Sinclair—she was betrothed to the son of a very powerful man."

Mercy's brows furrowed. "So?"

The man chuckled, shaking his head. "So... when Annabelle disappeared, it caused quite a problem. You see, her arranged marriage wasn't just about love—it was about sealing a business deal between two of the richest families in the territory. With her gone, that deal collapsed, and many very powerful men lost a lot of money."

Mercy swallowed hard.

"Some believed she ran away. Others thought she was kidnapped," he continued. "But regardless of what happened to the real Annabelle, those men still want their deal—and their money."

Mercy's chest tightened. "So what does that have to do with me?"

The man smiled. "Because someone heard whispers of a girl in these parts—a girl with Annabelle Sinclair's face."

The weight of his words hit her like a runaway horse.

That's how it happened. Someone saw her. Someone mistook her. And someone paid a lot of money to have her brought in.

She had been kidnapped over a business deal.

Her stomach twisted in disgust. "And what, exactly, do you plan to do with me?"

The man's smile widened. "Oh, Mercy... I plan to give you back to them."

# CHAPTER SIXTY-SEVEN

**M**ercy's blood ran cold at his words. Give you back to them. To men she had never met. To a life that wasn't hers.

She forced herself to keep her breathing steady, her expression unreadable, though panic clawed at her insides. The man before her—calm, calculating, dangerous—was no ordinary outlaw. He wasn't the kind of man who made idle threats or took unnecessary risks. Everything he did was precise, deliberate, and that made him more terrifying than any brute with a gun.

Her mind raced. If she was to survive this, she needed answers.

"Let me guess," she said, her voice steady despite the hammering of her heart. "You're planning to sell me to the highest bidder?"

The man chuckled, shaking his head as he leaned against the edge of the table. "Sell you? No, Mercy. Return you.

The difference is rather significant. Your value doesn't come from being a simple captive—it comes from who they believe you are."

Mercy clenched her jaw. "I'm not Annabelle Sinclair. You can't just parade me in front of them and expect them to believe it."

His dark eyes glinted with amusement. "Oh, but I can. And I will. You see, these men want to believe it. Annabelle's disappearance cost them power, prestige, and an empire that was supposed to be theirs. If I hand them someone who looks like her, who acts like her, who convinces them she is her... well, they'll take her without question."

Mercy swallowed. "And what if I refuse to play along?"

The man's smirk didn't falter, but his eyes darkened, the air between them turning heavy with unspoken threats. "You won't."

Silence stretched between them, broken only by the faint hiss of the oil lamp burning in the corner.

Mercy sat rigidly in the chair, her wrists still bound behind her. If she had the use of her hands, she might have gone for the lamp, smashed it against his head, and made a run for it. But tied up and locked in this room, she had no choice but to play his game—for now.

"What's in this for you?" she asked finally, searching his face for any sign of weakness.

He let out a low chuckle. "Ah, that's the right question." He stood and paced to the corner of the room, retrieving a crystal glass and a dark bottle of whiskey. He poured himself a drink, swirling the amber liquid before taking a slow sip.

"Power," he said simply. "The Sinclairs have been a thorn in my side for far too long. By returning their 'lost daughter,' I put myself in a position they can't ignore. I will be their ally, their savior—the man who restored their legacy. And once I have their trust..." He smiled coldly. "Well, let's just say, a man in my position does not waste such an opportunity."

Mercy felt sick. He wasn't doing this for ransom. He wasn't even doing it for the money. He was playing a much longer, more dangerous game.

She had to get out of here.

"You really think they'll believe it?" she said, keeping her tone even. "The Sinclairs? Annabelle's mother and father? You think a few dresses and fancy words will make them forget their own daughter?"

He took another slow sip of whiskey. "Grief makes people blind, my dear. And time makes the heart desperate. It has been long enough since Annabelle vanished—long enough that a father would rather embrace the lie than accept the truth. And a mother?" He set his glass down and met her gaze. "A mother will convince herself of anything, so long as it brings her child back."

Mercy's stomach twisted.

"And if they don't?" she challenged. "What happens when they see through it? What happens when they realize I'm not her?"

The man tilted his head, as if considering her words. Then, with a slow smile, he replied, "Then you die."

# CHAPTER SIXTY-EIGHT

**M**ercy's breath stilled in her chest. He had said it so casually, as if her life—or her death—was just another piece on his chessboard. He stepped closer, resting one hand on the back of her chair as he leaned down. His presence was suffocating, his breath warm against her cheek. "That's why you'll make them believe. That's why you'll play your part."

Mercy swallowed hard. "And if I do? If I become Annabelle for them? What then?"

He straightened, adjusting the cuffs of his coat, his expression unreadable. "Then you live the life she was meant to have. Marry the man she was promised to. Seal the deal that was broken." He turned, pouring himself another drink. "And you secure my future in the process."

Mercy's hands trembled against the rope binding her wrists.

Marry.

She hadn't even considered that part of it before. It wasn't just that they wanted her to pretend to be Annabelle—it was that they wanted her to become her. To step into her life, wear her name, walk her path. And that path led straight to a wedding altar.

Her mind spun.

"You expect me to just stand beside some stranger and let him put a ring on my finger?" she said, disbelief laced with fury.

The man smirked. "Not just any stranger. William Blackwood—the only son of the most powerful railroad magnate in the territory. A man whose family stands to gain as much from this arrangement as the Sinclairs themselves."

Mercy had heard that name before. Blackwood. Ruthless. Ambitious. His family owned nearly half the railways running through the West. If the Sinclairs and the Blackwoods had been set to unite their empires through marriage, then she understood now why Annabelle's disappearance had been such a catastrophe.

And why this man was so desperate to fix it.

"So that's it," she murmured. "You want me to fool them long enough to secure their wealth and power, and then what? You kill me in my sleep?"

His smirk deepened. "Not if you play your cards right."

Mercy exhaled sharply, her mind racing. She had no allies here. No one to run to. If she wanted to make it out of this alive, she needed to do what he did—play the long game.

Slowly, she lifted her chin. "You want me to be Annabelle?" she said. "Fine. But if I'm going to be her, then I want something in return."

His brow arched slightly, intrigued. "Oh?"

"You keep Jed and Tommy out of this. You let them go, unharmed, without ever coming after them again."

A silence stretched between them. He studied her, weighing her request like a merchant appraising a trade. Finally, he nodded once.

"Very well," he said. "You become Annabelle Sinclair. And I swear, by my word as a businessman, your friends will be left alone."

Mercy knew better than to trust men like him. But she also knew when she had no other choice.

She swallowed back the fear in her throat. "Then I guess I'd better learn how to be a Sinclair."

His smile widened, victorious. "That's the spirit."

And with that, her fate was sealed.

# CHAPTER SIXTY-NINE

The pine forest stretched endlessly before them, thick with tangled underbrush and the lingering dampness of the recent storm. The air was heavy with the scent of wet earth, pine resin, and the faint decay of fallen leaves, the wilderness a labyrinth of towering trees and shifting shadows. The deeper they moved, the denser the terrain became, the ground uneven beneath their boots, thick roots threatening to snare an unsteady step. Overhead, the sky remained a dull gray, the last traces of sunlight barely managing to pierce through the swaying branches, casting flickering patterns on the forest floor.

Jed pushed forward, his pace relentless but controlled, scanning their surroundings with the practiced eye of a man who had spent years navigating both the land and the dangers that lurked within it. Every few steps, he glanced back to check on Tommy, the boy struggling to keep up, his small boots crunching against twigs and loose gravel. Jed could hear his breathing, quick and shallow, but Tommy didn't complain, his jaw set in determination. He wasn't built for this kind of trek yet, but he was trying, and that was enough for now.

Gideon moved ahead, his steps soundless, his sharp gaze flitting between the trees like a predator tracking its prey. He moved with a quiet efficiency, his fingers brushing against the worn handle of his revolver at regular intervals, his every motion betraying the instincts of a seasoned hunter. Though Jed wasn't sure he fully trusted the man yet, there was no denying Gideon knew what he was doing. The way he examined the landscape, pausing now and then to listen, told Jed all he needed to know—this was a man who had spent years tracking dangerous men through even more treacherous terrain.

Suddenly, Gideon came to a halt. He crouched low, his eyes narrowing as he reached for something in the dirt. Jed was at his side in an instant, following his gaze to the patch of disturbed earth before them. Deep-set hoofprints, their edges still firm, stretched ahead, disappearing into the thick brush.

"They're moving fast," Gideon murmured, tracing the outline of the tracks with his fingers. "Steady pace, no sign of stopping for rest. They've got a destination."

Jed exhaled, his eyes following the trail ahead. "Means they got a reason to hurry."

Gideon shifted, his expression darkening. "Four riders at least. Heavy saddlebags." He glanced toward Jed. "That means supplies—food, water... weapons."

Jed's jaw tensed. He already knew what Gideon wasn't saying. The weight of those supplies wasn't just ammunition and provisions. It was a person.

"And a girl," Jed said, his voice low.

Gideon gave a tight nod. "They won't risk losin' her. She's worth too much."

Behind them, Tommy shuddered, his small fingers gripping the straps of his pack. His voice, barely above a whisper, broke through the silence. "What if... what if she's already gone?"

Jed turned his head sharply, his eyes locking onto the boy. He didn't hesitate. "She ain't." The words left no room for doubt.

Tommy swallowed hard but nodded, pressing his lips together. The boy had seen enough of the world to know the odds weren't always in their favor, but he also knew Jed wouldn't say it unless he believed it with his whole damn heart.

Gideon shifted, rising to his full height as he gazed toward the thinning trees ahead. "They're headin' toward the canyon."

Jed's breath left him in a slow, controlled exhale. "You sure?"

Gideon pointed toward the distant horizon, where the land began to shift, sloping sharply downward into a jagged valley. The canyon loomed in the distance, an open wound carved into the earth by time and erosion, its depths a treacherous maze of rock and shadow.

"Ain't nowhere else they'd be goin' in this direction," Gideon muttered.

Jed knew the place well. The canyon was rough country —unforgiving, nearly impossible to track through once a man got too deep into its winding passages. If the bounty hunters made it there before Jed and his group caught up, Mercy might vanish into the labyrinth of stone and dust, lost to them forever.

"We need to move," Jed said, his grip tightening around the barrel of his rifle. "Before they get too far ahead."

Gideon nodded, stepping forward, but before they could take more than a few paces, he froze.

Jed saw it at the same time.

Blood.

A single, dark stain in the dirt, smearing across the bark of a fallen branch, its edges still damp.

Jed's stomach turned to lead.

Mercy.

The world narrowed as he crouched beside the bloodstain, pressing his fingers into the dampened soil. The crimson smeared against his skin, still fresh. The metallic scent clung to the air, unmistakable, sending a ripple of something cold through him. She was hurt.

Tommy sucked in a sharp breath, his voice trembling. "She's bleeding."

Jed's fingers curled into a fist, his knuckles going white. She was alive. But bleeding meant pain, meant weakness. Meant she might not be able to run.

His gaze snapped back to Gideon. "How far ahead?"

Gideon's expression was grim as he examined the surrounding brush, his fingers skimming over another broken branch. "Not far. She's leakin', but she ain't dyin'—not yet." His voice was clipped, but Jed could tell he was holding something back.

Jed stood, his grip tightening on his rifle, his heart pounding a slow, controlled beat of urgency. He had wasted enough time. They had wasted enough time.

"Then we move," he said, his voice a low growl.

Without another word, they pressed on, the wilderness swallowing them whole.

# CHAPTER SEVENTY

The land before them plummeted into a deep, jagged chasm, the canyon stretching wide and treacherous beneath the dying light of the evening sun. Shadows lengthened like clawed fingers over the rock-strewn slopes, the sheer cliffs standing as towering, ancient sentinels over the narrow, winding trails that wove down into the depths. The walls of the canyon were a tapestry of time itself, layers of sediment exposed in rich hues of ochre and umber, the earth's history laid bare in striated rock. The wind howled through the ravine, carrying with it the scent of dust, dry brush, and something older—something almost primal.

Jed stood at the precipice, boots planted firm against the uneven ground, his rifle held loosely at his side, though his entire body thrummed with tension. He had traveled rough country before, but this land felt different, as though it had swallowed men whole and left nothing behind but bones and whispers. It was the kind of place a man could ride into and never return from. And somewhere down in that abyss, Mercy was waiting.

Beside him, Gideon crouched low, scanning the

winding switchback trails carved into the rock. His sharp eyes flicked to a plume of dust rising in the distance, just barely visible through the shifting light. The tracks of the bounty hunters had led them here, and now there was no doubt.

"They're down there," Gideon murmured, voice as dry as the canyon wind.

Jed narrowed his gaze, straining to make out the shapes moving far below. Against the ochre hues of the stone, dark silhouettes wove through the craggy pathways, shifting on horseback, their figures blurred by distance. Then he saw her —slumped forward in the saddle of one of the riders, her arms bound, her form too still. A sharp, searing bolt of rage coiled in his chest.

"She's still with 'em," Jed muttered, his voice low and taut with control. The fact that she was on a horse and not being dragged over the rocks like a discarded sack meant she was alive. But for how much longer?

A sharp intake of breath came from Tommy, who stood just behind them, his small fingers curling into the fabric of his coat. "So we can still get her back?" the boy asked, his voice laced with hope and fear.

Jed exhaled slowly through his nose, forcing himself to push past the urge to charge in guns blazing. "Yeah," he said. "But we gotta be smart."

Gideon let out a quiet breath, his fingers tightening on the rifle slung across his back. "They ain't gonna make it easy. That canyon's got a thousand places to hole up, and if they spot us before we get close, we're done for."

Jed knew he was right. The canyon wasn't just rough

terrain—it was a goddamn battlefield. The ridges, the rock overhangs, the natural stone pillars... all of it provided cover for a fight, and if the bounty hunters caught sight of them, they wouldn't hesitate to take advantage. It wouldn't take much for them to put a bullet in Mercy just to lighten their load, and Jed wasn't about to give them that chance.

His eyes swept the terrain, studying the ledges, the jagged switchbacks, the places where shadows could hide a man with a rifle. Rushing in would get them all killed. They needed to be deliberate. Calculated.

"We go down slow," Jed said finally, his voice measured. "We keep to the rocks, stay outta sight. Get close enough to take 'em before they get the chance to move her."

Gideon gave a tight nod, adjusting the strap of his rifle. "Then let's move."

The three of them picked their way down the canyon's edge, their boots displacing loose shale and brittle gravel, every step threatening to send a cascade of rock tumbling into the silence below. The air was thick with the scent of sunbaked stone and dry earth, the heat of the day still lingering in the cracks and crevices of the rock.

Jed moved first, keeping low, his rifle raised as his gaze flicked between the trail ahead and the unseen dangers that lurked in the valley below. Each movement had to be measured, every breath controlled. The wrong step could send them careening over the edge or alert the men below that their hunt had turned into a chase.

The walls of the canyon rose high around them, the passage narrowing as they moved deeper into the rugged terrain. The sound of voices carried through the rock, distorted by the natural acoustics, their words unclear but their presence unmistakable. The bounty hunters were close.

As they crept forward, the acrid scent of campfire smoke reached them, curling through the air like a warning. Jed pressed himself against a jutting rock, signaling for Tommy to stay put behind a narrow outcropping, his small frame easily concealed in the shadows. The boy nodded, his wide eyes darting between Jed and the unseen threat ahead.

Gideon moved beside Jed, inching forward until they had a clear view of the camp.

The bounty hunters had settled into a natural alcove, a small, sheltered pocket within the canyon walls. Their horses were tied haphazardly to a dead tree, their saddlebags heavy with supplies. Four men sat around a fire, passing a bottle between them, their postures relaxed, unaware of the danger stalking them from above.

And there she was.

Mercy.

Tied to a wooden post at the far edge of the camp, her head drooped forward, her body slumped in exhaustion. Her dress was torn and dirt-streaked, her face pale beneath the flickering firelight. She wasn't moving much, but she was breathing.

Jed's fingers curled around the grip of his rifle, every muscle in his body coiled, ready to spring. His mind screamed at him to act, to tear through the canyon and cut down the bastards who had done this to her. But before he could shift forward, Gideon's hand landed on his arm, a firm grip, shaking his head.

Not yet.

Jed ground his teeth, forcing himself to hold back. They needed the perfect moment, the right distraction. Rushing in too soon could cost them everything.

Then, before they could make their move, a sharp whistle cut through the canyon air.

Jed and Gideon stiffened as one of the bounty hunters jerked his head up, scanning the cliffs. The easy air of the camp shifted, tension rippling through them like a snake coiling before it struck.

"Riders," one of them muttered, his fingers already reaching for his gun.

Jed's pulse pounded.

More men were coming.

If they didn't act now, Mercy was going to be taken deeper into the canyon—and that would be the last time he ever saw her.

BREAK

Jed's grip on his rifle tightened as the sound of hoofbeats echoed through the canyon, a low thunder rolling through the narrow ravines, bouncing off the jagged cliffs like a warning bell. The distant riders were masked by the dust, their shapes indistinct against the fading light, but one thing was clear—they weren't part of the bounty hunters' camp. They were coming fast. And they weren't coming for a friendly visit.

The bounty hunters had heard it too. The easy, drunken air around the fire evaporated, replaced by sharp, sudden tension. One of them, a broad-shouldered brute with a thick black mustache and a mean glint in his eye, surged to his feet, the rickety wooden stool he had been perched on toppling backward. His hand went instinctively to his revolver, fingers flexing around the worn grip, his gaze flicking toward the canyon mouth where the sound had originated.

"That ain't Rourke," he muttered, his voice low and laced with suspicion. "We got company."

Jed knew they had mere seconds to act. The moment those men realized the real threat wasn't coming from the canyon entrance but from above, their advantage would be gone. He turned his head just enough to meet Gideon's gaze, giving him a sharp nod, silent but absolute.

"We take 'em now," he said, his voice barely above a whisper.

Gideon didn't hesitate. There was no time for doubt, no space for miscalculation. The moment the enemy was aware of them, the battle would turn into a bloodbath.

Jed rose smoothly from behind the rock, his rifle already trained on his mark. The mustached bounty hunter barely had time to react before the crack of the shot split the evening air. The impact was immediate and brutal—the man staggered backward, the force of the bullet ripping through him, his revolver slipping from his fingers as he collapsed into the dirt.

The camp exploded into chaos.

Shouts rang out, men scrambling for their weapons, knocking over bottles and kicking up embers from the fire. Gideon's rifle sang next, sharp and precise, sending two more bullets into the chest of a man who had nearly reached his holster. The bounty hunter crumpled where he stood, his body slumping against a rock, leaving a streak of blood against the pale stone as he slid down.

But the remaining men weren't greenhorns. They were seasoned killers, men who had survived shootouts and ambushes before, and they weren't about to go down easy. Gunfire erupted, bullets striking the rocks, ricocheting in sharp, whining bursts. Jed ducked, moving fast between boulders, his boots skidding over loose gravel as he closed the distance between himself and the camp.

"Mercy!" he shouted, his voice cutting through the chaos.

Through the shifting haze of dust and smoke, he saw her—tied to the post, slumped forward, her face pale, her wrists raw from struggling. She lifted her head at the sound of his voice, her wide, glassy eyes locking onto him. The exhaustion in them, the sheer helplessness, sent a fresh surge of fury burning through his veins.

And then he saw the movement.

A wiry bounty hunter with a deep scar carved down his cheek was already lunging for her, a glint of steel in his grip— a knife, poised and ready to slice through her throat before she could be taken from them.

Jed didn't think. He acted.

The crack of his rifle was lost in the chaos, but the result was immediate. The bounty hunter jerked as the bullet struck home, his knees buckling, his grip on the knife failing as it clattered uselessly onto the dirt. He crumpled against the post, his weight nearly dragging Mercy down with him before his body slid sideways into the dust.

But the fight wasn't over.

The last remaining bounty hunter—a **ruthless-looking man with a shaved head, cold eyes, and a rifle slung tight across his back—**had already bolted for the horses. Jed didn't need to guess what he was planning. The bastard wasn't running. He was heading for the reinforcements, riding out of the canyon to warn Rourke or worse—whoever had paid for Mercy in the first place. If he got away, it wouldn't just be another fight. It would be a war.

Jed didn't hesitate.

He swung his rifle up, steadying it against his shoulder. The man was fast, his boots kicking up dust, his hands already reaching for the reins, one foot in the stirrup. One more second and he'd be gone.

Jed exhaled and pulled the trigger.

The bullet found its mark. The bounty hunter pitched forward, tumbling from the saddle, his body hitting the earth with a lifeless thud. The horse whinnied, rearing back before bolting into the canyon.

Then, silence.

Smoke curled in the air, the scent of gunpowder thick, mingling with the sharp tang of blood and scorched embers. The canyon was still again, the only sound the distant echo of the last shot fading into the cliffs.

Jed let out a slow, shuddering breath and lowered his rifle. It was over.

His boots crunched against the dirt as he turned toward

the wooden post. Mercy was still there, bound and trembling, her breathing uneven. He dropped to one knee and pulled his knife from his belt, slicing cleanly through the ropes. The bindings snapped, and the moment she was free, she slumped forward, her body too weak to hold itself upright. Jed caught her before she could collapse completely, his arm wrapping around her, steadying her against his chest.

"I got you, kid," he murmured, his voice rough with something dangerously close to relief. "You're safe now."

But even as he said it, even as she clung to him, her fingers weak but desperate in the fabric of his shirt, he knew the words were a lie.

Because whoever had put a price on Mercy's head wasn't going to stop looking for her.

And that meant this fight was far from finished.

# CHAPTER

# SEVENTY-ONE

August 19, 1885 – Somewhere in the Arizona Territory

The wind screamed across the barren expanse, a restless, bitter thing that carried dust like shards of glass and the faint, metallic scent of impending rain. Dark clouds bruised the horizon, heavy and swollen, casting long, jagged shadows over the parched land below. The sun's dying light bled crimson along the edges of the sky, painting the desert in hues of fire and ash. This was a land carved by unforgiving hands—a place where bones disappeared into the earth, swallowed whole by time and silence.

Ellie McKenna rode with the storm at her back, her fingers clenched around the cracked leather reins, knuckles white beneath the grime of the trail. Her sharp blue eyes, cold and unyielding, scanned the jagged skyline where towering mesas rose like the ribs of some ancient beast. It had been weeks since Mercy was taken—weeks of dust-choked roads, dead ends, and shadows that vanished just when she thought she was getting close. But Ellie wasn't built to break. Not now. Not ever.

Beside her, Cullen Crowe McKenna rode in grim silence, his broad frame hunched slightly in the saddle, the brim of his battered hat casting his face in shadow. His revolver hung low on his hip, worn smooth from use, the handle dark with the sweat of calloused hands. There was a coldness in Cullen's eyes, something carved from loss and violence, but it was nothing compared to the fire simmering beneath Ellie's quiet rage. She'd bled for less before.

The silence between them stretched, brittle as glass. Finally, Cullen broke it, his voice low and rough like gravel beneath boots. "We're runnin' outta road, Ellie. If we don't find a lead soon—"

Ellie shot him a glare sharp enough to cut. "Then we keep ridin'."

Cullen huffed out a breath, shaking his head, but he didn't argue. He knew better. He'd seen that look before—the one that meant she'd ride straight into hell and drag the devil back out by the throat if it meant finding their daughter. He'd always been a hard man, but Ellie? Ellie was iron when it came to Mercy.

The land unfolded before them like an open wound, cracked and bleeding under the relentless sun. Dry riverbeds carved deep scars through the earth, their edges brittle and jagged. Cacti stood like silent sentinels, their spines brittle against the sky. This was Apache country—rugged, untamed, dangerous. But the land wasn't what haunted Ellie's thoughts. It was the men who had taken her daughter. Men who didn't care if she lived or died, so long as she served their purpose.

As they crested a ridge, a small trading post emerged from the heat-shimmered haze—a handful of weather-beaten buildings clinging to the dirt like they didn't belong. The roofs sagged under the weight of neglect, and the cracked windows reflected nothing but dust and regret. Smoke curled lazily from a crooked chimney, carrying with it the faint, greasy scent of roasted meat and old sweat.

Cullen clicked his tongue, urging his horse forward. "We'll ask around. Someone's gotta know somethin'."

Ellie said nothing, her jaw clenched so tight it ached. She was done asking. She wanted answers—or blood. Either would do.

The door creaked open with a reluctant groan, spilling weak daylight across the dusty floorboards. The room was dim, lit only by the dying glow of a single lantern hanging crookedly from a rusted nail. The air was thick with the sour stench of sweat, tobacco, and spilled whiskey—a mixture that clung to the walls like a second skin.

Behind the battered bar stood a man with the face of someone who'd stopped caring years ago. His apron was stained with old grease and darker things, and a shotgun rested within easy reach, propped casually against the shelves like an unspoken threat. His eyes flicked up as Ellie and Cullen entered, but he didn't bother with a greeting. Places like this didn't need pleasantries.

Their boots echoed on the warped wooden floor, dust rising with every step. Cullen moved first, his posture relaxed but his hand hovering near the worn grip of his Colt. Ellie followed, her eyes sweeping the room, noting every shadow, every face. Two men hunched over a game of cards in the corner, their laughter dying when she walked past. A woman with hollow eyes nursed a drink, her gaze distant, lost somewhere Ellie didn't care to know.

Cullen stopped at the bar, resting his forearm on the scarred wood. His voice was low, the kind that didn't ask for attention—it demanded it. "We're lookin' for someone."

The bartender snorted without looking up. "Ain't we all?"

Ellie stepped forward, her rifle slung casually over her shoulder, but her fingers were tense on the strap. She leaned in just enough to make the man look her in the eye. "Twelve-year-old girl. Taken by bounty hunters."

That got his attention.

The bartender's hand paused mid-wipe, his eyes narrowing slightly. He sized them up, his gaze lingering on the hardness in Ellie's face and the quiet threat coiled in Cullen's stance. He swallowed once, then jerked his chin toward the shadowed corner of the room.

"Man over there's been askin' 'bout the same girl."

Ellie's stomach twisted, a knot of dread tightening beneath her ribs. She turned slowly, her gaze following the bartender's nod.

In the far corner, half-hidden in shadow, sat a man slumped over a glass of something dark and cheap. His hat was pulled low, casting his face in darkness, but there was no mistaking the tension in his shoulders—the way a man sits when he's expecting trouble.

Cullen's fingers drifted toward his revolver, the

movement slow, deliberate.

The man lifted his head.

His face was a map of violence—a busted lip, bruises blossoming like dark flowers across his jaw, and eyes sunken with exhaustion. A bounty hunter, no doubt. But not one who'd walked away from his last job unscathed.

Ellie's pulse roared in her ears. She moved toward him without thinking, her boots striking the floor with purpose. She stopped just short of his table, her shadow falling over him like a blade.

"Start talkin'," she growled, her voice low, sharp enough to draw blood.

The man met her gaze, something dark flickering behind his swollen eyes. Regret, maybe. Or fear.

Either way, Ellie didn't care.

She was done waiting.

# CHAPTER
# SEVENTY-TWO

T he lamplight sputtered and hissed against the cracked glass of a dusty lantern, casting restless shadows across the warped wooden walls of the trading post. The place smelled of sweat, spilled whiskey, and the faint tang of blood—the kind that clung to the floorboards and never quite washed out. The bounty hunter sat slumped at a crooked table near the corner, a wiry man with hollowed cheeks, a busted lip swollen purple, and a bloodstained bandage wrapped tight around his upper arm. He looked like he'd crawled straight out of hell, and judging by the haunted flicker in his sunken eyes, hell had spit him back out with teeth marks.

Ellie McKenna didn't waste time on pleasantries. She stalked across the room with the coiled tension of a storm about to break, her rifle resting against her hip, her finger dangerously close to the trigger. The wooden floor creaked beneath her boots, but her presence made more noise than her footsteps ever could. She leaned in just enough to cast her shadow over him, her voice low and sharp as broken glass.

"Start talkin', or I start shootin'," she said, the words as calm and deadly as the cool barrel of her gun.

The bounty hunter exhaled sharply, the glass trembling slightly in his battered hand as he took a slow, steadying sip. The whiskey didn't seem to do much for his nerves. His gaze flicked between Ellie and Cullen—her husband looming like a dark specter just over her shoulder, broad and silent, his revolver within easy reach.

"You McKenna?" the bounty hunter rasped, his voice gravel-thick, worn down by dust and regret.

Cullen's jaw twitched, the muscle tightening like a cocked hammer. "That's right."

The bounty hunter nodded as if he'd expected that, his cracked lips pulling into something too hollow to be called a smile. His gaze lingered on Ellie, filled with something unexpected—not fear, not defiance. Pity. And that alone nearly made her pull the trigger.

"The girl," he muttered, fingers unconsciously brushing the blood-soaked bandage on his arm. "She ain't Annabelle Sinclair."

Ellie's stomach twisted, a cold knot forming beneath her ribs. She'd known it, of course. She'd known Mercy had been taken by mistake, caught in the snare meant for someone else. But hearing it confirmed by the bastard who helped steal her daughter made rage simmer beneath her skin, hot and sharp, coiling tighter with every heartbeat.

"Then why the hell did you take her?" Cullen's voice was

low, a dangerous growl that rumbled like distant thunder.

The bounty hunter sighed, shaking his head slowly, as if trying to shake loose ghosts that had been clinging to him too long. "It was supposed to be simple," he said, his voice brittle. "A job. Bring the Sinclair girl back, hand her over, collect the money. Easy." He swallowed hard, fingers tightening around the chipped glass. "But... things got messy."

Ellie's hand clenched at her side, nails digging crescents into her palm. "Messy?" she echoed, her voice soft, lethal. She took a step closer, enough for him to see the fury burning in her ice-blue eyes. "Try me."

The bounty hunter glanced down, his gaze distant, lost somewhere between guilt and memory. "Annabelle Sinclair was supposed to marry into the Broderick family—land barons, railroad tycoons. Her father arranged it to keep the fortune flowing. But before the wedding could happen, she disappeared."

Ellie felt her blood go cold, her breath shallow and sharp. "Disappeared?" she hissed. "Or was murdered?"

His expression flickered—just for a second—but it was enough.

Cullen leaned in, the menace in his voice as thick as the sweat beading on the bounty hunter's brow. "You know the answer, don't you?"

The bounty hunter licked his chapped lips, avoiding their eyes, staring down into the amber depths of his drink like it held absolution. "Annabelle's father, Franklin Sinclair, claims she ran away," he muttered. "Says she couldn't handle the pressure of the marriage."

Ellie's stomach twisted into knots. She didn't believe that for a damn second.

Cullen grunted, his fists curling into knots. "And what do you think?"

The bounty hunter swallowed hard, his throat working against words he didn't want to say. Finally, with a hollow breath, he whispered, "I think she's dead." He looked up, meeting Ellie's glare with a haunted gaze. "And I think her father paid to have it covered up."

The truth settled over them like ash after a wildfire—thick, suffocating, impossible to escape.

Ellie gripped the edge of the table so hard her knuckles turned white. "And now he's trying to replace her... with my daughter."

The bounty hunter gave a slow, reluctant nod. "They need an heir. If the Sinclair fortune dies with Annabelle, a whole lotta powerful men lose everything they've invested. Mercy was just a lucky find. She looked the part. That was all they needed."

Ellie's vision blurred with rage, her heart pounding like war drums. They had stolen her daughter, brutalized her, tried to erase her identity... all to cover up a murder and protect their empire of blood-stained wealth.

Cullen leaned closer, his voice a razor blade. "Where's the man who hired you?"

The bounty hunter shook his head, fear flickering in his eyes. "I don't know his real name. Just that he works for the Brodericks—the family Annabelle was supposed to marry into. They're the ones pulling the strings, funding all of it."

Ellie's heart hammered in her chest. The Brodericks weren't just powerful. They were untouchable. If they were still hunting Mercy, it meant her daughter wasn't safe—not even after escaping the bounty hunters. Not anywhere.

"Where were they takin' her?" Cullen asked, his voice sharp as the edge of a knife.

The bounty hunter hesitated, but the cold fire in Ellie's gaze told him he was running out of time.

"North," he croaked finally.

Ellie and Cullen exchanged a look, unspoken words passing between them. North meant deeper into Broderick territory. Into the lion's den.

Ellie's fists clenched around the stock of her rifle. "Then we ride north."

The bounty hunter let out a bitter laugh, shaking his head. "You won't make it far. They've got men in every town, every outpost. They own half the law west of the Mississippi."

Cullen snorted, pushing back from the bar with the lazy grace of a man who'd seen worse odds. "Good thing I never cared much for the law."

Ellie stood, slinging her rifle over her shoulder, her eyes cold as the steel she carried. "Let's go."

The bounty hunter raised his glass in a mock salute, his smile thin and twisted. "If you're ridin' north," he rasped, "I'd say you're ridin' straight into a bloodbath."

Ellie paused in the doorway, her silhouette framed by the dying light outside. She turned her head just enough for him to see the fire burning in her gaze.

"Then I hope they're ready to bleed."

# CHAPTER SEVENTY-THREE

August 20, 1885 – Somewhere North of Red Rock, Arizona Territory

The dawn crept over the jagged horizon like a fresh wound, bleeding hues of crimson and gold across the unforgiving landscape. The rising sun ignited the rugged terrain, casting long, fractured shadows over the brittle earth, where sparse tufts of dry grass fought against the relentless Arizona heat. The air itself seemed to shimmer, heavy with the metallic scent of dust and the faint, acrid tinge of smoke drifting from some distant wildfire gnawing at the hills. A storm was brewing, not in the skies, but in the hearts of those who rode beneath it.

Ellie McKenna tightened the leather straps on her saddlebag with hands calloused from years of hardship and loss, her face carved with determination. Her sharp blue eyes, as piercing as shards of glacial ice, scanned the barren horizon, hunting for signs invisible to the untrained eye. Grief had hollowed her once-soft features into something fierce and unyielding, but it was rage that lit the fire in her gaze. With a swift, practiced motion, she swung herself onto her horse, the creak of worn leather and the snort of the restless animal the only sounds breaking the dawn's fragile silence. Cullen Crowe McKenna mounted beside her, his broad frame a silhouette against the searing morning light, the brim of his weather-beaten hat casting deep shadows over a face etched with stoicism and scars—both old and new. His revolver rested within easy reach, as much a part of him as the grim resolve in his heart.

The bounty hunter's words from the night before echoed like gunshots in Ellie's mind, each syllable a spark to the tinder of her fury.

"They need an heir. Mercy was just a lucky find. She looked the part."

Her fingers clenched around the reins until her knuckles blanched. They had stolen her child to replace a dead girl, to polish a corpse with the illusion of life for the sake of wealth and legacy. This wasn't just about power or money anymore—this was about the twisted machinery of men who thought they could rewrite the living with lies carved into flesh and bone. If Mercy was still breathing, Ellie would burn the whole goddamn world to the ground to get her back.

The horses moved with relentless purpose, hooves pounding against the cracked earth, kicking up clouds of dust that clung to sweat-slicked skin. The landscape shifted around them, from the parched flatlands to rocky foothills, where jagged stones jutted from the earth like broken teeth. They crossed dry creek beds, their channels nothing more than veins of dust and memory, the ghost of water long since bled away.

They stopped only when the horses demanded it, pausing beneath the scant shade of withered trees or beside boulders scorched by the sun. Cullen would check his revolver with ritual precision, the cold steel a small comfort against the heat rising within him. "We're walking into a nest of vipers," he muttered, his voice low, gritty with dust and unspoken fear.

Ellie didn't spare him a glance. "Then we cut off their heads."

A muscle twitched in Cullen's jaw, the ghost of a smirk tugging at the corner of his mouth. "You always had a way with words."

Her reply was sharp and flat. "You always had a way with trouble."

He huffed a bitter laugh, his gaze fixed on the horizon. "And look where we are now."

Ellie's eyes narrowed, her grip tightening around the reins. "Not yet."

The words were a promise, not a warning.

Every mile dragged them deeper into the heart of Broderick territory, where the law bent under the weight of gold and blood, and names like Sinclair and Broderick were etched into the land with the same permanence as the scars on Ellie's heart.

Dusk bled across the sky when Ellie yanked her horse to a sudden halt, dust billowing around them like smoke. Cullen's mount reared slightly, snorting in protest, but she didn't flinch. Her gaze was locked ahead, where a gnarled tree stood twisted against the horizon, its blackened branches clawing at the blood-red sky like fingers reaching from a grave.

Three bodies swung from its limbs, the rope taut around their broken necks, creaking softly with each lazy sway in the breeze. They hung like grotesque fruit, faces bloated and purple, eyes wide and glassy in death's unblinking stare. The stench of decay seeped into the dry air, mingling with the faint copper tang of old blood.

Beneath them, nailed crudely to the tree, a splintered wooden sign swung in the wind, its message carved deep into the wood:

"NO TRESPASSERS. NO SURVIVORS."

Cullen exhaled sharply, his gaze darkening. "This is Broderick work."

Ellie slid from her saddle with a fluid motion, her boots sinking into the dry dirt. She approached the bodies without hesitation, her face an unreadable mask. The dead men wore the dusty remnants of bounty hunter gear—gun belts, worn leather vests, their weapons stripped, their dignity long gone.

She studied the bodies with clinical precision. One had a clean bullet hole centered between his eyes, the edges dark with powder burns. Another had his throat sliced from ear to ear, the wound jagged and sloppy. The third had been left to strangle, his face bloated and tongue swollen, his boots scraping faint tracks in the dirt where he'd fought against the inevitable.

Ellie didn't feel pity. Not for them.

"Someone got to them first," she murmured, crouching

to inspect the sign's crude carvings, her fingertips brushing over the blood-dark grooves.

Cullen dismounted, scanning the surrounding landscape, his hand never straying far from his revolver. "Mercy?"

Ellie's heart twisted, but she shook her head. The work was too clean, too calculated. This wasn't Mercy's doing.

She straightened, her gaze cutting to Cullen. "This isn't just a warning. It's a message."

"For us?"

Her jaw clenched. "For anyone who comes looking."

Cullen stalked forward and ripped the sign from the tree with a single, furious motion. The wood splintered in his fists before he tossed it into the dirt, his expression dark with fury.

"Let's keep moving," he growled.

Ellie mounted without another word, her eyes lingering on the swaying bodies one last time. The men who did this were still out there. And so was Mercy.

By the time they reached the outskirts of the next town, the moon hung low and heavy, casting pale light over the dusty streets and dilapidated buildings. The town was a husk of itself, shadows swallowing the alleys, the faint flicker of lanterns casting more darkness than light. It was too quiet—the kind of silence that didn't come from peace but from fear.

Ellie felt it like a weight in her chest.

They rode in slow, every creak of saddle leather and soft clop of hooves sounding unnaturally loud against the oppressive stillness. Cullen's rifle rested across his lap, his eyes sharp and alert.

Then Ellie saw it.

A body slumped against the saloon doors, blood dark and sticky beneath him, pooling into the cracks of the wooden porch. A knife protruded from his chest, buried to the hilt, pinning a folded piece of parchment against the torn fabric of his shirt.

Ellie dismounted without hesitation, her boots hitting the ground softly as she approached the corpse. Cullen followed, covering her with his rifle as she crouched beside the body, fingers deftly pulling the blood-soaked note free. She unfolded it slowly, the paper stiff and tacky with dried crimson.

The message was simple, scrawled in dark ink with lines smudged by blood and rough handling:

"TO THE ONES HUNTING FOR THE GIRL—TURN BACK NOW. SHE BELONGS TO US. IF YOU DON'T STOP RIDING, YOU'LL HANG JUST LIKE THE MEN ON THE ROAD."

Cullen ripped the note from her hands, crumpling it with a snarl. Ellie ignored him, her attention shifting to the knife still warm from the last life it claimed. She pulled it free, studying the polished steel, the fine craftsmanship... and the insignia etched into the hilt.

A single, unmistakable letter:

B.

Broderick.

Ellie rose slowly, her blue eyes burning with a fury that

felt cold as ice.

"They know we're coming."

Cullen spat into the dirt, his grip tightening on his rifle. "Then let's make 'em regret it."

Without another word, they mounted up, the sound of hooves echoing through the dead town like the drums of war.

# CHAPTER SEVENTY-FOUR

August 21, 1885 – Northern Arizona Territory

The night stretched over the land like a black shroud, heavy and oppressive, the darkness broken only by the flickering glow of the moon slipping through torn clouds. The desert air was thick with the scent of dust, sweat, and the faint metallic tang of old blood that clung stubbornly to the wind, a grim reminder of the town they had left behind. Ellie McKenna rode in a silence that was sharper than any blade, her body tense, her mind a furnace of fury and fear. The letter pinned to the chest of that dead man in the blood-soaked town replayed in her thoughts like a curse carved into stone: Turn back now. She belongs to us.

The reins in her hands felt like iron chains, her knuckles bone-white from the pressure of her grip. Every jolt of her horse beneath her was another beat of a war drum, pounding a relentless rhythm against her chest. Mercy's face haunted her vision, threaded between the jagged silhouettes of distant rock formations and the ghostly outlines of twisted trees. Her daughter wasn't some coin to be bartered, some heirloom to be passed between greedy hands. She was hers, flesh and blood, carved from Ellie's own heart. And there wasn't a force in this cursed land strong enough to keep them apart.

Cullen Crowe McKenna rode slightly ahead, his broad shoulders hunched beneath the weight of silent rage. The brim of his hat cast a shadow over eyes that burned with unspoken grief and wrath, his revolver resting casually on his thigh as if daring the night itself to test his patience. His horse moved with the ease of familiarity, hooves striking the ground in steady, unbroken beats.

"We ride straight through," Cullen muttered, his voice gravel rough from dust and unspoken words. "No stops. No distractions."

Ellie didn't respond, didn't need to. Her silence was an answer carved from stone, as unyielding as the cliffs looming on the horizon. They weren't running anymore. They weren't chasing ghosts or shadows. They were the storm now, and their fury would not be gentle.

The land unfolded before them in harsh, unforgiving stretches—vast plains baked under a relentless sun, scarred by dry creek beds and jagged rock formations that clawed at the sky like the ribs of ancient beasts long buried beneath the desert sands. It was a land that remembered every drop of blood spilled upon it, and it whispered those memories through the dry winds that battered their faces.

Ellie's sharp eyes caught it first—a wagon, broken and

slumped against the earth like a wounded animal. Its wheels were splintered, one axle snapped clean through, leaving the frame tilted at an awkward, defeated angle. The faint, sickly-sweet stench of decay reached her before they even drew close, seeping into her lungs, sour and unrelenting.

Cullen pulled his horse to a stop, his revolver already in hand as he scanned the perimeter. Ellie dismounted without a word, her rifle steady, boots crunching softly against the brittle dirt. The silence was unnatural, heavy, as if the earth itself was holding its breath.

The bodies were there, slumped like discarded dolls against the wagon's side. Two men, their throats opened wide, dark blood dried into the dust. Their hands were bound tightly behind their backs, the ropes cutting deep into lifeless flesh. Cullen crouched beside one, his fingers tugging at the collar to reveal a brutal brand seared into the man's skin—the unmistakable crest of the Broderick family, burned in like a mark of ownership.

Cullen exhaled sharply. "Broderick men."

Ellie didn't respond, her gaze drifting over the wreckage. Crates spilled open beside the wagon, their contents a grim inventory of violence—boxes of ammunition, rusted knives, flasks of whiskey, blood-streaked linens. This wasn't just a supply run. This was preparation for war.

Then, a sound. A faint rustle from the brittle brush nearby.

Ellie swung her rifle up, her body coiled like a spring. Cullen was already moving, his revolver raised.

A blur darted from the brush—small, quick, desperate.

Ellie fired a warning shot, the bullet biting into the dirt inches from the figure's feet. The runner stumbled, collapsing forward with a choked gasp, hands thrown up in surrender.

A child.

No older than Mercy.

Ellie's heart kicked against her ribs, her rifle unwavering as she approached. The girl was thin, her face streaked with dirt and sweat, dark eyes wide and glassy with fear. She clutched her side where fresh bruises bloomed beneath torn fabric.

Cullen lowered his gun slightly, his voice rough. "What the hell?"

Ellie didn't lower her weapon. "Who are you?"

The girl coughed, her voice a fragile whisper. "They... they killed my family."

Ellie felt the words like a knife to the chest. The girl pointed a trembling finger toward the wagon. "They burned our home. Killed my ma. Took my brother."

Cullen's jaw clenched as he exchanged a dark look with Ellie. This wasn't an isolated horror. The Brodericks weren't hunting just Mercy. They were collecting, like vultures gathering bones, stealing lives for some twisted purpose.

Ellie knelt beside the girl, her voice softer but no less fierce. "Where did they go?"

The girl's lips trembled. "North."

Ellie's stomach twisted into knots. North was Broderick territory, where power and corruption grew like weeds, choking out hope.

Cullen cursed under his breath. "They're building something. Something big."

Ellie stood slowly, her eyes dark as the storm clouds gathering on the horizon. "Then we'll tear it down."

Her grip tightened on her rifle, the weight of grief and fury anchoring her heart.

They would burn for what they had done.

# CHAPTER
# SEVENTY-FIVE

August 22, 1885 – The Arizona Territory, Just South of the Broderick Stronghold

The Arizona sun bled crimson over the jagged horizon, casting long, skeletal shadows across the unforgiving terrain. The desert was a harsh, merciless canvas, painted with the hues of dust, bone, and blood. The wind howled through the canyons like a wounded animal, carrying with it the acrid scent of sweat, copper, and the faint whisper of gunpowder—the lingering ghosts of violence that clung to the land like a second skin.

Jed McCallister wiped the sweat from his brow, the gritty residue of dust smearing against his weathered skin. His heart thundered in his chest, not from the exertion of the relentless ride, but from the fear coiled deep within—the fear that they were running out of time. Mercy rode beside him, her small frame hunched in exhaustion, fingers white-knuckled around the saddle horn. Her eyes, dark pools shadowed by fatigue and haunted by memories too heavy for her years, flickered with a stubborn spark of defiance. Behind them, Tommy clung to his mount, his face pale and drawn, his silence a fragile shield against the terror lurking just beyond the dust cloud that chased them.

They were still running.

But the hunters weren't far behind.

Gideon rode up alongside Jed, his sharp gaze flicking toward the horizon, where the sun's dying light bled into the jagged teeth of the distant cliffs. His words were low, a growl swallowed by the wind. "They're closing in. If we don't find cover by nightfall, we'll be picked off in the open."

Jed didn't bother to respond. He already knew. The Brodericks wouldn't stop. Not until Mercy was dead—or worse. And Jed wasn't going to let that happen. Not while he still drew breath.

The first shot cracked through the desert air, sharp and sudden like the snap of brittle bone. Jed's horse reared, hooves flailing against the sky, and he fought to keep control, his muscles screaming in protest. Mercy let out a choked cry, clutching at the saddle as Jed yanked the reins hard, forcing the panicked animal back into motion.

Gideon was already turning, rifle up, eyes narrowing to slits against the swirling dust. "Riders," he barked. "Four of 'em. Fast."

Jed twisted in the saddle, his breath catching at the sight—dark figures cresting the ridge, their silhouettes sharp against the bleeding sky. Long dusters billowed like the wings of carrion birds, rifles glinting with deadly promise. These weren't just bounty hunters. These were Broderick men—predators sent to finish what the others had failed to do.

"Keep her low. Keep her moving," Jed growled, shoving Mercy toward Tommy. His fingers gripped his rifle with a familiarity born from necessity, the weight of it grounding him as he turned back to face the oncoming storm.

The first shot was his—clean, precise. The lead rider jerked backward, blood blossoming from his shoulder as he tumbled from the saddle, a ragdoll swallowed by dust. The second man swerved, his horse screaming in protest, but Gideon's shot was faster. The bullet struck true, slamming into the man's chest, sending him sprawling.

Gunfire erupted around them, the air thick with smoke and fury. One of the Broderick men—a scarred bastard with a cigar clenched between his teeth—lined up a shot, his rifle aimed square at Mercy.

Jed's heart seized.

But before he could react, Mercy did.

She jerked the reins hard, her horse veering wildly, the shot missing by inches. Jed felt a searing pain rip across his shoulder—a grazing hit—but he didn't stop. Couldn't stop. All that mattered was keeping her alive.

Jed spurred his horse hard, leading them into the jagged maze of rock formations where the terrain turned treacherous. The ground beneath them was a battlefield of loose gravel and sharp edges, the narrow paths snaking between sheer cliffs that promised death with a single misstep.

"Follow me!" he roared, his voice lost to the chaos.

Tommy clung to Mercy, his small hands gripping her tightly as they navigated the deadly labyrinth. The riders were closing fast, their horses foaming at the mouth, driven by bloodlust and the promise of a Broderick payday.

Then Jed saw it—a narrow gap in the canyon wall, barely wide enough for a single horse. A choke point. A death trap.

Or salvation.

"Go through!" he barked, pushing Tommy and Mercy ahead. They disappeared into the shadows, their figures swallowed by the stone maw. Gideon followed, his revolver blazing, buying them precious seconds.

Jed was the last.

The riders surged after them, fury etched into every line of their faces. One horse slipped on the loose rock, its rider thrown violently against the canyon wall with a sickening crunch. The others didn't falter.

Jed spun in the saddle, rifle up, heart a drumbeat of rage and desperation. The shot was clean, brutal. The second man's throat exploded in a spray of crimson as he tumbled from his mount.

The last rider pulled back, his horse rearing, fear finally outweighing ambition. But his eyes met Jed's, and in that brief moment, a silent promise was exchanged.

This wasn't over.

When they finally stopped, the world had gone dark. The moon hung like a pale sentinel, casting long shadows that stretched across the wounded land. The only sounds were the ragged gasps of breath, the soft whimper of wind through the canyons, and the distant echo of death that still lingered in the rocks.

Mercy sat trembling, her face streaked with dirt and dried tears. Tommy was beside her, his wide eyes hollowed by fear and exhaustion. Gideon lit a cigar with steady hands, his face unreadable in the flickering light.

Jed collapsed onto a rock, his shoulder burning from the wound he'd ignored. It didn't matter. None of it mattered.

Mercy was alive.

For now.

Gideon broke the silence, his voice low and dark. "We've got a problem."

Jed didn't move. "Just one?"

Gideon exhaled smoke, his eyes glinting like steel. "We took out their riders. But that means they know exactly where we are."

Jed felt the weight of those words settle like lead in his chest.

Gideon leaned forward, his voice a growl. "They're not gonna send bounty hunters anymore, McCallister. They're gonna send an army."

Jed met his gaze, his jaw set like stone.

It was time to stop running.

It was time to start fighting.

# CHAPTER
# SEVENTY-SIX

August 23, 1885 – Near the Broderick Stronghold, Northern Arizona Territory

The morning sun clawed its way over the jagged ridges of the Arizona wilderness, casting molten streaks of gold and crimson across a sky bruised by the remnants of night. The air hung heavy with dust and the faint metallic tang of blood—the lingering echo of violence etched into every brittle shard of rock and bone-dry crevice. Each breath Jed McCallister took tasted like ash, mingling with the copper sting of sweat dripping into the shallow groove of the wound on his shoulder. The fabric of his shirt clung to his back, soaked through from days of relentless pursuit, the ache in his muscles now as familiar as the beat of his own heart.

They had been running for two days straight, slipping through narrow gullies and treacherous canyons, their horses driven to exhaustion under the scorching blaze of the Arizona sun. The land itself seemed to conspire against them, each rock and shadow whispering warnings they had no choice but to ignore. Mercy rode silently beside Jed, her small hands gripping the reins with a white-knuckled ferocity that belied the hollow exhaustion carved into her young face. Her dark eyes, once vibrant with curiosity, were dulled now—haunted windows reflecting memories too dark for someone so young. Tommy rode behind, his usual nervous chatter replaced by a brittle silence that pressed against Jed's heart harder than any bullet ever could.

Gideon pulled alongside Jed, his horse snorting, flanks heaving with exertion. His sharp gaze swept the horizon, pausing on the distant rise where heat shimmered like a mirage over the cracked earth. His words came low and tight, a grim confession swallowed by the whisper of the desert wind. "We're runnin' out of ground."

Jed didn't answer. He didn't have to. The walls were closing in, invisible hands tightening around their throats with every mile. The Broderick men were relentless, a shadow always at their backs, drawn not by duty but by something darker—a hunger for power, for control, for blood.

The first gunshot cracked through the morning haze, sharp as a whipcrack and just as unforgiving. Jed's horse reared, muscles coiling in panic, but Jed fought it down with a harsh tug on the reins. Mercy let out a startled cry, clutching at the saddle horn, her wide eyes snapping to Jed with raw fear. Another shot followed, the bullet whining past Jed's ear, embedding itself in a nearby rock with a vicious thud.

"Down!" Jed barked, instinct overtaking thought. He swung off his horse, landing hard on the unforgiving earth, rifle already in his hands. Gideon was beside him in a heartbeat, his revolver drawn, eyes narrowed against the glare of the sun.

Out of the dust, six riders emerged—ghostly figures cloaked in shadows, their faces hidden beneath wide-brimmed hats and the grit of the desert. But these weren't Broderick men.

They were Apache.

Their leader rode at the front, a tall figure with deep-set scars carved like ancient runes across his weathered face. A necklace of bones hung around his neck, rattling softly with each movement. The others fanned out behind him, armed with rifles, tomahawks, and the kind of cold, unwavering intent that didn't leave room for negotiation.

Jed kept his rifle low, his finger brushing the trigger, but he didn't fire. Not yet.

Gideon tensed beside him. "This just got worse," he muttered, the words barely more than a breath.

The Apache leader halted his horse, his gaze cutting through the dust and heat to land squarely on Jed. Silence fell, thick and oppressive, broken only by the ragged breathing of horses and the distant, restless murmur of the desert wind.

Then the man spoke, his voice rough as gravel, but clear enough to cut through the tension like a blade. "You are McCallister?"

Jed swallowed hard, his grip tightening on his rifle. "Yeah."

The man nodded slowly, as if confirming something unspoken. "Then you ride toward death."

Jed exhaled sharply, a bitter laugh escaping before he could stop it. "Been ridin' that way for a while now."

Without another word, the Apache leader reached into a leather satchel slung over his saddle and pulled out something dark and heavy. He tossed it at Jed's feet, and it landed with a sickening, fleshy thud.

A severed head.

Jed's stomach twisted, bile rising in the back of his throat. The face was twisted in a final grimace of agony, eyes wide and glassy. One of Broderick's men.

The Apache leader leaned forward slightly, his dark eyes gleaming with something ancient and unforgiving. "This one promised gold. Promised land. Lies." He spat into the dirt. "They do not own this land. They cannot pay with what is not theirs."

Jed understood then. The Brodericks had tried to buy off the Apache. It hadn't worked. Now, there was another war brewing, layered atop the one Jed was already fighting.

Mercy's voice broke the silence, small and fragile. "What do they want?"

The Apache leader's gaze shifted to her, and Jed felt his heart seize. His hand moved instinctively toward his gun, but the man didn't reach for his own weapon. Instead, he gave a slow, deliberate nod.

"They hunt you, girl. For gold. For power. We hunt them."

Jed swallowed hard. "And us?"

The leader smiled then—a thin, humorless curve of his

lips. "You are in the way."

With a swift motion, he pulled a long knife from his belt and held it out to Jed, hilt first.

Jed hesitated, then took it, the weight of the blade heavy in his hand.

"What's this?" he muttered.

The Apache leader met his gaze, his expression unreadable.

"A choice."

Then, without another word, the war band turned and vanished into the desert, swallowed by dust and shadow as if they had never been there at all.

Silence settled like ash in their wake, the desert stretching endless and empty before them. Jed stared at the knife in his hand, its blade catching the fading light, gleaming with silent menace. It wasn't a threat.

It was a message.

Gideon let out a slow breath, breaking the silence. "Well. That was unexpected."

Tommy looked pale, his wide eyes reflecting the fear none of them dared to voice. "Are we gonna die?"

Jed tossed the knife into the dirt, the blade sinking deep into the cracked earth.

"Not tonight."

But the next time the Apache found them, there wouldn't be another warning.

Jed clenched his jaw, staring down the road that led

north—toward the Broderick stronghold, toward Ellie and Cullen, toward the final reckoning.

No more running.

It was time to end this.

For good.

# CHAPTER SEVENTY-SEVEN

August 24, 1885 – The Arizona Territory, Near Broderick Land

The dawn bled across the desert like an open wound, staining the horizon with streaks of crimson and gold. The air was thick with the stale scent of death, mingling with the faint aroma of gunpowder and the sharp tang of sweat soaked into the dust-choked earth. The land was quiet, save for the occasional mournful howl of the wind snaking through the canyons, carrying whispers of bloodshed on its breath.

Jed McCallister stood over the twisted bodies sprawled across the dirt, his fingers clenched tight around the stock of his rifle. His breath came slow and measured, but his heart roared in his chest like a war drum, each beat a reminder of how close death had stalked them through the night. The Apache war band had vanished as swiftly as they had come, leaving behind only the raw evidence of their ferocity—fresh corpses, blood soaking into the thirsty ground, and the brittle silence that followed violence.

But they'd left something more valuable than carnage: an opportunity. A crack in the Broderick armor. A chance.

Gideon stood a few paces away, his boot nudging the body of a fallen Broderick enforcer, flipping it over with casual disdain. The dead man's eyes stared blankly at the rising sun, his mouth frozen in a final, soundless scream. Gideon spat into the dirt, his face carved with exhaustion and dark amusement. "Well, that's a damn sight I never expected," he muttered, his voice gravel against the brittle quiet.

Jed didn't answer. His gaze was locked on Mercy.

She sat stiffly in the saddle, her posture rigid, her face pale beneath a mask of dust and dried sweat. Her dark eyes were hollow, not with fear, but with something colder—the dawning realization of what survival truly cost. She stared at the bodies without flinching, her small hands clenched around the saddle horn until her knuckles turned white.

She wasn't a child anymore.

Tommy sat beside her on his own mount, his face drawn and pinched, fingers twisted into the reins like lifelines. The boy who once filled the silence with nervous chatter was gone, replaced by someone quieter, someone carved from the same ruthless survival that haunted Jed's own reflection.

Jed exhaled slowly, the weight of responsibility anchoring him in place. He couldn't let them stall. They had to keep moving, to outrun the ghosts that followed them and the men who wanted to bury them.

"We ride through the night," he said, his voice a rasp of

determination.

Gideon raised a brow, his mouth quirking into a half-smile that didn't reach his eyes. "You thinkin' we go straight into Broderick land?"

Jed's jaw clenched, the answer already carved into the marrow of his bones. "No more running."

Gideon grinned like a wolf catching the scent of blood. "Now that's the McCallister I know."

The horses thundered across the desert, their hooves pounding out a relentless rhythm against the cracked earth. Dust rose in choking clouds behind them, swirling like ghosts in the dim light. The night was heavy, the sky smeared with bruised clouds that threatened a storm. But the real tempest was already brewing—in their hearts, in the path ahead, in the promise of violence waiting just beyond the horizon.

Jed rode at the front, his wounded shoulder screaming with every jolt, but he didn't slow. Couldn't slow. The pain was a small price to pay for what lay ahead.

Two hours before dawn, they crested a rocky ridge overlooking Broderick land. The compound stretched out below them, an ugly scar carved into the desert's face. It wasn't just a ranch; it was a fortress. Wooden fences reinforced with iron stakes, guard towers rising like skeletal fingers clawing at the sky, and barns sprawling like bloated corpses across the land. Fires burned in controlled pits, casting flickering shadows over the men who patrolled the grounds with rifles slung over their shoulders and death etched into their faces.

It wasn't a homestead.

It was an army.

Gideon let out a low whistle, his breath misting in the chill morning air. "Well, hell."

Jed didn't respond. He didn't need to. They were outnumbered, outgunned, and out of time.

A rustle in the brush snapped Jed's attention to the shadows behind them. His rifle was up in an instant, finger poised on the trigger.

But he didn't fire.

Because the Apache had returned.

The Apache leader emerged from the darkness like a phantom, his horse stepping silently over the rocky ground. This time, he wasn't alone. Twenty warriors followed, their faces painted with streaks of ash and blood, rifles slung across their backs, tomahawks gleaming at their sides like hungry teeth.

Jed kept his rifle raised, his heart thudding like war drums in his chest. The Apache didn't raise theirs. They didn't need to.

The leader spoke first, his voice a harsh whisper against the morning wind. "You plan to fight."

Jed didn't flinch. "I don't have a choice."

The man studied him, his dark eyes reflecting both judgment and understanding. Then he nodded. "Then we fight with you."

Jed frowned, suspicion flickering in his chest like a match strike. "Why?"

The Apache leader shifted his gaze toward the Broderick compound below. "These men came into our land. They steal.

They kill. They promise gold and leave graves. Your daughter is not the first they've taken." His gaze returned to Jed, sharp as flint. "But she will be the last."

Jed felt something twist in his chest—hope, maybe, or the ghost of it.

He lowered his rifle. "Then we ride at dawn."

The night stretched long and thin, taut with the tension of what was to come. Fires burned low, casting flickering halos around the gathered men. The Apache sharpened their blades in silence, while Gideon checked his revolver with meticulous care. Jed sat apart, the weight of his choices pressing down like the desert sky.

He found Mercy near the edge of camp, staring out over the dark horizon, her face illuminated by the faint glow of distant firelight. He crouched beside her, his voice low, meant only for her.

"You ready for this?"

She didn't look at him. "I don't know."

Jed rested a calloused hand on her shoulder, squeezing gently. "That makes two of us."

After a long silence, she turned to him, her dark eyes older than her years. "Do you think we'll make it?"

Jed didn't lie to her. He couldn't. He gave her the only truth he had left.

"We don't have a choice."

And as the first light of dawn crept over the horizon, painting the world in shades of red, they prepared to ride into the mouth of hell.

# CHAPTER SEVENTY-EIGHT

August 25, 1885 – The Arizona Territory, Near Broderick Land

The night stretched its dark fingers across the broken land, shrouding the battered landscape in a heavy, restless stillness. The echoes of battle lingered like phantoms, etched into the scorched earth and carved into the jagged silhouettes of rock formations scattered across the desert floor. The fires smoldered in the ruins of the Broderick compound, casting flickering shadows that danced like specters, their ghostly shapes writhing with each curl of acrid smoke that drifted into the star-pinned sky. The air was thick, oppressive, laced with the iron tang of blood and the bitter residue of gunpowder, a testament to the lives lost beneath the relentless Arizona sun.

Jed McCallister sat with his back pressed against a sun-bleached boulder, his rifle resting heavily across his knees. The weight of it was a familiar comfort, as natural to him as the ache in his bones, a dull throb that pulsed with every heartbeat. His muscles were taut with exhaustion, stretched thin from days of relentless pursuit and the brutal toll of survival. Sleep was a luxury he could no longer afford, not with death lurking just beyond the horizon, waiting for the dawn.

Across the dying embers of a modest fire, Gideon rolled his shoulders, the leather of his coat creaking softly in the oppressive quiet. His face was etched with lines carved by hardship and dust, his expression shadowed beneath the brim of his hat. "Feels like the right kind of night to die," he muttered, stretching his legs out, his voice a low rasp swallowed by the night air.

Jed took a slow drag from his cigar, the ember glowing briefly like a distant star before fading back into darkness. "Then don't," he replied, his voice a gruff whisper, edged with weariness and defiance.

Gideon snorted softly but offered no retort. Words felt hollow in the face of what was coming.

Around them, the camp had settled into an uneasy stillness. The Apache warriors moved like shadows beyond the fragile glow of the fire, their silent vigilance a testament to battles fought long before Jed's war had begun. Cullen stood apart, his figure rigid against the backdrop of darkness, arms crossed tightly over his chest as he surveyed the distant compound. His silence was heavier than the air, filled with unspoken words and unfinished reckonings.

Ellie sat with Mercy cradled against her side, her fingers threaded through her daughter's tangled hair, stroking absently as if afraid that letting go might shatter the fragile reality of having her back. Mercy's eyes were open, dark orbs reflecting the dim firelight, too old for her years, shadowed by horrors that should never have touched her. Tommy lay nearby, wrapped in a threadbare blanket, his small body curled into itself, the faint rise and fall of his chest the only sign that sleep had claimed him despite the darkness crouched around them.

The fire cracked and hissed, sending tiny sparks spiraling upward, lost quickly in the vast emptiness overhead.

Then came the sound—faint at first, a distant rhythm that grew steadily louder.

Hoofbeats.

Jed's hand moved instinctively to his revolver, fingers curling around the grip with practiced ease. Cullen's head snapped up, his eyes narrowing to slits as he scanned the shadows. Gideon was already on his feet, shotgun in hand, his stance coiled and ready.

The steady drum of hooves echoed through the canyon, slicing through the fragile silence like a blade. Figures emerged from the darkness, their forms blurred by dust and distance, riders moving with purpose, their silhouettes etched in silver by the sliver of moonlight that crept over the horizon.

Jed's breath hitched, his heart pounding a grim cadence in his chest.

Even before the riders drew close enough to see their faces, he knew.

Relief and dread warred in his chest, a bitter concoction that settled like lead in his gut.

Because riding toward them was Ellie's worst fear and her only hope.

Cullen Crowe McKenna.

Ellie surged to her feet, her hand tightening around Mercy's shoulder, but the child was already moving, breaking free with a sudden cry that shattered the brittle quiet.

"Mama!"

Mercy ran, her small feet kicking up dust, arms outstretched, her voice trembling with the raw edge of relief and heartbreak. Ellie followed, her legs unsteady, driven by instinct and the primal pull of a mother's love.

When they collided, it wasn't graceful. It was desperate and messy, a tangle of limbs and sobs as Ellie dropped to her knees, clutching Mercy so tightly it seemed she might never let go. Her hands framed her daughter's dirt-smeared face, thumbs brushing away tears, her voice a broken whisper.

"I'm here. I'm here, baby. You're safe."

Jed turned away, his throat tight, his gaze finding Cullen across the fire. For a long moment, neither man spoke. Then Cullen dismounted, his boots hitting the earth with a dull thud. He stood tall, dust and sweat streaking his face, his revolver resting heavy at his hip. His eyes locked onto Jed with a look that held too many words unspoken.

Jed had imagined this moment a thousand times.

It was never like this.

Cullen stepped forward, his voice low and rough. "You kept her alive."

Jed shrugged, rolling the cigar between his fingers. "Ain't that what you pay me for?"

Cullen huffed out something between a laugh and a

growl. "I ain't paid you a damn thing."

Jed smirked. "Guess you still owe me, then."

For a heartbeat, it was almost like old times.

But they weren't those men anymore.

Jed extended his hand.

Cullen hesitated, just a breath, then gripped it, firm and solid.

The past didn't matter anymore.

All that mattered was the war ahead.

They gathered around the fire, the flames casting flickering shadows over faces carved from stone and resolve. A rough map was spread across the dirt, marked with hastily drawn lines and crude symbols. Cullen traced the perimeter of the Broderick compound with a calloused finger.

"They've got at least thirty men, maybe more. Guards on the towers, sharpshooters in the hills, patrols circling like vultures."

Jed studied the layout, his mind already shaping the chaos to come. "So we go in quiet."

Cullen snorted. "Ain't never known you to be quiet, McCallister."

Jed smirked. "Fair point."

Gideon leaned over, his fingers tapping the crude outline of a supply shed. "How much dynamite we got left?"

Cullen arched a brow. "You plannin' on blowin' the whole damn place up?"

Gideon grinned, sharp and feral. "Depends how much

you got."

Ellie looked up from where she sat, Mercy tucked against her side, her voice steady despite the exhaustion etched into every line of her face. "Then we use it."

Jed felt the words settle like a stone in his chest.

This wasn't just about survival anymore.

This was the end.

The final fight.

Mercy shifted, her small hand curling into a fist, her gaze hard and unflinching.

Jed met Cullen's eyes, a silent agreement passing between them.

"We ride at first light," Jed said.

Cullen nodded, his jaw tight with determination. "Agreed."

The Apache leader stepped forward, his shadow stretching long and thin across the dirt, his voice low and certain.

"Then tomorrow, they die."

# CHAPTER
# SEVENTY-NINE

August 26, 1885 – The Arizona Territory, Broderick Stronghold

The desert was a vast, indifferent expanse in the hour before dawn, a place where death had come and gone so often that the land itself seemed stained with the memory of blood. The sky was stretched taut and thin, an endless canvas of deep indigo slowly bleeding into a bruised violet at the horizon where the first streaks of light crept in like the sharp edge of a knife. The silence was oppressive, a thick, suffocating blanket that weighed heavy on the men crouched in the shadows. It wasn't peace. It was the kind of stillness that only settled right before hell was unleashed.

Jed McCallister crouched low behind a jagged outcrop of stone that jutted like broken teeth from the canyon's rim. His revolver was loaded, his rifle slung across his back, and his mind was sharp, honed to a single, lethal focus. The waiting was the hardest part, the stillness before the storm, when every breath felt too loud, every heartbeat like a drumbeat in a funeral procession. He inhaled slowly, the dry air filling his lungs, tasting of dust and distant smoke. The anticipation coiled in his gut, hot and restless. This was the moment he had been moving toward with grim inevitability.

Beside him, Cullen Crowe McKenna was a silent silhouette, his figure carved from shadow and grit. His eyes were locked on the Broderick compound below, unblinking, filled with the cold calculation of a man who had buried too many pieces of his soul under the weight of violence. Cullen was a man forged in the crucible of war, his edges sharp, his silence louder than any battle cry.

The Apache warriors were specters in the twilight, their war paint streaked with ash and blood, blending seamlessly into the jagged rocks. They moved like the wind, soundless, their presence felt more than seen. These were men who understood the language of death, who spoke it fluently without needing words.

Ellie sat near the fire, her face ghostly in the faint glow, pressing a trembling kiss to Mercy's forehead. Her hands were steady, but her eyes betrayed the storm beneath. Mercy nodded, her small face carved with a maturity born from horror. She wasn't the fragile child Jed had first met. The desert had claimed her innocence and replaced it with something harder, something unyielding.

Gideon shifted his weight, the leather of his coat creaking softly in the predawn silence. "I ever tell you how much I hate waiting?" he muttered, his fingers dancing along the worn grip of his shotgun.

Jed didn't look at him, his smirk a fleeting shadow. "You ever shut up?"

Gideon chuckled darkly, but the sound was thin, brittle against the looming dread.

Cullen exhaled, his voice a gravel scrape in the silence. "We do this quiet. Take the outer guards first. Ellie lights the fuse."

Jed nodded, his eyes never leaving the ridge. "Two men on the eastern wall. Snipers in the towers."

"You take the left. I'll take the right," Cullen replied, his grip tightening on his rifle.

The plan was simple. It had to be. Because complicated plans left room for mistakes, and mistakes got people killed.

A lone guard stumbled out from the shadow of the bunkhouse, yawning, stretching his arms wide as if the dawn was his to command. His rifle hung loose over his shoulder, his posture lax with the arrogance of a man who didn't believe death could find him here.

Jed exhaled slowly, his finger steady on the trigger. He had one shot.

The bullet ripped through the dawn, a sharp crack that shattered the fragile silence. The guard dropped instantly, his skull a ruin of bone and blood, his body crumpling like a discarded rag.

No scream. No alarm. Just the quiet, efficient end of a life.

Cullen fired a heartbeat later, his target collapsing against the barricade, a crimson spray marking the wooden planks. The Apache moved with deadly grace, slipping through the shadows, their blades flashing briefly before sinking into flesh. The guards never had a chance to cry out.

Then the explosion tore through the eastern wall.

The dynamite roared like an angry god, ripping apart stone and wood, sending debris flying in jagged arcs. Fire belched skyward, painting the dawn in hues of orange and red. The ground trembled, the shockwave rolling through the compound like a beast unleashed.

For a heartbeat, everything was silent.

Then the screaming began.

The Broderick men stumbled from the wreckage, coughing, choking on smoke and dust. Confusion etched into their blood-smeared faces. Jed and Cullen didn't give them time to recover. Their rifles spoke first, sharp reports cutting through the chaos.

Jed's revolver bucked in his grip, each shot precise, each target falling like dominoes. Blood painted the dirt, dark and thick, mingling with the rising dust. The Apache warriors surged through the breach, their war cries sharp and raw, blades flashing with ruthless efficiency. No mercy. No hesitation.

Gideon laughed, a wild, unhinged sound, as he fired his shotgun into the chest of a charging man. The impact sent the body sprawling, limbs twisted at impossible angles. Cullen moved like a force of nature, his revolver an extension of his will, each shot finding its mark with terrifying accuracy.

Ellie fired from cover, her aim true, her face set in grim determination. She was a mother fighting for her child, and there was no fiercer warrior in the world.

Mercy was nowhere near the fight. Just like they planned.

Because this wasn't a battle. This was a reckoning.

The doors of the main house burst open, and there he was.

Robert Broderick.

His fine waistcoat was stained with blood, his face slick with sweat and rage. He stood on the porch of his crumbling empire, a gold-plated revolver in his hand, the embodiment of arrogance and decay.

He wasn't running.

He was smiling.

Jed's stomach twisted. He knew that smile. It was the grin of a man who believed he couldn't lose.

Broderick raised his gun, his eyes locking onto Mercy.

Ellie froze, her breath a ragged gasp.

Jed moved first.

His revolver roared, the bullet striking true, punching through Broderick's chest with a sickening thud. The man stumbled, his smile fading, his body crumpling like paper as he tumbled down the steps.

His gold revolver slipped from his fingers, his final breath a wet, gurgling rasp.

Jed lowered his gun, his chest heaving.

It was done.

The Broderick empire was ash and blood.

But as the dust settled, as the fires smoldered in the ruins of what had been, Jed saw something that made his blood run cold.

Mercy held a letter, her small hands trembling as she offered it to him.

"I found this inside," she whispered.

Jed took it, the wax seal unbroken.

When he opened it, when his eyes scanned the words etched in dark ink, a new fear settled in his gut.

Because this wasn't over.

Not even close.

# CHAPTER EIGHTY

August 26, 1885 – The Arizona Territory, Broderick Stronghold

The fires had burned low by the time the dust settled, leaving the Broderick compound a hollow shell of what it had once been. The smoldering embers glowed faintly amidst the wreckage, casting twisted shadows that danced like dying spirits. The acrid stench of blood, sweat, and scorched wood hung thick in the air, mingling with the faint metallic tang of spent gunpowder. Smoke curled lazily toward the darkening sky, a final, ghostly breath exhaled by the fortress of a man who thought himself untouchable.

Jed McCallister stood at the foot of the grand staircase, now splintered and half-collapsed, his revolver still drawn, the steel cold and heavy in his calloused grip. His pulse pounded like a war drum beneath his ribs, each beat echoing the relentless chaos that had come before. His breath was slow, measured, the ragged control of a man too accustomed to violence. His sharp gaze was locked on the last man left breathing—Robert Broderick.

Broderick lay crumpled at the base of the staircase, slumped against a shattered railing, his once-pristine waistcoat now a patchwork of grime, ash, and blood. The golden revolver that had been his symbol of power rested uselessly in the dirt beside him, its polished surface smeared with the stains of his downfall. His breaths came in shallow, labored gasps, rattling in his chest like the last echoes of a dying storm. Despite it all, he wore a crooked smile, the grin of a man too arrogant to accept defeat even as death crept over him.

Jed hated that smile.

"You think you've won?" Broderick rasped, his voice little more than a whisper, raw and jagged like broken glass. He lifted his chin slightly, though his body trembled with the effort. His fine leather boots were scuffed, soaked with dust and blood, the filth of the battlefield mocking the luxury he once commanded. Here, in the dirt, he was no different from any other man Jed had sent to the grave.

Jed tilted his head, his grip tightening around the revolver's handle. "Ain't no winners in this kind of fight."

Broderick let out a weak, wheezing chuckle, coughing until blood trickled from the corner of his mouth, dark and thick. "You don't even know what you've done, do you?" His gaze drifted, settling on Mercy, who stood framed in the doorway of the burning house. Her small fists were clenched, her dark eyes hard with a fury that no child should carry.

Jed's jaw tightened. He didn't like the way Broderick looked at her, as if she were still a pawn in a game long lost.

Cullen stepped forward, silent as a shadow, his revolver loose in his grip. He'd seen enough men die to recognize when death had already claimed its prize. But Ellie stood stiff near the rubble, her rifle still raised, her knuckles white, her breath sharp and uneven as her eyes burned with the raw edges of exhaustion and rage.

Jed took a step forward, the crunch of ash beneath his boots the only sound. "I'd say you got one breath left, Broderick. Use it well."

Broderick's grin twisted into something darker, his voice a rasping hiss. "You think Mercy's safe now? You think this is over?" His words were a venomous coil, slipping between blood-streaked lips.

Jed's finger twitched on the trigger.

Broderick coughed again, blood bubbling at the corner of his mouth. "You took down one man," he gasped. "But there's another. Bigger. Smarter. Richer. And he doesn't leave loose ends."

His head lolled back against the broken wood, his strength fading, but his grin remained. "You should've let me take care of her when I had the chance."

Jed fired.

The bullet struck Broderick square in the chest, the impact jerking his body back against the splintered railing before he crumpled, lifeless. The smile was gone, wiped clean by the finality of death. His dark eyes, once filled with cruel amusement, stared blankly at nothing.

Jed lowered his gun, exhaling a breath he hadn't realized he'd been holding. It wasn't relief that filled his chest—just the cold, hollow certainty that came with a kill long overdue.

Ellie slowly lowered her rifle, her body swaying slightly as the adrenaline ebbed. Cullen rolled his shoulders, his face unreadable, a man too familiar with the echoes of war.

Mercy moved first.

She stepped forward, her small figure dwarfed by the ruins around her, her boots light in the dust. She didn't flinch at the sight of Broderick's corpse, didn't recoil from the blood pooling in the dirt. Instead, she knelt beside him, her fingers brushing the ground, lifting something small and folded, its edges smudged with soot.

A letter.

Her hands trembled slightly as she held it out. "I found this inside," she whispered, her voice fragile against the crackle of dying flames.

Jed took it, his fingers rough against the delicate parchment. The wax seal broke easily under his thumb. The paper was crisp, expensive—the ink dark, unmarred by time.

He read.

And his blood ran cold.

It wasn't from Broderick.

It was addressed to Jed.

The signature at the bottom was clear.

Franklin Sinclair.

Jed's pulse quickened, his heart a drumbeat in the stillness. He read the words again, slower this time, but the meaning didn't change.

The girl was never meant to survive. We cannot allow loose ends.

Cullen stepped closer, his brow furrowed as he scanned the letter over Jed's shoulder.

Ellie's breath hitched.

Mercy's small fists clenched at her sides.

Jed folded the letter carefully, tucking it into his coat pocket. His jaw tightened, his gaze meeting Cullen's.

"It means we ain't done yet."

Cullen nodded, his expression darkening.

Ellie swallowed hard, her eyes flickering to Mercy, then back to Jed.

Mercy simply nodded, her face carved from stone.

Jed adjusted his hat, the weight of the revolver still heavy in his hand.

Sinclair was waiting.

Denver was waiting.

And this time, there wouldn't be any loose ends.

# CHAPTER
# EIGHTY-ONE

August 27, 1885 – The Arizona Territory, On the Trail to Denver

The morning after the siege was thick with an unsettling quiet, a silence that settled like dust over the battered remains of what once was. The sky stretched wide and indifferent, painted in pale hues of orange and pink, its beauty a stark contrast to the carnage below. The fires had died out, leaving only smoldering ash and the scent of charred wood mingled with blood. The Broderick compound was nothing more than a skeleton of greed and violence, crumbling under the weight of its sins.

Jed McCallister sat on the outskirts of the makeshift camp, his back against a weathered boulder, a cigar resting between his fingers. He wasn't smoking it—just rolling it back and forth, watching the brittle leaves catch the morning light. His mind wasn't on the fire's warmth or the hushed voices behind him. It was on the letter tucked in his coat, its words etched into his skull like a brand. The letter that proved Robert Broderick had been nothing more than a puppet. The real monster was still out there.

Franklin Sinclair.

The name alone coiled in Jed's chest like barbed wire. Sinclair wasn't a man who dirtied his hands with blood; he hired others to do it for him, wrapping his cruelty in the velvet of wealth and influence. But now, his name was carved into Jed's ledger, and that debt was coming due.

Inside the camp, Ellie lay beneath a thin blanket, her body stitched with fresh wounds and the shadow of fever. Her breathing was shallow but steady, each exhale a fragile promise. Mercy hadn't left her side, her small hand clutching Ellie's as if she could tether her mother to life through sheer will alone.

Cullen sat nearby, his rugged features carved with exhaustion, his hands stained with blood that wasn't all from the fight. He'd done what he could to stop the bleeding, but there were battles even he couldn't win with a gun. His jaw clenched tight as he dabbed a cool cloth against Ellie's burning skin, the flicker of fear in his eyes betraying the stoicism he wore like armor.

"How bad is it?" Jed asked, his voice low, stepping into the fragile space beside Cullen.

Cullen didn't look up. "She'll live."

Jed studied him. "But?"

Cullen's exhale was sharp, bitter. "But she needs rest. We can't keep pushing." His gaze flickered to Mercy, then back to

Jed. "You know it as well as I do."

Jed nodded slowly, his jaw tight. "Ain't got much choice."

Ellie stirred, her lips parting, voice a brittle whisper. "No stopping."

Cullen's face twisted with frustration. "Ellie—"

She gripped his hand weakly. "We ride… tomorrow."

Jed couldn't help the faint smirk tugging at his mouth. "Tough as ever."

Cullen muttered a curse under his breath but didn't argue. They both knew she was right.

That night, as the fire dwindled to embers, Jed watched Mercy. She sat alone, a knife in her lap, the blade catching the flickering light as she dragged it slowly across a whetstone. There was precision in her movements, a grim focus that had no place in the hands of a child.

Jed approached, lowering himself beside her with a quiet sigh. "You're gettin' real good at that."

Mercy didn't look up. "I have to be."

Jed watched the tight set of her jaw, the anger simmering beneath her young face. "Ain't a good thing, carryin' that much hate."

She paused, her fingers curling around the knife handle. "They took me. They hurt Mama." Her voice was soft, but beneath it was steel. "They deserve it."

Jed exhaled, shaking his head. "Ain't about what people deserve, kid. It's about what you can live with."

Her eyes met his, dark and fierce. "I'll live with it."

Jed didn't argue. Because maybe, after everything, there was no stopping it.

Later, with the night stretched thin and the stars cold above them, Cullen sat beside Ellie, his fingers brushing strands of her sweat-damp hair.

"You ever think about what happens after?" she whispered, her voice hoarse.

Cullen stared into the darkness. "After what?"

"After Sinclair. After all the killing."

Cullen exhaled, a brittle sound. "Ain't much after. Just different ghosts."

Ellie managed a faint smile. "Always the optimist."

His gaze shifted to Mercy, curled up by the fire. "She's changing."

"I know."

Ellie's hand found his, her grip weak but determined. "Promise me something."

Cullen swallowed hard. "What?"

"If we don't make it… you keep her safe. You keep her from turning into us."

Cullen was silent for a long time, the weight of her words anchoring him. Finally, he nodded. "I'll try."

By dawn, Ellie was in the saddle, pale and fragile, but her grip on the reins was steady.

Jed mounted his horse, adjusting his hat. "You ready for this?"

Cullen swung up beside him. "Always."

Gideon grinned, loading his shotgun. "Let's ride into that city and burn it to the ground."

Mercy said nothing. She just tightened her grip and stared ahead.

They rode out, the dust rising behind them like a storm.

Denver was waiting.

Sinclair was waiting.

And this time, they weren't running.

This time, they were coming for blood.

# CHAPTER
# EIGHTY-TWO

August 28, 1885 – The Edge of the Colorado Plains

The desert stretched before them, an endless expanse of scorched earth under a sky that bled crimson and gold. The sun sank low on the horizon, dragging with it the last fragile threads of warmth, leaving behind a world bathed in bruised purples and shadows that crept like silent hunters. The wind carried whispers of dust, grit, and something darker —a scent tangled between rain and blood, so faint yet sharp enough to stir the ghosts buried deep in Jed McCallister's mind. He couldn't tell the difference anymore, not with the taste of vengeance lingering on his tongue like old whiskey.

They had ridden hard since dawn, their horses' flanks slick with sweat, muscles taut with the strain of distance and urgency. North. Always north, toward Denver, drawn like moths to the flame of Franklin Sinclair's empire. The

Brodericks were nothing but ash and memory, their legacy written in blood and burned into the dirt. But Sinclair still breathed, and as long as he did, none of them could rest. This wasn't over. Not until the last bullet found its mark.

Jed adjusted the reins, his gaze flicking over his shoulder to the small, battered procession trailing him. Cullen rode with a posture carved from stone, his revolver resting easy at his hip, but there was something brittle beneath his stoicism—a tension that coiled tighter with each mile, fed by loss and an unspoken fury. Ellie rode in the center, her face pale under the brim of her hat, the bandages peeking beneath her shirt a testament to wounds both fresh and festering. She didn't speak much, but her silence spoke volumes, her jaw set with the same stubbornness that had kept her alive through worse.

Mercy clung to her mother's side, her small hands gripping the saddle horn, knuckles white against the leather. She wasn't a child anymore, not after what they'd taken from her. The fear was gone, replaced by something colder, something that shimmered like frost in her dark eyes. Jed saw it every time she looked at the horizon—the simmering rage of someone who'd been broken and stitched herself back together with threads of vengeance.

By dusk, they reached the skeleton of a forgotten town, its bones bleached and brittle under the dying light. Crooked buildings leaned against the weight of time, windows shattered like hollow eyes watching their approach. The wind moved through the empty streets, carrying whispers of lives long gone, the faint clatter of broken shutters the only greeting.

They made camp near an old well, its stones cracked and crumbling, the fire they lit casting flickering shadows that danced like phantoms against the rotting wood. The horses stood restless, their ears twitching at sounds only they could hear. Jed crouched near the flames, the warmth doing little to thaw the chill coiled in his chest. His eyes scanned the darkness, instincts prickling with something he couldn't name.

Ellie sat close to Mercy, pressing a damp cloth to her forehead, though whether for fever or comfort, Jed couldn't tell. Cullen crouched beside them, his hand resting lightly on Ellie's knee, grounding her in a way words never could. Their exhaustion hung heavy, woven into the quiet between them.

Then came the first shot.

A sharp crack that split the night.

The Trap is Sprung

The bullet punched into the firewood pile, splinters exploding into the air. Jed was moving before the echo faded, rolling behind an overturned wagon as a second shot rang out, snapping past his ear.

"Ambush!" he roared, his voice cutting through the chaos.

Gunfire erupted from the rooftops, muzzle flashes stuttering like lightning against the dark. Shadows peeled from the buildings, figures clad in dusters and scarves, their rifles gleaming as they poured lead into the camp. These weren't bounty hunters. These were soldiers—men trained for death.

Sinclair's men.

Jed returned fire, his revolver barking in quick, measured bursts. One figure crumpled, then another, but they kept coming, relentless as a flood. Cullen was beside him, his face carved from stone, his gun spitting fire with ruthless precision. Ellie dragged Mercy behind the well, her rifle steady despite the blood staining her bandages. Gideon laughed as he fired, the wild, reckless sound of a man who had danced with death too many times to be afraid.

Then Jed saw him.

Stepping from the shadows, boots crunching on dirt, was a face Jed thought long buried.

Malcolm Broderick.

Jed didn't lower his gun. Neither did Malcolm.

"Fancy seeing you again, McCallister," Malcolm drawled, his smirk twisted and sharp.

Jed's jaw clenched. "I'd say the same, but I don't like lyin'."

Malcolm chuckled, his fingers flexing on the grip of his revolver. "Still got that mouth on you. Shame you never learned when to shut it."

His gaze slid to Cullen, then Ellie, lingering on Mercy with something dark in his eyes. That was when Jed knew. This wasn't revenge. This was business. Sinclair's business.

"You're workin' for Sinclair," Jed muttered.

Malcolm's grin widened. "Pays better than my brother ever did."

Cullen's knuckles whitened on his gun. "You sold your own blood for coin?"

Malcolm shrugged. "Family's dead. Doesn't matter much now."

Jed fired first.

The bullet hit Malcolm square in the chest, the impact jerking him backward. But he didn't fall. He stumbled, snarled, and fired back, his shot wild, missing Jed by inches. The firefight roared to life again, deafening in the narrow street.

The town became a slaughterhouse.

Bullets tore through rotting walls, shattering glass and bone alike. Jed moved through it like a ghost, his revolver an extension of his fury. Cullen fought with the precision of a man who had nothing left to lose, each shot a testament to the grief carved into his heart.

Ellie held her ground, her rifle steady despite the tremor in her limbs. Mercy stayed low, her knife clenched in small, white-knuckled fists, her eyes cold and empty.

Gideon fell first—a shot to the chest. He died laughing, blood bubbling from his lips, his last breath a curse spat at the sky.

Jed didn't stop.

Malcolm lunged in the chaos, his knife flashing. Jed met him head-on, their struggle brutal and close, fists and fury colliding until the blade found flesh. Jed roared, the pain sharp and blinding, but he didn't fall.

He pulled the trigger.

Malcolm's body jerked, the bullet tearing through him. He collapsed into the dirt, gasping, his blood dark against the dust.

Silence fell, broken only by the ragged gasps of the living and the soft, final sighs of the dying.

Jed stood over Malcolm's corpse, his chest heaving, blood dripping from the knife wound in his side. Cullen knelt beside Ellie, his hands slick with blood that wasn't his own. Mercy stared at Malcolm's body, her face unreadable.

Jed exhaled, his breath a shudder in the cold morning air.

Sinclair knew they were coming.

Denver was waiting.

And the road ahead was paved with blood.

# CHAPTER EIGHTY-THREE

The desert stretched endlessly, an unforgiving wasteland painted with the dying hues of a bleeding sun. The sky bled crimson and gold, casting long, jagged shadows across the barren plains as if the land itself bore the scars of every sin committed beneath it. The horizon wavered in the heat, a mirage of false hope that mocked them with every mile. The dust was relentless, clinging to sweat-slicked skin, grinding between teeth, filling lungs until every breath felt like inhaling ash. They carried the echoes of battle with them, the ghosts of the Broderick compound lingering in the folds of their clothes and the corners of their minds, as persistent as the dust and twice as heavy.

Ellie rode slumped in the saddle, her body a fragile shell wrapped in grit and stubbornness. The wound in her side, hastily stitched by Gideon's rough hands, was a festering thing, pulsing with fever and defiance. Her skin had turned pale, stretched tight over sharp cheekbones, her breath a shallow whisper of what it once was. Mercy rode beside her, small hands clenched around the reins with a grip fierce enough to make her knuckles whiten. She watched her mother with the same intensity a predator watches prey, not out of malice but sheer, unrelenting fear—fear that if she looked away, even for a heartbeat, Ellie might slip into the dark and never come back.

Jed rode ahead, his gaze a blade, cutting across the horizon, searching for threats woven into the landscape. The weight of Franklin Sinclair's name settled over him like a noose tightening with every mile. Denver loomed ahead, not just a city but a battleground stitched together with greed, corruption, and blood money. Sinclair waited there, his influence sprawling like a cancer, and Jed knew this fight would be different. This wasn't about survival anymore. This was about reckoning.

When the horses could carry them no further without rest, they found shelter in the skeletal remains of an outpost, little more than crumbling walls and a dry well. The shadows grew long, the night creeping in like a thief, and with it came the cold. Cullen and Jed lifted Ellie from her saddle with the careful reverence of men cradling dynamite, her body limp but her jaw clenched, refusing to give voice to the pain carved into her bones. They laid her on a threadbare blanket inside the shack, Mercy immediately dropping to her knees beside her, pressing a damp cloth to her mother's fevered brow. Her hands were steady, too steady for a child who had seen too much, endured too much.

Outside, the fire flickered weakly against the encroaching dark. Tommy sat curled near the flames, a silent witness to horrors too vast for words. His eyes were wide, but there was nothing childlike left in them. The boy had retreated inward, his silence louder than any scream, a testament to the damage that didn't bleed.

Jed lingered in the shadows, his eyes not on the horizon but on Mercy. She was changing. It was in the set of her shoulders, the hardness creeping into her gaze, the way her small fists clenched when she thought no one was looking. Earlier, he'd found her sitting alone, sharpening a knife with meticulous precision. There was nothing playful or curious about it. Her movements were deliberate, practiced, filled with intent.

"You plan on using that?" Jed had asked, his voice low, rough with something that wasn't quite judgment.

Mercy had paused, her gaze lifting to meet his, dark eyes unblinking. "If I have to." No hesitation. No fear. Just cold, hard certainty.

"They took me," she had whispered, her attention returning to the blade. "They hurt Mama. They killed people who didn't deserve to die."

Jed had leaned forward, elbows resting on his knees, the firelight casting shadows across his worn face. "And what happens if you kill someone? You think that makes it right?"

Her fingers tightened around the knife. "I don't care if it's right."

Jed had seen that look before. In men with too much blood on their hands. In reflections he avoided. But in a girl so young? That was something else. Something far more dangerous.

"You ain't gotta be like them," he'd said softly.

Mercy had met his gaze again, her expression unflinching. "Maybe I do."

Now, as she sat beside Ellie, her small hand clutching the fabric of her mother's dress, Jed knew the truth. Mercy was standing on the edge of a precipice, and one more push might send her plummeting into darkness she'd never climb out of.

Cullen sat across the fire, silent, the flickering flames casting his face in harsh relief. He hadn't said much since Ellie made him promise something he wasn't sure he could keep. They'd been alone when she asked, her voice ragged, her breath thin.

"We should've never let her see this," Ellie had murmured, her gaze distant, fixed on ghosts only she could see.

Cullen had swallowed hard, his jaw clenched. He knew exactly what she meant.

"You see her hands?" Ellie had whispered.

He had. He'd seen how Mercy gripped that knife, not like a tool but an extension of herself. He'd seen the calculation in her eyes, the absence of hesitation.

"She's turning into us," Ellie had rasped, her voice barely more than a breath.

Cullen had looked away, unable to deny it.

After a long silence, Ellie had turned her head, her fever-bright eyes locking onto his. "If we don't survive this..."

Cullen had gone still.

"...Promise me she won't turn into a killer."

The words had hung between them, a fragile thread stretched taut. Cullen wanted to lie, to offer comfort wrapped in false promises. But he couldn't. He didn't know if he could save Mercy from what the world had already carved into her heart.

All he could give Ellie was the truth.

"I'll try," he'd whispered.

By dawn, Ellie was back in the saddle. Pale. Hollow-eyed. But upright, her grip on the reins unyielding. That was enough. It had to be.

Jed swung onto his horse, adjusting the brim of his hat, his gaze cutting to Cullen. "You ready for this?"

Cullen rolled his shoulders, fingers brushing the revolver at his hip. "We were born ready."

Jed snorted. "You were born an asshole."

Cullen's lips twitched into something that wasn't quite a smile. "A talented asshole."

Gideon laughed sharply, slinging his shotgun over his shoulder. "Enough talk. Let's ride into that city and burn it to the goddamn ground."

Mercy said nothing.

She just tightened her grip on the saddle horn, the knife strapped to her thigh like it belonged there.

And then they rode.

Denver loomed ahead, a city built on blood and greed.

Sinclair was waiting.

And one way or another, this was going to end.

# CHAPTER EIGHTY-FOUR

The wind was a living thing as they approached the outskirts of Denver, a vicious, howling force that carried with it the stench of coal smoke, sweat, and something metallic—blood, maybe, or the promise of it. The horizon was jagged with rooftops and smokestacks, a city carved out of ambition and greed, its skyline smeared against a sky bruised with storm clouds. Denver sprawled wide and mean, a beast of brick and steel, its heart pulsing with commerce and corruption. The streets were veins, pumping life through a body already rotting from the inside out.

Jed McCallister's gaze wasn't on the city, though. His eyes were fixed on the figures standing sentinel at its gates. A line of men stretched across the dirt road, a wall of flesh and steel, armed with rifles and shotguns, their silhouettes sharp against the fading light. These weren't the usual drifters and hired guns. These were professionals—killers by trade, men who'd long since forgotten what it felt like to hesitate.

At their center stood Franklin Sinclair, the architect of their suffering, dressed in a black suit that seemed to repel the dust swirling around him. His blond hair was slicked back, his pale blue eyes sharp and glinting with the cold amusement of a man who thought he had already won. He didn't flinch as Jed and the others rode closer, didn't shift his weight or adjust his grip on the cane he carried like some twisted symbol of authority. He just stood there, a viper coiled in human skin.

Jed's fingers itched around the grip of his revolver, the urge to end this now thrumming through his veins like wildfire. But he didn't draw. Not yet. Cullen's horse danced beneath him, sensing the tension, nostrils flaring. Cullen's face was carved from stone, his jaw clenched tight enough to crack. Ellie sat stiff in the saddle despite the fever hollowing her out from the inside, her rifle resting across her lap, eyes dark with the kind of focus that only comes when death feels close enough to touch.

And then there was Mercy.

She rode beside Ellie, her small frame rigid, hands wrapped around the hilt of the knife strapped to her thigh. She wasn't a child anymore, not where it mattered. Her gaze was steady, her jaw set with a resolve that made Jed's chest ache. He'd seen that look before—etched into the faces of men who had survived too much and lost even more.

Gideon broke the silence, his voice a low rasp. "Well, shit. They were expectin' us."

Jed's lips curled into a humorless smile. "Ain't that a surprise."

They rode closer, the distance shrinking until Jed could see the smug twist of Sinclair's mouth, the way his fingers drummed lazily against the polished wood of his cane. Jed pulled his horse to a stop just a few feet from the line of guns, dust settling around them like ash after a fire.

Sinclair tipped his hat with mock courtesy. "McCallister."

Jed didn't blink. "Sinclair."

Sinclair's gaze swept over the group, lingering on Cullen, then Ellie, and finally settling on Mercy. His smile deepened, a snake's grin. "I must admit, I didn't expect her to make it this far."

Jed felt Mercy tense beside him, her breath sharp in the heavy air. Cullen's hand hovered near his holster. Ellie's grip tightened on her rifle, the knuckles white against the dark wood.

Sinclair's voice was smooth, dripping with condescension. "You've made quite the mess. Broderick was a blunt instrument. But me?" He tapped the ground with his cane. "I don't make mistakes."

Jed's jaw clenched. This man wasn't here to negotiate. He was here to gloat, to revel in his perceived superiority. But Jed wasn't interested in words.

"You've got a lot of men, Sinclair," Cullen said, his voice a low growl.

Sinclair nodded, as if proud. "I do."

Jed's smile was thin and sharp. "Pity they're all gonna die."

The amusement flickered in Sinclair's eyes, just for a heartbeat, before that smug mask slid back into place.

"McCallister, you and I both know this is a losing battle." He gestured toward the city behind him. "Denver is mine. Every lawman, every judge, every goddamn banker. You don't piss in this city without me hearin' it hit the dirt."

He leaned forward slightly, his voice a hiss. "I own it all."

Jed's grip on his revolver tightened. "Funny. I don't feel owned."

Sinclair chuckled softly. "That's because you're still breathing."

His hand shot up, a signal.

And the world exploded.

Gunfire tore through the air, a symphony of violence that shattered the tense quiet. Jed was off his horse before the first bullet whizzed past his ear, rolling into the dirt and coming up firing. Cullen's revolver barked beside him, each shot precise, deadly. Gideon's shotgun roared, the force of it sending men sprawling, blood painting the dust in vivid arcs.

Ellie stayed in the saddle long enough to put two bullets through the skulls of men who thought they could flank her, then slid to the ground, propping herself against a crate, her rifle steady despite the fever burning through her veins.

And Mercy—

Jed caught a glimpse of her through the chaos, moving like she was born in it. She was small, fast, a shadow with a blade, cutting through the legs of a man twice her size. He went down screaming, clutching at the ruin of his thigh. Mercy didn't hesitate. She drove the knife into his throat, her face blank, eyes dark and endless.

Jed didn't have time to process the chill that ran through him. Sinclair was still standing.

Amid the carnage, Sinclair hadn't moved. He watched, calm, detached, as his men died around him. Then, with the ease of a man picking up a glass of whiskey, he grabbed Mercy.

One moment she was fighting. The next, Sinclair had a gun to her head, his arm locked around her throat. The battlefield froze. Ellie's scream cut through the noise, raw and ragged. Cullen's gun was up, but his hands were trembling with rage.

Jed felt his heart stop.

Sinclair smiled, his teeth bright against the blood-spattered street. "I think we've had enough fun for one day."

Mercy didn't struggle. She didn't cry. She just breathed —slow, steady, her eyes locked on Jed's.

Sinclair's grip tightened. "Tell me, McCallister. How much is she worth to you?"

Jed's gun was still raised. His hands were steady. But his mind was racing. Because there had to be a way out.

He wasn't going to let that bastard take her.

Not now.

Not ever.

# CHAPTER
# EIGHTY-FIVE

The air was thick with the iron tang of blood and the acrid sting of gunpowder, mingling with the dust kicked up by frantic feet and dying men. The silence that followed the last gunshot felt heavier than the battle itself —a suffocating, unnatural stillness broken only by the rasping breath of the wounded and the faint crackle of fires burning out along the street. Bodies were strewn like discarded rags, twisted in the dirt, their blood seeping into the thirsty ground, a grim tribute to Denver's corrupt heart. But none of that mattered to Jed McCallister. His focus was a single, brutal point of clarity: the gun pressed against Mercy's temple.

Sinclair's grip was iron, his face twisted in a mockery of calm, though sweat glistened on his brow beneath the brim of his pristine hat. His black suit, once a symbol of untouchable power, was now smeared with dust and blood—some of it his men's, some perhaps his own. Yet he still smiled, that smug curl of lips that had haunted Jed for too long, a grin carved from arrogance and cruelty. Sinclair believed he was still in control, that he held the final card. But Jed knew better. He felt it in the weight of his revolver, the familiar pressure against his palm, the whisper of fate wrapped around one last bullet.

Cullen stood to Jed's left, his jaw clenched so tight it seemed carved from stone, his revolver steady despite the tremor of fury that radiated off him. Ellie crouched behind a broken crate, her rifle trained on Sinclair, her hands slick with sweat, eyes wild with a mother's terror barely masked by the sniper's focus. Mercy didn't cry. She didn't plead. She stood rigid in Sinclair's grip, her small hands clenched into fists, her dark eyes burning with a defiance that made Jed's chest ache.

Sinclair's voice was low, smooth like oil over water. "McCallister, you and I both know how this ends. You're not fast enough."

Jed's thumb pulled back the hammer of his revolver with a soft, deadly click that seemed to echo through the silent battlefield. Sinclair's smile faltered—a flicker, almost imperceptible, but it was there. A crack in the mask.

Jed allowed himself a ghost of a smile in return. "Let's find out."

Time fractured.

Sinclair's finger twitched on the trigger, but Jed's bullet was faster—a streak of molten lead that found its mark with surgical precision. The impact snapped Sinclair's head back, his body spasming once before crumpling to the ground like a marionette with its strings cut. Blood bloomed from the perfect hole in his forehead, spreading in a dark halo around his skull.

But Mercy didn't fall. She remained upright, her chest heaving, staring down at Sinclair's corpse with something more than shock. Something darker.

Jed approached slowly, his heart pounding like a war drum. "Mercy—"

Before he could finish, she moved.

The knife gleamed in her hand, a flash of silver stained with old blood. She plunged it into Sinclair's chest with all the force her small body could muster, her face a mask of raw, unfiltered rage. She didn't stop after the first stab. She twisted the blade, yanked it free, and drove it down again. And again. The wet, sickening sound of steel meeting flesh filled the void left by gunfire.

Jed didn't stop her. No one did.

Finally, Mercy pulled back, her hands slick with crimson, her breath coming in ragged gasps. She looked up, her eyes locking with Jed's, dark and hollow.

"I had to make sure," she whispered, her voice small but steady.

Jed swallowed hard, his throat dry as ash. "I know, kid."

Ellie was there in an instant, gathering Mercy into her arms, her body shaking with the force of her sobs. Cullen holstered his revolver, his gaze lingering on Sinclair's broken form, then shifting to Mercy with a haunted look that spoke of promises made and already broken.

Gideon exhaled a sharp breath, muttering under his breath as he kicked Sinclair's gun aside. "Well, I'll be damned. Guess that's that."

Jed holstered his weapon, his shoulders heavy with exhaustion, but he knew better. This wasn't over.

Not yet.

Across the street, shadows moved—figures emerging from the alleys, rooftops, and the broken doorways of Denver's rotting heart. Men drawn by the noise, by the promise of unfinished business. Sinclair's personal army, or what was left of it. Hardened killers with nothing left to lose, fueled by vengeance and greed.

Cullen sighed, reloading his revolver with the weary precision of a man who had done this too many times. "Guess we ain't done yet."

Jed's grin was sharp, feral. "Wouldn't want it any other way."

Ellie pressed a kiss to Mercy's blood-smeared temple, whispering something soft before pulling her daughter behind the wreckage of an overturned wagon. She wiped her face with trembling hands, then gripped her rifle like it was an extension of her soul.

The gunmen opened fire, and Denver burned with the fury of the damned.

The final fight had begun.

# CHAPTER
# EIGHTY-SIX

The dawn crept over Denver with the reluctant grace of a dying flame, casting long shadows across streets slick with blood and strewn with the bodies of men who had thought themselves invincible. The air was thick with the stench of charred wood, gunpowder, and the copper tang of death, lingering like a ghost that refused to be exorcised. The fires had not died with Sinclair; they had only found new breath, fueled by the hatred left behind in the hearts of men too stubborn to let the past die. But Jed McCallister didn't have the luxury of mourning. His hand was steady, his heart a metronome set to the rhythm of survival, and his mind was a blade honed on the whetstone of vengeance.

The first shot rang out, shattering the fragile silence, a sniper's bullet whistling past Jed's ear and embedding itself in the splintered wood of an overturned cart. Jed's reaction was instinctual—a fluid, practiced motion as he snapped his rifle to his shoulder and fired. The bullet found its mark with brutal precision, punching through the sniper's skull and sending his lifeless body tumbling from the rooftop like a discarded rag doll. The thud of his corpse hitting the ground was a starting gun, and the race to the grave had begun.

The streets erupted into chaos, men pouring from alleys and doorways like rats fleeing a sinking ship, their guns barking with fury. Jed moved through the storm like a phantom, his revolvers barking in time with the beat of his heart, each shot a note in a symphony of violence. The air was alive with the hiss of bullets and the screams of the dying, the ground slick with blood and spent casings. Beside him, Cullen was a force of nature, his revolver never pausing, his face a mask of grim determination. Gideon, mad as ever, laughed between shots, the sound sharp and wild, a counterpoint to the gunfire.

Ellie fought like a woman possessed, her rifle a deadly extension of her will, each shot finding its mark with surgical precision. Her eyes were hollow, dark pools reflecting the fires burning around them, but her hands never wavered. She was a mother protecting her child, and there was no fiercer warrior. Mercy, no longer just a child, moved with the lethal grace of someone who had been forged in fire. She was swift and silent, her knife flashing like a serpent's fang, striking with deadly accuracy. She had been a girl once, but Denver had stolen that from her. Now she was something else—something sharp and dangerous.

The battle raged, minutes stretching into eternity, until the streets grew quiet once more, save for the crackle of dying flames and the ragged breath of the few left standing.

The bodies of Sinclair's men littered the ground, their blood mingling with the dust, a grim testament to the cost of power and the price of vengeance.

Jed stood amidst the carnage, his revolver still smoking, his chest heaving with exertion. His eyes scanned the wreckage, landing on Mercy. She stood over the body of a man twice her size, her knife buried deep in his chest, her hands slick with blood. She was trembling, not from fear, but from the adrenaline still coursing through her veins. Jed approached slowly, his heart heavy with something he couldn't name.

"Mercy," he whispered, his voice rough.

She didn't move. Didn't acknowledge him. She just stared down at the man she had killed, her expression unreadable. Then, slowly, she released the knife, letting it fall with a soft thud to the blood-soaked ground. She turned to Jed, her dark eyes meeting his, and for a moment, he saw the child she had been. But it was fleeting, gone in the blink of an eye, replaced by something older, something broken.

Ellie was there in an instant, pulling Mercy into her arms, holding her close as if she could shield her from the world with nothing more than sheer will. Cullen stood nearby, his face a mask of exhaustion and grief, his revolver finally lowered. Gideon lit a cigarette with shaking hands, his laughter gone, replaced by a hollow silence.

As the sun climbed higher, casting its indifferent light over the battlefield, Jed knew it was over. The men who had hunted them were dead. Sinclair was gone. But the scars would remain, etched into their skin, their hearts, their souls.

Jed looked at Mercy, her small hand clinging to Ellie's, and felt the weight of what they had done, what they had become. He holstered his gun, his shoulders heavy with the knowledge that victory had come at a cost none of them could afford.

"Let's go home," he said softly, though he knew there was no home to return to. Only the road ahead, paved with fire and blood.

# EPILOGUE

The desert never forgets. It holds the echoes of screams and gunfire, the ghosts of men who thought they could carve their names into its unforgiving skin. But the desert swallows them whole, leaving nothing behind but bones bleached white by the relentless sun and stories whispered on the wind.

The year was 1885, and the West had already bled more than it could bear. Men with money and men with guns ruled with the same currency—fear. Empires were built on stolen land, watered with the blood of the innocent, and fed by the broken bodies of those too stubborn to die quietly. Denver was no different. A city dressed in the illusion of progress, its heart blackened by corruption and greed, pumping poison through the veins of every street and alley.

Franklin Sinclair was the kind of man who didn't need to pull a trigger to kill you. He owned men the way ranchers owned cattle—branded, broken, and easily replaced. He didn't fear outlaws or lawmen because, in the end, they all served the same god he did: power. But even gods bleed when you cut deep enough.

Jed McCallister was never a hero. He didn't ride for justice or vengeance, though both had clung to him like shadows in the years since the war ended. He was a man shaped by violence, carved from the same rough stone as the killers he hunted. But even a man like Jed knew there were debts that had to be paid in blood. And when Sinclair made the mistake of stealing a child—of turning Mercy into a pawn in his brutal game—Jed didn't see it as a mission.

He saw it as a reckoning.

They rode into Denver under a sky the color of old bruises, the horizon burning with the promise of violence. Cullen Crowe McKenna, haunted by ghosts only he could see, rode with a gun in one hand and regret in the other. Ellie, fierce and unyielding despite the wounds that marked her skin and soul, carried her rifle like an extension of her rage. And Mercy, too young to hold so much darkness, carried the weight of every life stolen from her in the curve of her small, blood-streaked hands.

What followed wasn't a battle.

It was an execution.

The streets of Denver ran red, the echoes of gunfire ringing louder than the church bells meant to drown them out. Men screamed. Men begged. Some fought. Most died. The city watched in silence, its heart exposed, raw and rotten beneath the polished veneer of civility.

When the smoke cleared, the bodies were stacked like cordwood, and the only thing left standing was the truth: power doesn't protect you from death. It only delays it. And for men like Sinclair, delay had run out.

Jed never spoke much about what happened that day. The

blood washed away, the bodies buried, but the memories lingered, stitched into the scars left behind. Some said he was a hero. Some said he was worse than the men he killed.

But the desert doesn't care about stories.

It only remembers the blood.

# AFTERWORD

As this journey through fire and blood comes to a close, I find myself reflecting on the unyielding spirit of the American frontier—a time and place where survival was never guaranteed, and love often came at great cost. Ellie Calhoun's story is one of unwavering resolve, a mother's unbreakable bond, and the scars left by both vengeance and hope.

My hope is that this tale not only transported you to the unforgiving landscape of the Llano Estacado but also resonated with the timeless struggles of love, loss, and redemption. Thank you for taking this journey with me. May the echoes of the West stay with you long after the final page.

# ACKNOWLEDGEMENT

This novel would not have been possible without the support, inspiration, and guidance of so many. To my family and friends—your unwavering belief in me kept me going through every challenge. To my editor and publishing team—your insights and dedication brought this story to life.

To the historians and storytellers who have preserved the rich history of the American West—your work inspired every page of this book. And finally, to my readers—thank you for embarking on this journey through fire and blood with me. Your support means everything. Thank you all from the bottom of my heart.

# ABOUT THE AUTHOR

## Kimberly St. Clair

Kimberly St. Clair is a writer with a passion for historical fiction, particularly stories that explore the lives of early settlers and the incredible resilience required to survive in a harsh and unforgiving world. Through her writing, Kimberly seeks to bring the past to life, weaving together the struggles, triumphs, and emotions of those who shaped the landscape we know today.

With a deep love for storytelling, Kimberly writes with the belief that every individual's journey—no matter how small or difficult—is worth telling. Her work is inspired by the untold stories of survival, love, and the unyielding human spirit.

When she's not writing, Kimberly enjoys immersing herself in history, connecting with nature, and exploring the complexities of human relationships. She believes that literature can build bridges between people, offering connection and understanding through the written word.

For now, Kimberly prefers to keep her personal life private, focusing instead on the stories she brings to the world. She hopes that her readers find as much inspiration and strength in these tales as she has in writing them.

# BOOKS BY THIS AUTHOR

## We Will Not Be Forgotten

We Will Not Be Forgotten – Book Description

In the harsh and unforgiving Kansas plains of 1885, Clara and Jack face a battle for their very survival. As pioneers struggling to make a living from the parched earth, they must endure the brutal realities of the American frontier—land that promises prosperity, but too often delivers hardship. We Will Not Be Forgotten is a gripping historical novel of love, resilience, and hope in the face of overwhelming adversity.

Set against the backdrop of the late 19th century, the story follows Clara and Jack, a young couple who dream of building a future on the untamed land of Kansas. But their dreams are nearly crushed when a relentless drought ravages their crops, decimates their cattle, and threatens to wipe out their livelihood. As their ranch is pushed to the brink of destruction, Clara's strength is tested like never before. With each passing day, the stakes grow higher, and Clara finds herself struggling not only against the elements but also against the fear of losing everything she and Jack have worked for.

Survival on the frontier is never easy, but Clara's determination to persevere and protect her family drives her forward. Alongside Jack, their friends, and neighbors,

Clara faces hardships that would break even the toughest of pioneers, but she remains steadfast in her belief that they can rebuild and overcome any challenge.

As Clara and Jack navigate the unrelenting drought and the challenges of early settler life, their bond deepens, and they discover that survival is about more than just the land. It's about love, community, and the unwavering belief that together, they can face whatever the future holds.

With vivid descriptions of the American plains and meticulous historical detail, We Will Not Be Forgotten takes readers on an unforgettable journey through the life of pioneers fighting to create a new life in a land full of promise and danger. Clara's journey of personal and familial growth is one of transformation, as she faces the harshest trials a person can endure, only to emerge stronger and more determined to protect the future of her family.

For fans of historical fiction, early settler novels, and stories of perseverance and survival, We Will Not Be Forgotten offers an emotional and powerful experience. This is a tale of love, of community, of strength, and of resilience—one that will resonate with anyone who has ever fought for their dreams, no matter the cost.